A Time To Forgive

Tricia Linden

Kingsburg Press

San Francisco, California

Kingsburg Press
P.O. Box 475146
San Francisco, California, 94147
www.KingsburgPress.com

A Time To Forgive is a work of fiction. Names, characters, places, and incidents are a product of the author's imagination. Locales and public names are sometimes used for atmospheric purposes. Any resemblance to actual people, living or dead, or to businesses, companies, events, institutions, or locales is completely coincidental.

Editor: Barbara Millman-Cole
Cover Design: Killion Group
A Time To Forgive / Tricia Linden – 2nd ed.
previously published as Away Over Yonder

ISBN- 13:978-1-946177-06-3
ISBN- 10: 1-946177-06-7
eBook ISBN: 978-1-946177-07-0

Other Works by Tricia Linden

The MacNicol Clan Through Time

A Time To Begin – Book 1

A Time To Return – Book 2

A Time To Belong – Book 3

A Time To Forgive – Book 4

.

.

.

Dreaming In Moonlight

.

.

.

Jules Vanderzeit novels

set in the Gilded Age of New York

Until We Meet Again

Until Their Hearts Desire

.

Coming Soon: Until You Love Me

Dedication

To Dolores Geiger,
my supportive mother.
Thank you for your encouragement
as I travel this road.

CHAPTER 1

Breanna stopped brushing the gelding's warm chestnut hide for a moment and listened as the rumble of a motorcycle reached her ears. The sound was definitely a motorcycle—not a car or a truck—and not only was the sound notably distinctive, it was unexpected. Far enough from the beaten path to make unknown visitors a bit of a concern, Over-Yonder ranch sat nestled against the foothills of Diablo Valley at the end of a long and narrow country road.

Sunnyside, the horse she was brushing down, turned his ears, pointing them in the direction of the roadway, his big brown eyes watching her.

"You hear it, too, don't you, boy?" Bree spoke to the horse, rubbing his long brown nose. They had just finished his morning exercise, and she was in the process of rubbing him down, first along his back and then down each leg. Front to back, left to right, the process always stayed the same. She had rescued Sunnyside from an abusive owner, and this daily routine was part of his treatment.

Bree registered the sound of the motorcycle growing closer as she methodically completed her task. It would take a lot more than the lure of an approaching visitor to pull her away from Sunnyside. For the moment, this horse was her priority. Nothing and no one was more important.

She had just finished brushing Sunnyside and was setting aside her tools when she heard the motor bike roll into the parkway in front of the stables and come to a stop. Bree turned to give the horse a parting hug. "You're loved, Sunnyside. Now and always, you are safe, and strong, and loved." Bree gave the horse a final pat.

Sunnyside bobbed his head in approval and nickered, nudging her gently away with his nose. She could almost hear him say, "I'm all right now. Go greet your visitor." Sensing his contentment, she smiled.

As she headed down the shed row toward the front entrance, she dusted off her hands along the front of her snug-fitting jeans before she rolled the long sleeves of her plaid flannel shirt up to her elbows. In a futile effort to contain her wayward curls, she ran her fingers through her thick copper-red hair and readjusted the elastic band holding it away from her face. Though it was a never-ending battle to contain her hair, she refused to admit defeat.

When she reached the shadowed entrance at the wide double doors of the stables, she stopped to observe her visitor. The rider had already dismounted from his bike and was removing his helmet, a sleek black orb with a tinted face plate that when worn would obscure his features.

Still standing in the shadow of the doorway, she watched as he set the helmet on the seat of his bike and ran his fingers through his dark auburn hair, releasing his disheveled curls from the dreaded curse of helmet hair. His profile revealed a strong, nearly straight nose, bold cheekbones, and a well-formed jaw.

Bree watched a moment longer as the man unzipped his black leather jacket and tucked his shirt into his faded black jeans. The tight fit of his dark tee shirt revealed the type of rock hard muscles that came from long hours of hard work. He was one nice-looking man.

After she finished checking out the man, she checked out his bike, a sleek black-and-gray Ducati Multistrada. The model looked to be a few years old, but the Italian motorcycle was in mint condition. He obviously took good care of his toys. His Ducati was one nice-looking bike.

She judged her visitor to be in his late twenties, maybe six or seven years older than her. When he started to walk toward the front of the ranch house, Bree stepped out into the bright sunlight and shouted, "Can I help you?"

The man turned with a startled jerk. Squinting, he reached a hand up to shield his eyes from the glare of the sun. "Sorry, I didn't see you standing there."

"Looking for someone?"

"Yeah, Breanna Ellers. Know where I can find her?"

Bree walked forward to greet him. "I'm Breanna Ellers."

The man fished a card from his back pocket and looked it over, then looked back at her. "You're Breanna Ellers, the animal trainer?"

"Yeah, that's me," she confirmed. He was holding one of the business cards her cousin Jack had designed for her and insisted on handing out to everyone he met. Jack also had a habit of leaving them at every pet and feed store in the area, which meant this guy could be anyone.

Her visitor looked skeptical. "It says here you have twelve years of experience."

"That's right. I trained my first puppy when I was ten years old." She moved closer so he wouldn't have to squint into the sun.

3

"Professionally?" He raised a doubtful brow. She noted how he gave her a quick once-over.

"Did I get paid? Sure, there's always a reward." She'd been down this road before. It was always the same until they saw what she could do. "I take it you're in need of a trainer?"

He took a few steps toward her, stopping with the bike still between them. "I've got some horses that are giving me trouble. Frank McGregor said you could help."

Her face relaxed into an easy grin. "You know Franklin?"

"Yeah. He gave me your card, but…" He flipped the card back and forth against his other hand.

"Let me guess. He didn't tell you my age."

"Nope, never mentioned that." The man gave her his first honest smile.

"That sounds like Franklin." The elder man was like a grandfather to her, part of a strong network of friends and family she had created to replace the family she had lost back home on Skye.

Though it was still early spring, the day was unseasonably warm, and the sun was approaching its zenith. She motioned over to the covered patio at the back of the house. "Why don't we go sit down in the shade? It's a little hot to be standing out here in the sun. Especially with you all dressed in black."

Now it was her turn to give him the once-over. For a second, he reminded her of a dark warrior, ready to ride into battle, mysterious and romantic. She quickly reined in her overactive imagination, but she couldn't dismiss the thought, not completely.

"All right," he nodded, stepping around his bike.

"Would you like something to drink?"

"Cold water would be nice." He met her halfway as they walked toward the table and chairs under the latticed awning.

As they drew closer, she noticed his stunning hazel eyes. Swirls of browns and greens created a kaleidoscope effect, mysteriously drawing her in. She drew in a quick, sharp breath while her heart pumped iron for a few fast beats. For a brief moment, his eyes reminded her of William Gregory, a boy from back home on Skye; but William was dead. He had died when he was only twenty, fighting to protect her ma. She blinked hard and shook her head, willing the image to fade as quickly as it had appeared.

Still dazed, she looked down and noticed the man had reached out his hand. "I'm Alex. Alex Connor," he said.

"I'm...I'm pleased to meet you, Mr. Connor," she stammered.

"Just call me Alex," he said. His beguiling smile washed over her like fresh sweet cream.

"And you can call me Bree." She shook his hand, fighting back her memories. This man wasn't William, and she was no longer in Scotland. She needed to relax.

"Here, take a seat while I get us both something cold to drink." Hoping he hadn't noticed her sudden flare of nerves, she stepped quickly through the back door and into the kitchen, seeking refuge within its cool, shadowy interior. Leaning against the kitchen counter, she forced herself to remain calm.

Bree hadn't felt this way since she arrived in California nearly four years ago. No man had affected her this strongly since William. She hadn't believed a modern man could. These men seemed wimpy and weak compared to the warriors she had grown up with on Skye. But Alex didn't appear wimpy or weak. He looked like a man who didn't back down from a challenge, and something told her she was about to be challenged in ways she wouldn't expect.

~~~

Alex watched as Bree disappeared into the darkness of the house. *Damn.* She looked good coming and going. Not at all what he had expected, and that had thrown him for a loop. He had expected to meet an old crone who didn't know how to use the internet considering she hadn't responded to any of his emails. Instead, he had encountered a pretty, young woman who grabbed the attention of body parts well south of his brain.

Damn McGregor for not telling him. It felt like he'd been set up. Too late now, he'd just have to make the best of it, which was fine with him. Right now, the best of it was looking pretty darn good.

Thankfully, he hadn't completely lost his mind. When he learned she was the horse trainer he was looking for, he remembered one vital piece of advice McGregor had shared with him. "I don't recommend telling her you're a MacDonald, at least not right away. Not if you want her help." Frank had refused to explain why, except to say there was some old family history.

Instead, Alex had opted to use his middle name, Connor, which was also his mother's maiden name. All through college, he'd been a charmer and a partygoer and had learned how to tell folks whatever they needed to hear to get what he wanted. He wasn't above using a fib or a little white lie if it served his purpose, not that he liked it. For some reason, lying to Bree felt wrong, as though she deserved better from him.

Unfortunately, old habits were hard to break, and even with good intentions tap dancing on his shoulder, he had felt compelled to hide his true identity. At least until he knew what she had against the MacDonalds. It didn't seem fair she should have the chance to dismiss him before he had a chance to win her over with his charm. After all, his charming ways had gotten him through college, and he trusted they would get him through this.

Sooner or later she'd find out he was a MacDonald; he couldn't keep it a secret forever, not if they were going to work together. But that could wait. First, she had to agree to take the job and prove to him she could do it. There was still a chance this would turn out to be a wasted trip and he'd be heading back to Placerville before sunset.

Skeptical, he wondered if she were really as good as McGregor claimed. Doing the math, he figured she couldn't be much more than twenty-two years old. That seemed a little young to be calling herself a professional animal trainer. Even if he did overlook the dubious advertising claim of twelve years of experience, he wasn't convinced a woman this young could work magic with his horses.

In her riding boots, she stood nearly as tall as him, and he tapped in at six foot one. She was slim, with an athletic build, but not overly skinny. That was nice. On the whole, she looked as though she could hold her own in a game of beach volleyball. Funny how that image had sprung to mind—including sand, surf, and a tight bikini— considering she didn't look or sound like a typical California girl. It was obvious she was Scottish, through and through. Along with her pale, freckled skin, mass of coppery curls, and moss-green eyes, she had the sweetest Scottish brogue he'd ever heard outside Inverness. But her last name didn't fit. Ellers was an English name, as far as he knew, which meant the Scottish blood must come from her mother's side of the family.

She soon came back out with two large tumblers filled with ice water and set one in front of him before taking the chair across from him.

"So why do you need a horse trainer?" she asked, getting right to business. She sat back in her chair, looking relaxed. He did the same.

"My dad and I have a small ranch near McGregor's place up in Placerville where we raise Clydesdales. We've got half a dozen horses that are used to pull wagons. Our biggest coach runs four to a hitch with two standbys for rotation. Two of my best Clydes have been misbehaving, and I can't keep running the business without them."

"Sounds like a good-sized operation. What are the wagons used for?"

"The big rig is a fully restored stage coach. It's mostly used to work rodeos and county fairs, that sort of thing. We also have a few smaller rigs—a nine-passenger surrey and a couple of smaller carriages for weddings and such. It's a pretty successful business, and it usually pays the bills, but I can't keep running it with just the four. I need my full team to keep it going."

Alex was making the enterprise sound better than it was. The business was knee-deep in debt after his dad had taken out a second mortgage to buy and restore the stage coach, and the project was eating up every spare cent of profit. He needed to get the operation back up to full capacity, or he risked losing it all. It was already bad enough that he had given up his expensive apartment and was back living at his dad's ranch; not a happy place to be. The operation was hard work, but he loved those Clydesdales. They were a noble breed of working horses.

He worried if he appeared desperate, she wouldn't agree to help. As it was, he really couldn't afford to pay her until the team was fully restored and making good money. Even then, it probably wouldn't be until well into the summer season when they had their biggest jobs working the county fairs.

"I'm glad to hear you don't want to overwork your horses. It sounds like they're your bread and butter," Bree said.

"Yeah, you could say that."

"What do you think happened to your horses?"

"I wish I knew. For a while, everything was going great, but recently, Malt and Barley have been acting unpredictable. They've been giving my carriage drivers a hard time, refusing to perform like they should. I can't risk having them misbehave around the public. These are big animals. Someone could get hurt, and then I'd lose my business."

It had only been in the last year, since his dad's health started deteriorating, that he had gotten involved in running the day-to-day operations. When he looked back through the books, it seemed the company had done well for several years, but recently, after the economy had taken a nosedive, so had their business. Still, he had managed to keep it together until his two best Clydesdales had started to act up. Malt and Barley were beautiful draught horses, and he wanted to keep things going, but there wasn't much use for them if they couldn't pull their weight, and that meant pulling a wagon full of paying customers.

"I'll have to meet them before I can agree to take on the job," she said.

"You mean the horses?"

"Of course." She gave him a duh-what-did-you-think kind of look. "I have to know if I can work with them."

That sounded rather suspicious. Maybe she was hedging her bets in case the job was more than she could handle. "You think you can tell just by seeing them?"

"I'll know in the first meeting whether or not I can help." She took a sip of water, looking quite pleased with herself.

"Really?" he asked, raising a skeptical brow. "How do I know you have what it takes? Shouldn't I see some references or something?" He had come here expecting to interview her, and yet for some reason, it felt as if she were in control.

"I can show you a reference." She stood up from the table. "Here. Turn your chair around."

"Why?" he asked, rising from his seat.

"You need to be facing the stables."

He repositioned his chair then sat down again, facing toward the back yard and the stables beyond.

Bree walked to the edge of the patio and turned to face him, her back to the yard. As soon as he was settled in his seat, she put two fingers to her mouth and let out a high, shrill whistle. A second later, a border collie came running from behind the stables. Before the dog crossed the yard, Bree raised her left hand up at a forty-five-degree angle, like a signal to stop. The collie stopped in his tracks, his tail wagging. With her back still turned toward the dog, she lowered her hand to a straight-out position. The collie sat back on its hind legs. Without looking back to see if the dog had obeyed, she lowered her hand toward the ground, and the dog dropped to his front paws. Next, she raised her hand back to the straight-out position and waved it from side to side. The dog sat up and turned his head, looking left and right. Then, she brought her hand back up to the forty-five degree angle and waved it forward. The dog took off running toward her again. Just as he reached the cement slab of the patio, she turned around and opened her arms to greet him.

"Good doggie. That's my good Laddy." She ruffled his fur, giving him an affectionate hug. The dog's tail wagged a rapid beat.

Alex was darn impressed; although, he tried not to show it. "How do you know what the dog did? Maybe he just ran across the yard when you weren't looking."

She looked up from praising the dog, grinning from ear to ear. "If he had, you wouldn't be asking me that question."

CHAPTER 2

B ree admitted she was intrigued but only to herself. She liked the idea of working with Clydesdales. They were a hardy breed of Scottish draught horse, typically standing over fifteen hands high, and one of her favorites. However, when she started thinking about the logistics of taking a job outside Diablo Valley, she doubted it would work. Unfortunately, she had too many obligations to be away from the ranch for more than a day or two.

Under her guidance, Over-Yonder was becoming a sanctuary for abandoned horses, which she trained for use as therapeutic riding horses for children with learning disabilities. So far, she only had two qualified horses and five students, but the program was gaining success. The biggest share of her income came from her other clients, mostly dog owners who wanted individualized training for their pets. That was where her special talent—her gift—helped the most.

"So how do you see this working?" she asked. "Since your horses are in Placerville and I'm down here." From experience, she knew the ride to Placerville was at least two hours, often longer, depending on traffic.

"I was thinking you could take a trip up there to check them out and let me know what you think. Maybe give me an estimate of your charges. After all, I have no idea how long you'll need to retrain them, or fix their problem, or whatever it is you do."

"I try to heal them, if I can." Taking the job seemed totally out of the question, but she couldn't resist the idea of working with the Clydesdales. It was too good to pass up. In a rush, she said, "It'll probably take a few hours before I'm sure. I'll need to make an evaluation, and I'll need you to cover my expenses up front. Are you all right with that?"

Alex sat quiet for a moment, considering. "If you don't mind riding on the back of my bike, I can drive you up and back. You know, before we commit to anything." He shrugged, as though it was no big deal.

She saw right through him. He was short of cash. That wasn't surprising, considering his team wasn't working at full capacity.

Bree continued to think it over. She liked the idea of working with the Clydesdales, it would be nice to visit with Franklin, and Alex was easy on the eyes. Still, she needed income for the ranch, and it didn't look as if Alex could pay as well as she had hoped. What could it hurt to take a look? Curious to know what had happened to his horses, she figured a night away from the ranch would be a nice little break.

"Okay, I'll make the trip, but I'll ride my own bike. While I'm there, I can stop in and visit Franklin, maybe spend the night at his place. I haven't seen him in a while. It'll save you the return trip, and I'll be more comfortable."

"You ride?" he asked, looking somewhat impressed.

It seemed he was easy to impress considering how he had reacted to her little dog show with Laddy. "Yeah, I ride. I've got a 1982 Triumph Bonneville I inherited from my dad."

"You're freaking kidding me, right? You have a classic Bonnie?" His expression progressed from somewhat impressed to downright stunned.

Grinning with pride, she said, "Yeah, and in mint condition, along with a 1975 Ford Mustang, candy apple red. They belonged to my dad."

"Really? That's awesome. Your dad must love antiques."

"You could say that." She indulged in a little chuckle, thinking just how much her dad had loved old things and living in the past. He'd been happy to give her what he called "his good, old-fashioned dependable machines." For her, the idea that a car or motorcycle was built in a particular year was a fascinating connection to a time she had never known.

"I love 'em, too—the classics, I mean. Think maybe you'll let me see them?" It was obvious he would love to test drive her toys.

"Sure, they're parked in the garage. They came with the ranch. Well, the ranch isn't really mine, not yet, but I run the place."

He gave her a questioning look. "What about your parents?"

"My parents passed away some time ago, but I still have family. My aunt and uncles actually own the ranch."

Only a few knew of her true family background, and it was best to keep it that way. As far as most people were concerned, she was officially the adopted daughter of Daniel Ellers, not his daughter by birth.

According to public records, Daniel Ellers had traveled to Scotland and the Isle of Skye when he was thirty-one years old. A few months later, he died unexpectedly from a heart attack, but before his death, he had arranged to adopt Bree and had asked to be buried on the Isle of Skye. At least, that was the story according to the public records.

It was a well-kept family secret that her real parents were Daniel Ellers and Kayla MacNicol. Very few people knew Daniel Ellers had actually traveled through time to the late thirteenth century and had stayed in the past to marry Kayla MacNicol, the love of his life, and that Breanna had been born in 1308.

After her mother died during a battle with the MacDonalds, her dad had arranged to return to his time in the twenty-first century with the help of Moezell, a powerful faerie. It was Moezell who had taken Daniel back in time to meet Kayla, and the faerie had promised she would send him back to the future, to the moment he had left, whenever he asked. After Ma had died, Bree's father had wanted to go back to see his sister and tell her what happened. Bree had agreed to travel with him forward in time so he wouldn't be alone. She was his youngest daughter and only eighteen years old. At the time, it had seemed like a good idea.

After her dad passed away on the Isle of Skye, Bree agreed to move to California with her Aunt Teressa and Uncle Robert. It was a devastating time for her, and they were the only family she knew. It took several months for her to adapt to her strange new life, but eventually she moved to Over-Yonder, her father's ranch, hoping someday she could make it her own.

"I'm sorry to hear about your parents. Do you live here by yourself?" Alex looked a little uncomfortable, as if realizing for the first time they were alone.

"No, I have housemates—my cousins, Jack and Jenny. They help me run the ranch when they're not busy with their jobs. I also have an aunt and uncle who live in Berkeley. So no, I'm not alone." Although sometimes it felt that way, especially when she had first arrived in California. She had to keep reminding herself she chose to accompany her dad to the future. Besides, there was no one left for her back home on Skye.

"When would you be available to make the trip over to Placerville?" Alex asked.

Bree considered her schedule. It was Wednesday afternoon, and she had appointments booked through to Friday morning, plus the therapeutic riding class on Saturday morning. She could probably reschedule the Friday morning appointment, but she couldn't miss Saturday. "I could leave Thursday evening as long as I return Friday night. I have a nine o'clock riding class on Saturday. Other than that, it would have to be a day trip on Sunday. That's my only real day off."

"Sounds like you keep yourself pretty busy."

"It pays the bills, and this is a big place. There's always a lot to do."

"I don't need to get back home right away. Maybe I should stay here and wait for you. It's only one night." Alex twisted in his seat. "I mean, it's obvious you could use some help around here. Then we could ride to Placerville together. Consider it a down payment for you agreeing to take the job. I'll just need a place to stay. What do you think?"

For some reason, his offer sparked a defensive reaction in Bree, as if she were some kind of hard-luck case. "First off, I didn't agree to take the job, only to meet your animals. And second, if this is about being paid . . ."

"Hey, I'm not asking to be paid. I only asked for a place to stay. I offered to help. On a ranch this big, surely you can spare a bed, but hey, if that doesn't work for you, I can just leave." Alex raised his hands as though he were being robbed and sounded as defensive as she felt. Apparently, finances were a touchy subject for both of them.

Bree lowered her hackles and was surprised to find herself agreeing to his plan. "No, it makes sense." A thought suddenly occurred to her. "By the way, does Franklin still drive that old, beat-up, puke-green pickup truck?" she asked.

Alex gave her a skeptical look. "Are you sure we're talking about the same McGregor? I've never seen Frank drive anything other than an old vintage Ford pickup he painted orange about a dozen years ago. It runs like a top, and he keeps it shined up like a new copper penny."

"Yeah, that sounds like Grandpa. I was just checking." It occurred to her she should call Franklin before she let this go too far and put it on her list of things to do as soon as she got the chance. If nothing else, Jack and Jenny would be home soon to provide backup if needed.

Alex relaxed into an easy grin. "Guess I can't blame you. Here I am asking to stay the night, and you don't know me from Adam."

"Yeah, and I don't know who Adam is either. So, anyway, there's a spare room in the house. It's mostly used for storage, but there's a bed. I have to warn you, I'm not much of a cook. Jenny does most of the cooking around here when she's not busy at culinary school. Usually it's leftovers from one of her class assignments."

"That's fine with me. Besides, I'm a pretty good cook myself. Maybe I can add that to my list of services."

The way he looked at her, with his half-lidded hazel-green eyes, Bree wondered what other *services* he would like to add to that list.

~~~

Alex wondered if he would regret offering his services as sweat equity in exchange for overnight lodging. He had acted on impulse when he made the offer, and now he was having second thoughts. Maybe it was wiser to head back home instead of hanging around Over-Yonder. He had a business to run. He didn't need to hire himself out to another struggling rancher. Even if she was young, pretty, and intriguing, he shouldn't be wasting his time. Besides, she

16

was barely old enough to drink, and he'd be turning thirty in another year.

He had too many problems of his own to be taking on hers, but he had let his dick do the talking, and he wasn't about to withdraw his offer. It certainly wasn't because he wanted to muck out stalls or fix broken fences. He did enough of that working for his dad. They had two hired hands who worked on the ranch, but lately he worried if they needed closer oversight than he could give them. Mostly he had concerns about Howard. The driver had only been with the company for a couple of years, and there were times when Alex questioned his judgment. Though he trusted his other handler well enough, Roy was nearing retirement and only worked part-time.

If McGregor hadn't convinced him Breanna Ellers was perfect for the job, he wouldn't have even taken the time to come to Over-Yonder. The idea was hard to believe, and he still wasn't one hundred percent convinced, but he was willing to take a chance. Because that's what he did; he took chances. Without even thinking about what he was doing, he had offered to stay and help Bree with her ranch. No, this wasn't what he had planned, but now that he was here, he was determined to make the best of it.

This trip was supposed to be a one-day turn-around. Alex had come to Diablo Valley to visit the owners of Conroy's Horse and Cattle Feed Company to settle a past due account and arrange for enough credit to get him through the next six months. It irked him that his dad refused to take on this annoying little task, but lately, it seemed when it came to running the family business, it was all up to him. If he didn't do it, it wouldn't get done. He could have settled the account by simply mailing in a payment, but he knew his request for credit would be a lot harder to refuse if he was there in person, using his charm and their long-standing business connection to convince them to keep the account open.

He'd have to call his uncle and ask him to cover for a couple of days. Wayne would probably give him a hard time about it, but that was nothing new. For as long as Alex could remember, he'd been with MacDonald's Clydesdales and Carriage, and besides being his dad's brother, he was the company's foreman. Maybe he should just send his uncle a text message so he wouldn't have to hear one of his lectures.

The idea of texting reminded him Bree hadn't bothered to answer his email messages asking for more information and to arrange an appointment. Frank had warned him she wouldn't. He'd said she was a bit of a recluse and kind of old-fashioned. From the way Frank talked, Alex had expected to meet an old crone. Instead, he was greeted by a beautiful young woman barely old enough to legally enter a bar.

"Hey, I wanted to ask, why didn't you respond to any of my emails? You know, it's not a good way of doing business."

"Oh, that. As you can imagine, our internet isn't very good out here, and well, you see, computers and I don't get along very well. It's a curse I inherited from my dad. He never liked them, either. My friend Jenny has been trying to bring me into the twenty-first century, God bless her soul, but I'm afraid it's a losing battle."

"Maybe I can help. I'm a wiz with computers." He loved the internet and technical gadgets. He couldn't imagine going anywhere without his smart phone. It was his connection to the world.

Bree shrugged, looking too darn cute for her own good. "You can try, but I can't promise anything. Computers are a time-suck. I've spent hours trying to learn how to surf the web. Other than a lot of funny pet videos, I don't see the point."

"You've got to be kidding. You can find anything you want online."

"Yeah, I know, but first you have to know what you're looking for."

"Most times it helps if you know what you're looking for, but sometimes you can find stuff you didn't even know you wanted. That's what makes it so exciting."

"Usually I don't."

"You don't find it exciting?" Alex asked.

"I don't know what I'm looking for. Besides, most of the time I'm pretty happy with what I have."

Alex wasn't convinced. "Everyone wants something, and it's all on the internet."

"So I've heard." Bree glanced at her watch. "I'd like to sit and talk about your horses some more, but I've got to get going. After tending to horses all morning, I need to get cleaned up." She glanced down at her dirty work clothes. "I've got a client coming in for a session, and I have to get ready."

"Will it take long? Maybe I can help," he asked, thinking it would be helpful to see her at work.

"You want to help me get ready?" Bree looked as if she might jump out of her skin if he said yes. Alex almost laughed out loud. It was obvious she had misunderstood. But laughing at her wouldn't be nice.

"No, I meant help you with your client," he said, with a cocky grin.

"Thanks, but I don't need any help. I work alone." She lifted her chin, sitting up a little straighter.

"Can I watch?" He was being bad, and he knew it, but he was having way too much fun to stop.

"Watch? You want to watch me work?"

"I'll stay out of your way. I'd like to see how you do what you do."

"No, you can't watch. It'll make my client nervous." She pushed back her chair and stood up from the table. Suddenly she was all business again. "Look, you said you wanted to help out around here. The deck and sun porch need some minor repairs. There are some boards that need replacing and the railing wobbles. There's a stack of lumber next to the workshop, and you'll find any tools you need inside. If you were serious about your offer to help, you can start there."

"I was serious," Alex assured her. "And don't worry. I'll stay out of your way. Just let me know when it's time for dinner, either to make it or to eat it," he said, grinning. Sparring with her was kinda fun. One minute she seemed mature and confident, and the next she became curiously innocent. He couldn't tell which way her wind would blow at any given time, but either way, she was incredibly intriguing, and a joy to observe.

CHAPTER 3

Alex was sorting through the lumber when he heard a pickup truck pull into the driveway. He continued to work at his task, selecting the boards he needed to repair the deck, as he watched an older woman step out from the driver's side. Bree was right there to meet her. She had changed into a lightweight summer dress with a full skirt that just touched her knees and had swapped out her riding boots for little yellow flats. Her shapely legs seemed to go on forever.

The older woman walked around to the passenger door, opened it, and then just stood there. From his vantage point, he couldn't see who was inside the truck or why they weren't getting out. As she approached, Bree said something to the woman, who was waving at the passenger to get out. Nothing happened. Finally, the older woman stepped up to the door, reached inside, and emerged with a non-descript midsized dog in her arms. It was probably a mutt. The poor creature looked scared out of its wits. Even from twenty yards away, he could see the dog shaking in its owner's arms. Not a good partnership from the look of things.

Bree took the pet owner with her dog over to the grassy lawn spread out between the ranch house and the stables, disappearing from view. Since the workshop was on the far side of the stables, if he wanted to watch the action, he needed an excuse to move to that section of the property. He stuck a hammer in his back pocket, grabbed a bag of nails he had found in the workshop, and hefted a board over his shoulder. Time to get to work on the deck. It had a great view of the back yard.

Alex watched Bree as she crouched down in front of the little mutt. She petted the dog's head, scratching his ears and stroking his neck. Bree called Laddy over to join them, and together they went through a series of hand signals and maneuverers with the pet owner mimicking her gestures. After each maneuver, the pet owner followed her actions, encouraging the mutt—the pet owner called him Otis—to do as Laddy had done. They were playing a game of doggy see, doggy do, and as far as he could tell, for the most part, it was working.

Sometimes Laddy would go right and Otis would go left, or Laddy would go left and Otis would go backward. More often, Laddy would sit still and Otis would run off in another direction. The mutt definitely lacked discipline, and Alex figured it was going to take more than one lesson to instill the concept into the rambunctious dog's head.

Alex was wrong.

Surprisingly, with Bree's diligent and repeated efforts, Alex watched as the dog made progress. Several times throughout the session, Bree crouched down in front of Otis and talked directly to the dog as though he were capable of understanding her, and each time he showed signs of improvement. Not surprisingly, it didn't always stick, at least not completely. Apparently, Otis's attention span had limitations, and after a while, he slipped back into carelessly wandering off into his own la-la land.

Bree worked with the owner and dog for the next hour, giving them only a short ten-minute break halfway through the lesson, during which time Otis ran happily about the yard, investigating every new and unusual scent he could find. It appeared Otis was a happy dog, just not very smart.

When the lesson was over, she invited the dog owner—Alex had overheard her name was Edna—to the covered patio for a glass of lemonade.

Throughout the entire training session, Bree had appeared professional, knowledgeable, and darn good-looking. More than once, he appreciated the occasional gust of wind that fluffed the hem of Bree's skirt, affording Alex a clearer view of her long, shapely legs.

Even with the distractions, he managed to replace several rotting boards in the deck and shore up the unstable railing by adding additional bracing on each side. All in all, it was a fairly productive afternoon.

He returned the tools to the well-organized workshop and was cleaning up his workspace, restacking the unused boards, when Bree came looking for him.

"Well, I see you got a lot done after all," she said, sounding slightly condescending with a snarky grin.

"Glad you approve."

"Even though you were watching my training session the whole time."

"It's called multi-tasking. Can't blame a man for admiring the view." Alex raised a brow in jest, and she smiled back.

"I'll be starting dinner soon. Maybe you should stop now and go wash up."

"I was just thinking the same thing. I'm almost finished. Maybe I should change. I have an extra sweater in the pack on my bike."

She looked him over. He followed her glance and realized he was covered in sawdust, sweat, and dirt. It was going to take more than a clean sweater to make him look presentable.

"I still have some of my dad's things in the room where you're staying. If you want, you can borrow something of his. You know, while we throw your clothes in the wash."

Alex wanted to set her at ease. "That's fine with me," he said. "Show me the way."

~*~

As soon as she heard the shower running, Bree rushed to the phone to call Franklin. Alex hadn't given her a reason to doubt his story, but she'd feel better getting a confirmation from her old family friend.

Franklin answered on the third ring, "McGregor's Tree Farm."

"Hey Grandpa, it's Bree."

"Bree, my darling, to what do I owe this pleasure?" Franklin said in his thick Scottish brogue. It warmed her heart just to hear his voice.

"I wanted to check on something. I met Alex Conner today. He said you recommended me to work on his horses."

"Alex Conner?" Franklin sounded as though the name were unfamiliar. It had her worried.

"Yeah, don't you know him? He says he has a horse ranch near you. They raise Clydesdales."

"Oh, yeah, Alex, now I remember. Clydesdales and Carriages. I talked to him about you, gave him one of your cards."

Bree breathed a sigh of relief. "That's what he said. I guess he sent me an email, but I must have missed it. When I didn't respond, he came to Over-Yonder to find me."

"The boy's got gumption, I'll give him that. So, what did you think? Are you going to take the job?"

"I'm thinking about it, but it sounds like his business may be a little tight on money. I can't afford a charity case."

"I wouldn't worry about money too much. Alex always pays his bills. I'd trust him on that. But his horses sure could use your special touch."

"I'm thinking of going up tomorrow to take a look. Thought I'd stop by and stay the night at your place if that's all right with you." She knew Franklin wouldn't refuse her, and would probably use any excuse he could to get her to visit.

"Sounds good to me. You know you're welcome here anytime. I'll have the guest room ready for you."

"Thanks, Grandpa, that'll be nice. I'll look forward to seeing you."

"Me too, Lassie. See you soon."

Bree hung up feeling a whole lot better about the man taking a shower in her bathroom. She wasn't used to being around men her own age, unless they were family, and though she tried to hide it, Alex made her nervous. Not in a bad way, but nervous nonetheless. Why was he so nice and friendly when they had only just met? And why did he ask so many questions, as if they were the best of friends? Most of all, why did he have to be so darn good-looking? This would be a whole lot easier if he were some old fart her grandpa's age, instead of the sexy, young, naked man she was imagining in her shower right about now.

Maybe she should talk to her aunt. Aunt Teressa would know what to do. She always knew how to handle people. It was part of her job as a relationship coach.

She'd been aware of Alex watching her training session with Edna and Otis, two of her more challenging clients, and it had made

25

her job even more difficult. She repeatedly tried to forget he was there, and repeatedly she had failed. And each time, Otis had used her distraction to go his own way.

Edna had really wanted a pet dog, and she really loved Otis, but she needed to learn how to work with him. When the older woman rescued the young pup from the animal shelter, she had told Bree, it was a case of love at first sight. Even with her strong initial attraction, Edna found she had very little patience for his antics, and Otis had too little discipline to stay focused on one task long enough to please her. That's where Bree came in.

Bree knew Otis meant well, he truly did, and he was truly grateful to Edna for rescuing him from the shelter, but to him, the world was just one big, happy playground to explore, and as much as he loved Edna, he loved exploring even more. She had no doubts they would soon form the bond they needed to settle into a successful working relationship. There was already a lot of love between the two; they just needed time.

She was still staring into the pantry, her eyes glazed over looking for something to fix for dinner, when Alex walked in, freshly showered, wearing a pair of her dad's blue jeans and an old denim work shirt. His feet were bare. Though the jeans were a little loose and hung low on his hips, for the most part, they were a pretty good fit and looked darn good on him. The sight of Alex in her father's clothing made her remember how much she missed her dad.

These old clothes came from a time in his life that was unknown to Bree, and like historical artifacts from a bygone era, she had kept them as a record of the life her father had once lived, before he met her mother. Seeing Alex in his things, she tried to imagine her dad being young, and strong, and living in this house. She could almost imagine him walking into this kitchen while his mom fixed the family dinner. Even though she never met her twenty-first-century grandparents, she could easily imagine them through the vivid stories Da used to tell. The heartwarming image brought a smile to her face.

Coming out of her reverie, she saw Alex glance at the box of pasta and unopened jar of spaghetti sauce sitting on the kitchen counter.

"So, what's for dinner?" he asked.

"I haven't quite figured that out. I'm thinking spaghetti. It's fairly quick and easy."

"Mind if I take a look?"

"Be my guest," she said, waving him forward as she stepped back to get out of his way.

Alex rummaged through the pantry and started pulling out jars and cans. When he had finished, he came away with a handful of spices and a surprising array of canned vegetables that would never have caught her eye, including beets and mushrooms. She wondered what he planned to do with them. He set them on the counter then proceeded to look through the refrigerator.

"Have you got any sausage or hamburger meat?" he asked over his shoulder. "Never mind, I found what I need." He pulled a few more items from the recesses of the big silver box. Thankfully, Jenny tended to keep the kitchen well stocked. Bree just never knew what to do with it all. Her creative talent was with animals, not cooking.

"I saw some red wine in the pantry. Do you mind if I open a bottle? I'd like to use some in the sauce."

"Go ahead. Use what you need." Bree took a seat on one of the bar stools fronting the raised serving counter. "Mind if I watch? It only seems fair," she said, referring to his blatant observation of her dog training session.

"It would be my pleasure," Alex grinned. "I rather like having an audience, and we can chat while I cook. Would you like me to

27

pour you a glass of wine?" he asked, holding up a bottle of Napa Valley merlot.

Bree was about to say no—she didn't like to drink and dreaded the idea of becoming tipsy or losing control—but changed her mind. Having a glass of wine in front of her would give her a distraction, and it seemed like the sociable thing to do. She would just be sure to sip it real slow.

"Okay, just a little. The wine glasses are in that left-hand cupboard." She pointed at the cabinets next to him.

Alex proceeded to make himself at home in her kitchen. He pulled out pots and pans, knives and cutting boards, serving spoons and forks, usually finding what he needed without asking for directions. Bree was happy to sit back, relax, and enjoy the show.

"How did you learn to cook?" she asked, attempting to make small talk.

"My mom was a wiz in the kitchen, and I often sat and watched her; kinda like you're doing right now. After I moved away from home, I wasn't about to go hungry, and I couldn't afford to eat out all the time, so that meant fending for myself. I really enjoy it. You know, many of the great chefs are men; just watch the Food Network. It's a great source of inspiration."

"No, thanks. I don't watch much TV, and I'd never watch the Food Network if it wasn't for Jenny. It's one of her favorite channels. I'd rather watch a movie. Mostly, I don't like commercials; too much of an interruption." *Too much crap we don't need.*

When she first arrived in California, in the twenty-first century, she had spent a good amount of time watching movies—anything and everything. They were her crash course on American history and culture. Her Aunt Teressa had warned her they weren't real and certainly not all true, but they'd been a great indoctrination into modern American pop culture.

She particularly liked Westerns with ruggedly handsome cowboys and strong, independent women. They reminded her of the people she had known back home and their simpler way of life. Folks trained for conflict while striving for peace, much like her own clan. And technology was not yet a part of daily life. One exception to the similarities was that the harsh, dry, western plains of America were quite different from the lush, craggy hillsides of Skye. Rain was a regular occurrence on Skye.

"If you'd like, we can watch a movie after dinner. It'll be a nice way to relax," Alex said. He hardly looked up from cutting fresh vegetables for a salad.

"Sure, if we have enough time. What kind of movies do you like?"

"Just about anything, except those old black-and-white movies. It's such ancient history."

Bree smiled, thinking how ancient her own history was.

Alex continued, "I kinda go for the offbeat. One of my favorites is *Monty Python and the Holy Grail*."

"You've got to be kidding. That's one of my favorites. I love that movie. Did you know it was filmed at Castle Doune in Scotland?" Bree started quoting from the film. "'It was vicious rabbit, I tell you.'"

"'The Black Knight always triumphs. Come back, you pansies. I'll bite your legs off,'" Alex quoted back.

His imitation of a British accent cracked her up.

They exchanged a half-dozen more quotes before Bree held up her hands in surrender. "Okay, it's a deal. We'll have to watch it together. By the way, my housemates, Jenny and Jack, should be home soon. They'll probably join us for dinner. It looks like you're making more than enough."

"Thanks for telling me."

"I never worry about cooking for them. Jenny teaches culinary classes over at Diablo Valley College and usually brings home the sample dishes she makes for the class. What you're making looks pretty darn good. They just may want to join us."

Alex took her jar of spaghetti sauce and turned it into gourmet cuisine, adding sausages, mushrooms, spices, and a few other items she may have missed along the way. He made a fresh garden salad and added the canned beets on top to give it a flash of color. Now he was toasting garlic bread in the oven. The meal looked and smelled divine.

The pasta was boiling and the spaghetti sauce was still simmering when the phone rang. It was Jenny calling.

"Hey, Bree. I wanted to let you know Jack and I won't be home for dinner. We're meeting some friends after work, so you're on your own. Are you okay with that?" Jenny asked.

Bree glanced at Alex then turned away to hide her expression. She smiled. "Yeah, I'm okay. I've got it covered."

"I expect we'll be home by nine, maybe ten at the latest. Remember to leave the lights on," Jenny said, referring to the outside lights lining the long, dark driveway.

"Sure. No problem." Bree paused a moment, considering what to say. "Um, just so you know, we have a visitor. Franklin sent him; they're old friends. He needs help with some horses. I put him in the guest bedroom, the one we use for storage. It's just for one night." She tried to sound nonchalant. She also hoped Jenny wouldn't ask too many questions, not with Alex standing so close. Maybe it was just her imagination, but she was sure she could feel his eyes on the back of her head.

"Are you okay? Should we come home?" Jenny sounded concerned. Bree understood. She was twenty-two years old and had lived with Jack and Jenny for nearly four years, but this was the first time she had ever allowed a man, much less a near stranger, to spend the night at the ranch.

"No, really, I'm okay. Right now he's cooking dinner." Bree felt better when she heard Jenny's lighthearted chuckle.

"That's my girl. Put the old guy right to work. Don't worry, we won't be late."

Bree didn't correct Jenny's assumption that Franklin's friend was an older man. "I'm fine, Jenny, really. I'll see you when you get here."

Bree hung up the phone and turned back to face Alex. He was busy draining the pasta.

"I guess you heard. That was my housemate, Jenny. It'll just be the two of us for dinner." She surveyed the amount of food he had prepared. "Looks like there'll be leftovers."

Alex maintained a happy grin. "That's the good thing about spaghetti; it always tastes better the next day."

~*~

They sat on the sofa together to watch the movie. Close, but not too close. Bree sat cross-legged while Alex stretched out, propping his bare feet on the coffee table. Their shared enthusiasm for the off-beat humor of the British film created an easy bond between them as they laughed together in all the right places. The movie was nearly ended when Bree heard Jack's pickup pull into the driveway. She reached for the remote control and hit the pause button.

"Ready to meet my housemates?" Bree asked.

"Do I have a choice?" Alex asked, looking slightly pensive.

"Not unless you want to run and hide."

"'Run away, run away,'" Alex laughed, mocking a line from the movie.

"Too late for that." Bree turned to look over her shoulder as she heard the back door open. A draft of cold night air preceded Jack and

31

Jenny as they made their way into the warmth of the kitchen. Bree stood to greet her housemates and introduce them to Alex.

"Jack, Jenny, this is Alex Connor. He's a friend of Franklin's."

Alex also stood and reached out to shake their hands. "I've been looking for an animal trainer. I had to come in person, since she doesn't answer her emails."

Bree grinned and shrugged, not bothering to deny his statement.

"Yep, that's our Bree," Jenny agreed. "Pleasure to meet you."

"How do you know Frank?" Jack asked.

"My family has a horse ranch not far from his place," Alex replied.

"Long way to come to find a horse trainer, don't you think?" Jack looked as skeptical as he sounded. Bree wondered if her distant cousin was going to put on his dad hat. As Uncle Robert's first cousin, Jack's protective streak ran a mile wide where she was concerned.

"McGregor said she's the best, and who am I to argue?" Alex maintained his easy smile. It didn't look as though he were easily intimidated. Bree liked that.

"Are you expecting to stay here long?" Jack asked, looking less than friendly.

"Only until tomorrow . . . Then I'll head back to Placerville. Bree has agreed to take a look at my horses," Alex answered, looking confident. Before Jack could fire off another question, he added, "Bree tells me you both work at the local college."

"Yeah, I'm the maintenance manager for Diablo Valley College, and Jenny teaches cooking," Jack said, and then added, "I knew Bree's dad before he went to Scotland, and her uncle is my cousin."

Bree figured Jack's latter comment was his way of declaring his role as protector of her. She looked at Jenny, hoping her best friend would help her out. It looked as though the men were about to engage in a sparring match, and the last thing she wanted was for Jack to start interrogating Alex as if he were a boy who had come to pick her up for their first date.

Jack looked as though he was about to say something else when his wife spoke up. "I'm sorry we can't stay and chat. I have an early morning pastry class." Jenny reached for Jack's hand, giving it a tug, followed up with a rather pointed look.

Apparently, her cousin got the message. Reluctantly, he allowed Jenny to pull him down the hall toward their bedroom. Being an older married couple, they'd been granted the master suite, an arrangement dating back to when her father lived in the house, before he left for Scotland.

As they walked away, Bree heard Jack grumble. "I was just asking . . ."

"She can do as she wants. This is her house." Although Jenny tried to shush her husband, Bree could still hear their whispered comments, and she figured Alex could, too.

Bree watched Jenny maneuver Jack down the hall and through their bedroom door, taking one final look down the hallway to give her the thumbs up. She didn't have to ask to know Alex had seen everything.

"Well, that was awkward," Bree acknowledged.

"They mean well. I'm sure he's just looking out for you."

"Yeah. The Scottish tend to be a wee bit protective of their kin. No offense was intended, I'm sure."

"None was taken." They stood a moment longer in awkward silence before Alex asked, "Do you want to finish watching the movie?"

"Not really. It was almost over, anyway. Maybe we ought to call it a night. I've got to get up early in the morning." She picked up the remote control and clicked off the TV.

"How early?" Alex looked a little disappointed.

"With the sun. It's an old habit. There's too much to do around here to waste daylight."

"Yeah, I understand," Alex nodded.

They turned and headed down the hall. The first door on the right was the guest room where Alex was staying. "Do you have everything you need?" Bree asked.

"Yeah, I think I'm good for now."

His hand was on the knob, but he wasn't moving. Bree had the strongest feeling he wanted to kiss her. If she let him, she figured he probably would; but they weren't on a date, and becoming personal wasn't a good idea. Not if they were going to be working together. She needed to keep things strictly business and professional as much as possible. Letting him fix dinner and watching a movie together already felt more casual than she thought was appropriate.

She bid him good-night and walked to her room at the end of the hall. It took everything she had not to look back to see if he was watching.

Bree hadn't been in her room more than five minutes when she heard a light tapping, followed by Jenny slipping quickly through the door.

"That was a bit of a surprise. From the way you talked, I was expecting some old geezer," Jenny said.

"Funny, he said the same thing about me, but I never said he was old."

"Are you sure?" Jenny's eyebrows rose to new heights on her forehead.

"I said he's an old friend of Franklin's, not that he was old. I'm sure there's a difference."

"You knew exactly what you were doing, little miss innocent. Why didn't you tell me he's young and good looking?"

"He was standing right there when you called. What was I supposed to do?" Bree lowered her voice. "So you think he's good looking?"

"I'm married, not blind. What's his story?"

Bree grabbed Jenny's hands and pulled her to sit on the bed. It was time for some girl talk. Jenny was twelve years her senior and married, but she was also Bree's best friend.

"Alex has a team of Clydesdales he wants me to take a look at. A couple of them are giving him trouble, and he's hoping I can help. Clydesdales! Can you believe it, Jenny? I'm so excited."

"About him or the horses?"

Bree gave her a swat. "The horses, of course. They're an old Scottish breed, like war horses."

"I don't think anyone uses war horses anymore. Do you think they'll speak with a Scottish brogue like you and Cousin Robert?" Jenny gave her a slight poke in her ribs.

"Are you teasing me?"

"Sure I am. But what about you and Alex?" Jenny's expression turned serious.

"What do you mean?"

"He comes over here from Placerville, fixes you dinner, you watch a movie together, and he's staying the night. Looks to me like a bit more than strictly a business relationship."

Bree shook her head. "It's not like that. I get the impression his company isn't doing very well. I kinda felt sorry for him."

"That's just like you to take in any stray that comes along."

"He's not a stray. Alex has a home and a ranch. We're going there tomorrow after I finish with my clients. That reminds me, can you ask Jack to tend to the horses on Friday? I'll just be gone for one day."

"He'll do whatever you need. But back up for a second. Where do you think you're going?"

"Alex's horses are in Placerville. I'm going to ride there on Dad's bike. I can't leave until the afternoon, and I don't want to make the return trip on the same day. Don't worry; I'm going to spend the night with Franklin. I already called him, and he gave me the all clear on Alex. Besides, I haven't seen him in months. We're due for a visit." Bree scooted closer to her cousin. "Jenny, you should've seen. Alex has a black Ducati, a Multistrada. When he arrived, he looked like a hot warrior dude, all dressed in black."

Jenny chuckled and shook her head. "Yeah, right. And this is all strictly business."

CHAPTER 4

Alex awoke to a quiet house surrounded by the mellow sounds of morning, complete with chirping birds and curtains rustling at the slightly open window. As his eyes slowly adjusted to the light, he recalled exactly where he was and how he had gotten here. He smiled, rather pleased with his situation.

The night before, when they had said good-night, he had wanted to kiss Bree, and it almost looked as if she was going to let him, but then she had simply walked away. Actually, he had wanted to pull her into his bedroom and make love to her, but that wasn't going to happen, not yet, and especially not with Jack around, nor should it. Their relationship needed to be on the up-and-up, strictly business, at least for now. He didn't want to muck things up before she agreed to help mend his horses. After that, who knew? Maybe there'd be room for some extracurricular activity.

With that tantalizing thought, he got up and got dressed, putting on the freshly washed blue jeans and tee shirt he'd worn the day before. After grabbing a quick cup of orange juice from the refrigerator, he headed out to the stables in search of Bree. Just as he expected, she was already busy tending to her horses.

He'd only taken a few steps past the door when she turned to face him.

"Stay back," she ordered.

"Excuse me?"

"Stay where you are. Don't come any closer." She held a hand out to halt him with a look that indicated she meant business.

"Well, good morning to you, too. What did I do to deserve this?" he asked, bewildered by her sudden change of temperament.

"It's the horse. Sunnyside's not used to strangers. I don't want you to scare him." A reassuring softness returned to her voice. He felt his shoulders relax.

"I'm not going to scare your horse."

"You don't know Sunnyside, and he doesn't know you."

"I'll tell you what. How about if we just take it slow? Let him know I'm not a bad guy. If it looks like he's getting skittish, I'll back off."

Bree didn't answer him. Instead, she turned toward her horse. "How about it, Sunnyside? Would you like to meet Alex?" She stood facing the horse, petting the long white strip running down his broad nose. "He won't hurt you. You're safe here."

The horse fixed his big brown eyes on him, watching his every move. Alex felt slightly ridiculous, but flashed the horse a broad smile and held his hands out in front of him.

Bree turned back to him. "It's okay. You can approach."

Moving slowly, Alex spread his arms wide, showing his hands, palms out. "There now, boy. I mean you no harm," he spoke in soothing tones, taking one slow step forward. "You're a beauty. No wonder she fancies you." Alex took another measured step forward.

From the corner of his eye, he saw Bree's lips curve into a half smile. He was making progress.

Sunnyside didn't move, and yet Alex sensed the positive change. Still wary, the animal relaxed by small degrees as slowly, step-by-step, Alex advanced. When he was about halfway to the horse's stall, Sunnyside pulled back and snorted, his muscles flexed, ready to bolt if need be.

Alex stopped in place, standing his ground. "Need a minute, boy?" He kept his voice gentle as he focused on Sunnyside, not breaking their connection. "Take all the time you need."

The steed blinked and bobbed his head, giving Alex a signal it was all right to proceed.

Again, Alex stepped forward, closing the gap between them. Still showing his hands, palms out, he reached out to let the animal smell him before he stroked Sunnyside's neck and shoulders, feeling the powerful muscles taut beneath the bay's sleek and glossy coat.

"You take good care of him. He's a real beauty."

Bree beamed with the accolade even as she tried to appear modest. "It's my job. It's what I do." Then she leaned forward and whispered in Alex's ear. "Sunnyside's last owner beat him."

Alex registered the effect of her warm breath against his neck. *Nice.* He leaned over and placed a hand on her back, his touch light but sure, and whispered into her ear. "What happened?" Beneath his touch, he felt her quiver.

"See the scars on his neck, shoulders, and back?"

Alex nodded, taking note of the fading jagged lines marring Sunnyside's hide.

"They restrained him with barbed wire."

Stunned, Alex pulled back. "You're kidding."

She curtly shook her head, "No."

Seeing tears pool in her eyes, he reacted on pure instinct and pulled her into his arms. "He's safe now."

For one, brief, glorious moment, she seemed to welcomed his embrace. He felt her lush curves press enticingly against his body as he breathed in the fresh herbal scent of her shampoo. Heaven above, she felt good.

Then all too quickly, she stiffened and pulled back. Alex sensed her discomfort and dropped his arms to his side.

"What kind of heartless fool would do something like that?" he asked, taking a half step back to give her some space.

"The heartless jackass kind." Bree turned her back to him and began stroking Sunnyside's hide, restoring her well-established self-control.

Dang. She was darn good at maintaining her boundaries.

"Can he take a rider?" Alex asked. He wondered how much damage had been inflicted on the horse.

"He couldn't when he first arrived, but he can now. I'm the only who rides him. It's part of his daily exercise routine. We always take the same route up to the hills and back again as part of his treatment. The routine has helped him regain his confidence."

Pride. He heard it in her voice and saw it in her eyes. She took great pride in her accomplishment. From what he could see, it was justified.

"How about if I join you? Think he's ready for some company?" Alex asked.

Bree hesitated.

Alex addressed the horse. "What do you say, ole boy? Mind if I come along?"

Bree focused on the horse for a moment longer then flashed him a brilliant smile. "I think it's a real good idea."

~*~

Bree was impressed. Alex had done something no one but she had been able to do up to now. He had approached Sunnyside without the horse attempting to flee his stall. Even Jack maintained a respectable distance around the skittish gelding.

Alex had turned on some kind of innate charm, and Sunnyside had responded, accepting him as a friendly presence. She had sensed Sunnyside relax, even gain confidence as Alex approached. Rather like the instinctive master and beast bonding she had often observed when Scottish warriors prepared for battle with their most trusted war horse, she recognized she was witnessing a connection based on mutual respect and need between man and animal that reached back through time. She wondered if Alex was aware of his effect on Sunnyside, or if his affinity to the animal just came naturally. From what she had seen, warrior instincts had been bred out of most twenty-first century males.

She directed Alex to saddle Moonbeam, one of her other horses, while she finished working on Sunnyside. From the way the big fella pranced around, it was obvious he was excited about Alex's presence.

"There are about a half dozen horse paths running across the ranch, but we always take the same one. It leads to the top of the ridge. Are you okay with that?" Bree asked.

"Lead the way, and I'll follow," Alex said.

They mounted and rode across the lower pasture until they reached the switchback path hugging the foothills behind Over-Yonder Ranch. Under Bree's guidance, Sunnyside maintained a steady pace up the steep slope, not stopping until they reached the summit of the ridge. The view from the top was stunning. Looking east, toward the rising sun, she could see the whole of Diablo Valley spread out before them. This was her favorite spot.

"Nice view," Alex said as he drew up alongside her. "Not quite as grand as some I've seen, but it'll do."

Bree cast a sideways glance at Alex, choosing to dismiss his comment. Maybe Diablo Valley couldn't compare to the mountainous views around Placerville, but to her, this was a little slice of heaven. This was her home.

"Over-Yonder has its own brand of beauty," she said, defending her territory. "It's a rough and rugged ranch, living right next door to prim and proper suburbia. It makes for interesting neighbors."

"Which one are you?" Alex asked, leaning forward in his saddle.

Not sure she understood his question, Bree stared at him blankly.

"Rough and rugged, or prim and proper?"

"I don't think anyone would describe me as prim and proper," she said, laughing. "I guess that leaves rough and rugged."

Alex's smile took on a playful glint. "Umm, I'm not so sure. Maybe you're not prim, but you're certainly proper."

"What makes you say that?" His quick assessment surprised her.

"I don't know, a feeling, I guess. But hey, what do I know? I just met you. So yesterday, when I asked you about your qualifications, why didn't you tell me about Sunnyside?"

"I'm still working with him, and I didn't want to put him on display. Laddy's used to performing around clients."

He raised an inquisitive brow, an apparent habit of his. "You seem pretty modest for a professional animal trainer."

"I'd rather let the results speak for themselves." She felt a blush heating her cheeks and hoped he didn't notice.

"So tell me; how do you know McGregor?" he asked.

"He's an old family friend of my Aunt Teressa's. She's known him her whole life. We visit him at least three or four times a year, and we always go see him around the holidays."

"McGregor's a great old guy. He's got some strange ideas sometimes, but I've never known him to be wrong yet."

"I met him soon after I moved here from Skye. He's always been like a grandfather to me; pretty much the only one I've ever known."

She'd never had a chance to know any of her own grandparents. Her father's parents had died shortly before his fateful trip to Scotland, and her mother's parents had both passed long before she was born.

"When did you leave Skye?" Alex asked.

"When I was eighteen. After my parents died, I came here to live with my Aunt Teressa and Uncle Robert. I didn't have any other family left on the island." A thread of melancholy wove its way through Bree's heart. She had lost so much in her young life, first her mother and William in the raid by the MacDonalds, and then her father after following him to the future. It didn't seem fair.

Then again, no one ever said life was fair.

"I'm sorry for your loss. I know it's hard. My mother passed away a few years ago. Now it's just me and my dad, and he's not doing too well."

"No brothers or sisters?"

"One sister, but I'm my dad's only son. The last great hope of the—um—of my father rests solely upon my shoulders."

Bree surveyed his broad muscular shoulders straining against the sleeves of the denim work shirt. They looked like a sturdy place to rest.

~~~

Alex breathed a sigh of relief. That was close. Nearly forgetting McGregor's warning, he had almost said "the MacDonalds" but

43

thankfully, had caught his flub at the last moment. Though he was curious to know what she had against the MacDonald name, his curiosity would have to wait. He was too close to getting her to look at his horses to blow it now.

"By the way, I already called Franklin and told him I'll be coming over to spend the night. He's looking forward to my visit," Bree said.

"I'm sure he is. He's always telling me you don't visit often enough."

"Yeah, and I always tell him the road runs both ways. It's not easy to get him off his farm."

"Yeah, he's pretty attached to his little Christmas tree farm. So where to now?" Alex asked, pointing at the fork in the path.

"We head on back. I've got chores to do before my next client arrives." Bree started to guide Sunnyside toward the downward sloping path.

"Really? I was hoping to have a better look around." Alex felt a rascally urge to test her willpower, to see how far he could push her outside her comfort zone. He had a feeling her little morning routine with Sunnyside was as much for her benefit as it was for the horse. "Where does that road lead?"

Bree halted Sunnyside. "I thought you were going to follow my lead?" she argued.

"I did, but now I'd like to have a look around." He nudged his horse toward the higher path.

She held her ground, looking unsure about what to do next.

"You don't mind, do you?" he asked, halting his horse.

"It's just that I don't want you getting lost. I don't have time to go looking for you."

Alex had to restrain himself from chuckling. It would be mighty hard to get lost. His sense of direction wasn't that bad. After all, he knew east from west and north from south. He'd have to be pretty senseless not to know how to follow a horse trail back to her ranch.

"I guess I'm willing to take my chances," he said, spurring his mount a few steps forward. Turning back, he flashed her a playful grin "Sure you don't want to join me?"

"Oh heck, I better come with you." Bree pulled on the reins, directing Sunnyside up to the higher path. "Maybe it won't hurt for Sunnyside to have a break in his routine, just this once."

Alex turned away to hide his happy grin, pleased he had charmed her into accompanying him. "Yeah, I'm sure you're right," he said.

~*~

Bree spurred Sunnyside into an all-out gallop as they raced back to the stables. Thankfully, the horse loved it. She would too, if she wasn't in such a hurry to get back and get ready for her next appointment. As a rule, she hated to keep anyone waiting, but she especially didn't want to upset Sandra, her highest paying client. And she sure as heck didn't want to risk losing the income Sandra provided because some smooth-talking mountain man had kept her out on the trail for too long. *Darn that Alex*. He had caused her to lose all track of time.

When she pulled up to the paddock, Alex and Moonbeam were right behind. Jumping from her horse, she tossed him the reins.

"Here. Make sure you cool him down. Walk him, then brush him. I have to go get ready."

Alex was grinning from ear to ear, looking far too pleased. "Go ahead. I know how to tend horses."

"Just be glad Sandra's not here yet."

"You'll be fine. There's plenty of time."

Bree glanced at her watch. "Five minutes is not plenty of time." She raced toward the house. Luckily, there wasn't any sign of

Sandra's big black SUV coming down the long back road that led to the ranch, at least not yet.

She rushed to the bathroom to wash her face and hands, and then ran a brush through her hair, trying to make herself look presentable. Back in her room, she glanced again at her watch. Eleven o'clock. There wasn't enough time to change into clean clothes. Her jeans and plaid flannel shirt would have to do.

A minute later, she heard Sandra's SUV pull into the graveled drive next to the house. Heading for the back door, she met Sandra just as the stylish woman was climbing out of her car. Bree breathed a sigh of relief.

"Sandra, so good to see you," Bree greeted her client. "You're right on time."

"As always." Wearing designer shredded jeans with high-heeled boots and a flashy jacket, Sandra lifted the back hatch of the big SUV and out jumped two standard poodles, one black and one white. Bree was working with Sandra to prepare them for their next big show. They had already placed well in a local competition, and Sandra had high hopes they were her ticket to the Westminster Kennel Club.

Bree spent the next ninety minutes putting Maxwell and Montague through their paces with Sandra, listening to her client's concerns about their progress the whole time. Silently, she tapped into the dogs' thoughts and emotions, keeping track of their moods throughout the session. Verbally, as well as telepathically, she communicated reassurance along with her instructions to the proud dogs. As show dogs, they sometimes had a tendency to get a little too sure of themselves, and she repeatedly needed to remind them they had a job to do that went above and beyond looking good while they strutted around the course set up on the back lawn.

Midway through the session, Bree took a short break to rush over to the stables and check on her horses. She hadn't been able to watch Alex while he was out in the paddock cooling down Sunnyside and Moonbeam—she'd been too focused on the dogs—but now they were done with their cool down, and she wanted to make sure Sunnyside was all right. Coming to a halt at the stable doors, Bree watched as Alex checked out each horse, running his strong, callused hands over their muscles and down their legs, checking their joints, hooves and shoes. While silently observing him, she wondered if he were just being thorough or if he were checking her work. Either way, it was obvious he knew what he was doing.

When Bree turned away to return to the training session, Sandra was standing only a few feet behind her. "Where ever did you get him?" she asked, licking her lips. Her client seemed particularly interested in the way Alex was checking the horses' legs and running his hands over their bodies. In Bree's mind, the flashy dog owner was showing way too much interest in her temporary helper.

"He's only here for the day. He'll be heading back to Placerville by the end of the day." *Where he belongs*. Sandra was a dog breeder. What the hell did she need with a horse rancher?

Confident her horses were being well cared for, Bree turned her focus back to Sandra's dogs, taking their owner along with her. "Your dogs, Sandra, we need to focus on your dogs. Remember?"

"Oh, right, my dogs," Sandra agreed, finally pulling her eyes off Alex.

As soon as their session was over and they were headed down the driveway, Bree returned to the stables to check on Alex and was surprised by what she found. Alex had taken it upon himself to clean out the stables, mucking out a load of dirty straw and manure. Now he was laying down fresh hay in the feed troughs.

Alex's back was toward her, and he was speaking to Sunnyside as he pitched hay into his trough. He was telling the horse a story about his Clydesdales, saying he hoped Bree could help them as much as she'd been able to help him. The gelding was responding with rapt attention. Bree stopped to listen.

"Yep, if she can get my Clydes back in the harness, I'll be a happy man. They're too young and strong not to be working. I can't send them out to pasture. You understand, don't you, Sunnyside?"

Sunnyside snorted and stomped a hoof.

"Yeah, I knew you would. You've got a lot of spirit left in you. It'll take more than one bad trip to knock you down."

Bree came up behind Alex. "Can you hear him?" she asked.

Alex jumped, startled by her presence. Apparently, he hadn't heard her come in.

"Hear who?" Alex asked, looking around. It was obvious he had no idea what she meant.

"I heard you talking to Sunnyside."

"Oh, that. I always talk to my horses. I figure it helps set them at ease, and they seem to respond, even if they don't know what I'm saying."

Bree stepped forward, hearing Sunnyside's thoughts. "But they do know. Maybe not precisely, but in general, they understand your meaning. He knows you're someone kind, someone who can be trusted."

"I've always hoped so, but there's no way to be sure."

"Of course, there is, just listen."

"Listen to what?" From the look on his face, she could tell he was totally perplexed.

"The animals. They communicate with their thoughts and feelings, just like we do, even when we don't say anything. Earlier this morning, when you came into the stables, you knew Sunnyside was nervous. You sensed he needed reassuring as you approached, and you responded in kind, giving him the time he needed to be sure you meant him no harm."

"Yeah, I guess I did. But I've always had a way with horses, and animals in general."

"Alex, you have a gift. I don't know why you can't heal your horses yourself."

"No, it's nothing like that," he said, waving her off. "Anyone can do what I do. I need someone who's specially trained to help me with my Clydesdales."

"You're wrong. I've been around animals all my life. Few have your gift."

He turned to pick up the handles on the wheel barrel he had used to haul the hay. As he started walking toward the back of the building, he spoke over his shoulder. "You looked pretty comfortable with Miss Poodle dog and friends. They're show dogs, right?"

Apparently, Alex was uncomfortable with where the conversation was going and had decided to change subjects on her.

Bree picked up the pitchfork Alex left leaning against the wall and fell in step beside him. "Aye. They've already won some local competitions and placed well in a regional. Sandra's hoping to move their ranking high enough to get them into Westminster."

"That's gotta be good for you, right? The publicity will be good for your business."

"I hope so. Sandra said she already referred me to the owner of a border collie. It may have been just talk, but she said he recently lost his handler and was looking for another. I don't mind working with the dogs; they're great animals, so much love, but I prefer to work with horses. They're such big, gentle beasts with strong hearts and souls."

49

"Yeah, and they need less attention than most dogs." Alex tipped the wheel barrel up and leaned it against the wall under the hay loft where she usually kept it.

"You should have heard those two poodles bragging about how good they look," she said, laughing. They're as bad as their owner."

Alex lifted that inquisitive brow of his. "*Heard* them bragging?" he questioned.

Bree reined in her laughter. "You know, their body language and such. I listen to their body language." She pointed to her eyes.

She suddenly became too self-conscious to admit the extent of her gift, that she could actually sense the thoughts and feelings of her animals. Since he'd been so quick to deny his gift, she felt compelled to hide hers. In her experience, most people wouldn't accept something they couldn't understand. She'd been belittled before, called a charlatan and a kook, and she didn't want to risk hearing that from Alex. It looked as though he were one of those who didn't easily accept such gifts of nature, and she didn't want to expose herself to his ridicule.

"I'd rather work with horses," Bree said, redirecting the conversation. "But right now, they cost me more than they earn, so I need the dog training jobs to supplement my income."

"How do you manage to keep this place running?" Alex asked, turning serious. "It's gotta take more than a few doggy classes to pay for all this."

"My grandparents bought this farm several years ago. There's no longer a mortgage, just upkeep and taxes." She had learned a lot about taxes in the last four years. Apparently, like death, they were unavoidable. "Jack and Jenny pay rent and help out where they can. So do my uncles and Aunt Teressa. They set up a trust fund to cover the basic expenses, but there's always something more that needs to get done—like the deck you worked on yesterday." She flashed him a bright smile. "Thanks for your help."

"Ah, it was nothing. It was worth it to get to watch you in action." He was smiling again. Bree liked that.

"No, it was a lot, what you did, helping out a stranger like that. I really do appreciate it. And you're a hard worker. I'll give you a reference anytime, if you ever need it."

Now he was laughing. "Yeah? My dad would love to hear that. He thinks I'm a ne'er-do-well, his way of calling me a skater."

"You mean a lazy man, right?"

"Right."

"But that's not true. You've done more than I could ask, fixing the deck, making dinner, tending to Sunnyside and Moonbeam. I don't see you shirking your duties."

"Make sure you mention all that to my dad the next time you see him."

"I've never met your dad. Why would he care what I think?"

Alex shrugged, flashing a devilish smile. "It never hurts to get praise from a pretty young woman."

Bree swatted his arm. He was teasing her.

"Come on, I'm done for the day," Bree said. She turned and started to walk toward the house. "How about I fix us some lunch before we head out? I'd like to get started before it gets too late. I don't want to get caught in commuter traffic."

Alex fell into step beside her. "Let me fix lunch while you go get ready. I can heat up the spaghetti or make us some sandwiches. Which do you prefer?"

"Your spaghetti was darn good. I wouldn't mind more of that."

"Then spaghetti it is," he said.

Dang, she thought, *it sure is nice to have a man around the house.*

CHAPTER 5

Anxious as he was to hit the road, Alex had to sit and wait while Bree kept finding things she needed to take care of before she would leave. After lunch, she checked again to make sure all her animals were fed and watered before she started packing for her short overnight trip. Then she went from room to room to be sure she had everything she needed. If it were up to Alex, he would have packed his tooth brush and a change of clothes and called it done.

Alex also discovered that although Bree was a competent rider, she was also cautious and slow, consistently sticking close to the speed limit. It took them almost two and a half hours to make a drive he usually made in less than two. By the time they arrived at Frank's place, Alex was worn out.

He had sensed her excitement building as they neared MacGregor's. When they hit the last few miles of country road leading to his farm, she finally reached her comfort zone and let the bike fly, taking it up to eighty miles an hour.

Frank must have heard them coming. As soon as they pulled into his drive, he was out standing on his porch, waiting for them. Bree parked her bike, yanked off her helmet, and rushed to greet him. The barrel-chested old man swept her up into a generous bear hug, lifting her off the ground. It hit Alex square in the chest to see her so happy.

"Grandpa," she squealed with delight.

"Hey, how's my old Scottish lass? Look at you, riding that bike like a pro."

Frank's use of "my old Scottish lass" struck Alex as an odd term of endearment for one so young, especially since he thought of Frank as an old Scottish geezer. Although the man looked good for his age, McGregor had to be at least sixty, maybe closer to seventy years old. He wondered if Bree and her grandfather shared some kind of inside joke.

Looking up from Bree, Frank cast a questioning eye at Alex. "I take it your trip went well."

"Safe and sound," Alex replied.

"We didn't have any problems. Alex is a very safe rider," Bree assured him.

Alex nearly laughed out loud. He was sure her opinion would be different if she saw him riding alone, but he hadn't left her side during the entire ride and had let her set the pace.

"'Tis good you brought her safe to my door. If not, I would have hunted you down and skinned you like a rabbit."

"It's good to see you, too, McGregor." Alex grinned, accepting Frank's good natured, but wholly truthful barb.

"Let's not be standing out here all night. Come on in. I've got the kettle on for tea."

Alex had never known a time when Frank didn't have the kettle on for tea. However, the old Scot didn't serve gentile, front parlor tea. No, McGregor brewed it strong and drank it like coffee from a large commuter cup to keep it hot.

"Thanks, but I can't stay. I've got to go check on Dad. He's expecting me. I called him from the road at our last rest stop."

"That's a good son, to be so concerned," Frank nodded with approval. "How about you, Breanna?"

"Sure. Make mine English breakfast tea—and not so strong," she said.

"Like I don't know." Frank gave her another squeeze before he went into the house.

Bree, still standing on the porch, turned to Alex. "What about your horses? When will I see them?"

"It's getting late. You and Frank will want to visit. I'd rather we get started first thing in the morning, right after breakfast. I'll come by and get you, and we can ride over to the pasture together."

Bree nodded. "Okay. I'll be waiting."

As much as he wanted to linger, he knew his father was expecting him. His overnight stay at Bree's hadn't been planned, and he needed to get home to check on his dad. She looked so good standing there, all flushed and excited from their long ride. It hit him hard, how much he wished he could grab her and kiss her goodbye, but their relationship needed to be strictly business. At least for now, he needed to respect her boundaries.

He was just about to put his helmet back on when Bree surprised him. She ran off the porch steps and rushed over to give him a hug. Alex didn't know if it was a reaction from her excitement over arriving safe at McGregor's, or if she was showing him honest affection, but he wasn't about to ask questions; he would take what he could get.

She surprised him even more by delivering a full body hug, crushing her curvaceous form against his all too welcoming frame.

Dang, she felt good. Following her lead, he held her close, soaking up the pleasure of her embrace.

Holding her closed like this triggered an intense need in him. He longed to run his hands through her long, silky hair and let the copper-red tresses flow through his fingers. His hands ached to roam over her body, explore her feminine curves, discover her pleasures, and unleash her passions. His need to kiss her and claim her as his own nearly overwhelmed him.

But he resisted.

This type of desire was a dangerous thing. It threatened to take control. And Alex couldn't allow that to happen. If he pushed too hard, too fast, he'd risk losing everything he was working so hard to achieve. He'd risk losing her respect and his chance to save his family business from ruin. So he reined in his craving and harnessed his control.

"Thank you," she whispered into his ear.

"For what?" he asked, still holding her.

Bree pulled back far enough to see his face. "For coming to find me. For bringing me here. For everything."

"The pleasure was all mine." Alex couldn't contain the silly smile splashed wide across his face. He didn't even try.

She took a step back, breaking their connection. As much as he wanted to hang on, he let her go.

"I've a bit of a secret to confess," she said.

Unexpectedly, his abs tightened around his stomach, as if bracing for a punch, while he waited in silence for her to continue.

"Before today, I've never ridden more than thirty miles from the ranch."

He let out his breath. "You're kidding! Why didn't you tell me?"

"I didn't want you to try to talk me out of riding on my own. It was far too grand." She looked so happy, and yet, her smile was just shy of being mischievous.

"Why, you little sneak." He lowered his voice, glancing at the front door of the house. "Does McGregor know?"

Bree shook her head. "I don't think so."

"Well, I sure as hell don't want to be around here when he finds out."

She threw her head back and laughed. The sound was glorious, like tinkling confetti falling from the tall pine trees surrounding them. "Franklin will be okay. He trusts me."

"It's not you I'm worried about." He stood there for a moment longer before reaching for his helmet. "I'd best be going."

"I'm looking forward to seeing your horses," she said, sticking her hands in her back pockets.

"I'll be here right after breakfast."

Feeling more alive than he had in months, he rode the rest of the way home in record time. It wasn't because he was anxious to see his dad. Rather, after his long, slow ride with Bree, and after their stirring embrace, he needed to push his limits. He knew every curve of the narrow back mountain road and carved a fast track through the trail. The thrill of the short, hair-raising ride was undeniable.

Almost as soon as he walked in the front door of his father's ranch house, his bubble deflated. His dad had barely greeted him when he started in with the questions.

"So how did it go? Were you able to convince that horse trainer to take the job? How much is this going to cost me?"

That was just like his dad. Always thinking about the money. "We haven't talked price yet. First, she wants to see the horses." Alex shrugged out of his riding jacket and hung it over the back of the brown leather sofa dominating the living room before taking a seat.

Since his mother's passing, the house had taken on more and more of his dad's personality, leaving behind very little of his mother's soft touch. It seemed as though his dad had made a point of removing every frill or feminine memento of his deceased wife. Not because his dad hadn't loved her. Quite the contrary, Alex figured his dad couldn't stand the reminders that she was no longer there.

As Alex took in the predominantly dull brown décor and less than sparkling-clean housekeeping, he realized how much he missed his mother.

"*See* the horses? Then what? Is she going to charge based on their size?" his dad asked.

"She wants to evaluate them to see how much work they need before she agrees to take the job."

"Ha! She's looking for an excuse to negotiate a higher price. I knew I should have handled this myself." His father kicked down the footrest of his old brown recliner and sat forward.

Damn. The man knew how to push all his buttons, but Alex was determined he wouldn't let his dad get to him. Not this time. This time, he would prove he could handle the situation. He didn't want his dad, Angus MacDonald, to go anywhere near Breanna Ellers; at least not before she helped him with the Clydesdales.

"It's not like that. She wants to be sure she can really help them before she commits to taking the job. I think it makes good sense."

"Aye, so she can jack up the price." Angus jerked his thumb up in the air, as if to prove his point.

"Look, Dad, I've got it covered. I know how much we can spend." *And how much we can't.*

Restless, Alex stood and headed for the kitchen to examine the contents of the fridge. After his long ride, he needed a drink. His choices were limited to beer and cranberry juice. A half-empty bottle of whisky sat on the counter. It seemed his dad was always trying to either pollute his liver or clean it out. Alex chose a beer.

Turning around, he noticed his dad's limp looked more pronounced as he followed him into the kitchen. Angus took a seat on one of the bar stools, taking the weight off his bad leg as he stretched it out before him. "The old biddy better not try to swindle us, or you can send her packing."

"She's not an old biddy, and she's not going to swindle us. And who the hell talks like that? Really, Dad, lighten up. Miss Ellers will be okay." He was even more determined than ever to keep his dad away from Bree.

"So, when is she going to see the horses?"

"I'm taking her there first thing in the morning, right after breakfast." He took a swig of his beer. The cold brew felt good going down.

"Good. I'll go with you. We can ride over in the truck."

"No way, Dad." That was the last thing he needed, to have his dad pull up in the company truck with the name *MacDonald's Clydesdales and Carriages* painted large across its sides. "She prefers to work alone. Damn it, Dad, can you just trust me on this?"

"Now don't go getting your hackles up. Every day those horses are out in the field and not in the harness costs us money."

"Don't you think I know that?" Alex slammed the beer on the counter a little harder than he had intended.

"If this old biddy of yours doesn't work out, I'm calling George, like I should have in the first place."

"I already told you, she's not an old biddy, and I've seen her work. She'll be fine. George doesn't train horses, he breaks them."

"At least he gets results." Angus slapped his hand on the counter.

"Not the ones I want. I don't want their spirit taken from our Clydes."

"Spirit? Hell, you make it sound like they're our children. They're working horses. And they need to get working."

"And they will." Alex had had enough of this conversation. "I don't suppose you've started dinner."

"Of course not. I was waiting for you."

"Right. Of course you were."

Alex cooked up some gourmet hamburgers with sautéed mushrooms and prepared a fresh garden salad. He also boiled a couple of ears of corn to round out their meal. After that, he spent the rest of the evening avoiding his dad's questions about Bree and her horse training experience.

When he'd been down in Diablo Valley at Over-Yonder Ranch, hiring Bree to work with his horses had seemed like a good idea. Now that he was back home trying to convince his dad she was a good choice, he was having second thoughts.

What did he really know about her? She had printed up business cards claiming she had twelve years of experience, but that was based on her house-training a puppy when she was ten years old. It was a rather dubious claim and certainly not one his dad would buy into.

She had put on a nice little display of dog training with Laddy, but everyone knew training dogs was a lot different from training horses. Besides, he wasn't even sure his Clydesdales needed more training. They'd been trained to take the harness years ago, but lately they were refusing to behave as they should.

If Bree's efforts didn't produce the results they needed, his dad would ride his ass for months about his failed attempt to fix the problem. And he'd be right there with him, kicking himself for being swayed by a pretty face and a kind heart. She hadn't really claimed she could fix his horses, only that she would try. But he'd fallen for her fresh, innocent, country girl demeanor, and had gone skipping down the yellow brick road, wanting to believe she was the all wise and powerful Oz who could make things right.

~*~

Bree stood next to Franklin, her adopted grandfather, in his cozy country kitchen, cutting up vegetables for their dinner salad while he prepared fruit-covered tarts for dessert. Franklin preferred to eat fresh, local produce as much as possible. It was probably one of the things that kept him looking younger than his years. He was seventy-six but could easily pass for sixty-six if not younger.

Keeping her eyes focused on her chopping, Bree asked, "Grandpa, what do you think Alex would do if he knew about my past?"

"Are you talking about when you were born or how you were raised?" Franklin asked, answering her question with a question.

"Both, or either," she shrugged, hoping he wouldn't notice how important this was to her.

"If he wasn't already here, he'd run for the hills. There aren't many who can accept the magic of Skye," he said, referring to the Scottish isle where she was born. "They may enjoy the stories of the fae, but most modern Americans don't believe in them, not really."

"That's what I figured." Bree paused in her chopping and sighed. Franklin's answer was pretty much what she expected, even if it wasn't what she wanted to hear. "Back at the ranch I tried to talk to Alex about my gift, but I got the impression he doesn't believe in such stuff."

"Your ability to tap into the thoughts of animals is not something most folks can understand."

"I know. It's like if they can't do it, they don't think anyone else can, either."

Bree watched for a moment as Franklin spread pear wedges into a perfect fan shape atop a creamy custard tart. She felt the need to vent, and her grandpa was one of the few people she could talk to freely about her past. Even Jenny didn't know all her secrets. Other than her Aunt Teressa and Uncle Robert, only Franklin knew where she came from and how she had traveled though time with her father. They were the only ones who knew she was part fae and that a powerful faerie named Moezell was actually her distant cousin.

"For a minute, when I saw Alex talking with Sunnyside, I thought maybe he had the gift, too, but he denied it. He said it was all well and good to talk to animals, but he never heard them talk back."

"Sounds like you don't believe him."

"It's not that, but I wonder if he has more of a gift than he's admitting."

"Maybe he's not aware of his gift like you are. Some folks, like Alex, have a real good sense about animals, but not many are willing to accept an ability to hear their thoughts or read their emotions. To most folks, animals can't communicate."

"Maybe they're not willing to listen."

"Same thing. Either way, they've made up their mind that's not how it works."

"Sometimes it's hard to carry these secrets—that I was born in 1308 and can hear animals' thoughts."

Franklin stopped cutting the pears and pulled her close. "I understand, my sweet lass. It must weigh heavily on ye at times."

Bree shrugged, feeling better just being able to talk to someone about it. "Most of the time I don't think about it. But when I meet someone new, like Alex, I know I have to watch what I say. I don't want to say the wrong thing and sound all crazy."

"You're not crazy, and only a fool would think so."

61

"You know how hard I've worked to fit in," she sighed.

She could still remember her first year in California. It had taken everything she had not to crawl into a shell and stay there. The modern world was grand, but it was also overwhelming to a young Scottish girl raised in the fourteenth century. Everything moved so fast. Riding in cars and airplanes had often made her sick to her stomach. Her Aunt Teressa called it motion sickness. That was one of the reasons she liked riding the motorcycle; it was more like riding a horse. Bree felt in control of the bike, sitting out in the fresh air instead of inside a moving metal box.

But there was also the homesickness. Her longing to fit in often warred with her thoughts of returning home, back to where she came from in 1326.

After her father died, Moezell and her Aunt Teressa had both asked her to give it some time, and she had reluctantly agreed to one year. By the end of that first year, she was so excited about everything she was learning—and her emerging independence—she had readily agreed to stay, giving up her option of traveling back in time.

Now, nearly four years later, she knew there was no longer any reason to return. Even if she could go back, Skye was no longer home. Over-Yonder had become her new home, and she was committed to making it work.

As if reading her thoughts, Franklin spoke. "You belong here now, Breanna. The past is gone. 'Tis best to leave it that way."

Bree gave him a weak smile. "Don't worry, Grandpa. I'm not going anywhere."

"Och, I do worry about you. I was so proud when you managed to get your GED in just two years. But lately, it seems you've become too settled down there at Over-Yonder. Teressa tells me you hardly ever get out."

"I get out. I'm doing fine. Besides, the ranch keeps me busy. I have horses and dogs to train, and my riding class, and all the chores to keep the farm running. It takes a lot of work."

"You're too young to take this all on by yourself."

"I'm not by myself. Jack and Jenny help me. And Aunt Teressa and Uncle Robert come by all the time."

"That's not what I'm talking about, and you know it," Franklin said with annoyance. "For a little old Scottish lass, you've got a mighty stubborn streak in you."

"Like you don't? I must have learned from the best," she said flippantly.

"What? Ye think me stubborn?" Franklin's gray brows shot to the top of his forehead. She chuckled; he looked so comical.

"No, not at all, Grandpa." She shook her head with mock dismay. "And you never take whisky in your tea."

"Now watch your manners, little one. Don't you go getting sassy on me." The smile in his voice reached his eyes, causing them to twinkle with delight.

Bree had to laugh. They'd been down this road before, sparring and jesting, and neither ever conceded to the other.

"I don't know which is worse, a half-fae Scottish lass—" Franklin started to tease her.

"Or a full-blooded old Scottish mule," Bree interjected with a grin.

"In that case, little lassie, my money's on the old Scottish mule."

"Oh, Grandpa," she sighed. She hugged him again, letting the comfort of their connection surround her like a warm blanket of love.

"Don't ye worry, my sweet lass. Ye must believe everything's gonna be all right."

CHAPTER 6

Alex was still mired with doubts the next morning when he went to pick up Bree, unable to shake his fear of failure. He had hoped a good night's sleep in his own bed would clear his head, but the moment he saw his dad fixing their morning coffee, his worries came pouring back. Breathing deeply, he tried to brush his qualms aside, hoping Bree would give him a reason to believe she could handle the job. It sucked that his belief in her wasn't stronger than his doubts, but he needed more than a doggy show to be convinced she was up for the task of fixing what was wrong with his horses.

He had just stepped onto Franklin's porch when Bree greeted him at the door with a bright smile, her eyes lit with anticipation. She was dressed in dark denim jeans and a snug-fitting white tee shirt under a half-buttoned red-and-black plaid flannel shirt. Holding her motorcycle helmet in one hand and her leather jacket in the other, it was obvious she'd been waiting for him to arrive.

"Morning, Alex. I heard you drive up. I'm all ready to go. I'm really looking forward to seeing your Clydesdales." She sounded excited, like a kid getting ready to meet Santa Claus.

"Good." Alex forced a smile he didn't completely feel. "We can ride over together on my bike. The pasture's only a couple of miles from here."

It was probably a mistake asking her to ride with him. Having her body so close to his made him crave her touch. But he didn't have the time or patience to ride at her slower pace. The faster they got started, the faster he could go back to believing all would be well. He wanted to drop his doubts—really, he did—but right now the odds weren't feeling so good.

~*~

The first thing Bree felt was contentment. As she approached the two large Clydesdales grazing in the lush, grassy field, she sensed contentment; they felt safe and well cared for. These matching chestnut-brown Clydesdales, Malt and Barley, were large powerful beasts, standing just over sixteen hands high. They acknowledged her arrival alongside Alex with relaxed familiarity then went back to enjoying their breakfast. She sensed they looked upon Alex as a master, someone who could be trusted. That was reassuring. Bree looked back at him and smiled. She just wished he didn't look so glum.

She had sensed his change of mood as soon as he pulled into Franklin's drive. She'd been waiting for him, anxious to see him as much as she was to see his horses, but he'd been moody, or maybe just distracted. It was obvious something was bothering him. His demeanor was so different from how he'd been down at the ranch. At the ranch, he'd been happy, lighthearted, even flirty, but now he was all business. Hoping to shed the cloud that darkened his disposition, she had tried to lighten his mood, but she'd had no luck.

He had insisted she ride with him on his bike to the field where the horses were pastured, and she had agreed. Now he stood leaning on the fence, watching her as she approached his horses.

With slow, confident strides, she walked toward Malt and Barley. She could tell they were fairly accepting of strangers. Although their senses were on alert and they were clearly aware of her, they didn't show signs of wanting to flee, at least not yet.

There was also a feeling of restlessness. These were working horses in the prime of their lives, and they had a strong desire to be useful. Much like a thoroughbred felt the need to run or a sporting dog felt the need to hunt, these draught horses felt the need to be of service.

Bree believed all God's creatures, man and beast, had a purpose in their lives, a destiny that lived within them, and any attempt to deny or restrict their natural instinct would cause an imbalance. She'd seen it in humans as much as in animals. Animals were easy to understand; humans were more complicated. Most folks found it hard to understand their purpose or even be sure what it was, but it was always there, waiting to be exposed.

As for Bree, she could no more deny her psychic abilities than she could stop thinking. It was her calling; it made her who she was. Knowing she could read animals was the easy part. Knowing what to do with her abilities was usually the challenge.

A few feet away from the horses, Bree stopped, watching their reactions and assessing their emotions. As she reached further into the horses' thoughts, she felt them resist the intrusion ever so slightly, but it was to be expected from animals that hadn't been read before. Actually, she felt they were much more accepting of her psychic presence than most horses she'd met and wondered if it had anything to do with their ancient Scottish heritage.

Alex had said they were fighting the harness and acting up around strangers, so she focused on testing their reactions to those types of images. She projected a mental image of them being hitched to a wagon. Step by step, she walked them through the process, hoping to find what made them upset. First, she buckled them into the horse collar and traces that would bind them to the tongue of the wagon. Then she placed them at the front of a team of four, completing the hitch.

At each stage of the harnessing, they accepted the images she presented without balking or showing signs of resistance. Quite the contrary, she felt their growing excitement, as though they anticipated their return to service.

If the idea of being harnessed didn't incite fear in the horses, the root of their problems must be something else. This was going to be harder to find, since she didn't know where to look.

While maintaining her presence at the front of the imaginary scene, she mentally introduced the image of a driver climbing aboard the wagon and taking up the reins. For a moment, she felt them grow nervous, as if anticipating pain or discomfort. Their heightened awareness bordered on fear but was still under control. The horses lifted their heads and cocked their ears, listening. She felt them flex their large powerful muscles, ready to buck or bolt.

Next, she replaced the unknown driver with an image of Alex, wondering if his presence would calm the horses or increase their fear. As soon as her imaginary Alex spoke their names, she felt their fear subside. It was obvious they were comfortable with his familiar presence. Perhaps it was their natural fear of an unknown driver that had provoked their anxious reaction.

Wanting to test her theory, she replaced the image of Alex with Franklin at the reins. Again, she sensed the horses' heightened nervousness for an unfamiliar driver, but it was far less than what she had felt only moments before. They were wary, but with Franklin at the reins, she felt no undue fear or distress. It was possible the animals were picking up on her feelings of comfort with the two men. She knew a mental image was hardly a match for the real thing, but until she could put them into a real-life situation, she couldn't be sure. That would have to wait until later when she could arrange an actual hitching with Alex and his crew.

Finally, she brought in a crowd of onlookers, imagining the public milling about as they waited to board the passenger wagon. She tried to imagine a variety of tourists, everyone from older grandparents to young kids too antsy to stand still around the large, powerful beasts. Still, she didn't detect any undue problems. Their moment of fear had passed, and she hadn't been able to pin-point the trigger.

Tired from the strain of maintaining her connection, she allowed the image to fade away, breaking her psychic link to the horses. Stepping up to Malt and then Barley, she petted their large heads and rubbed their hides, creating a true physical bond with them. They'd been through a mental workout and needed a soft return to reality. She gave them love and acceptance and felt theirs in return.

After standing in the field with the Clydesdales for over half an hour, she felt drained and tired from the intense concentration required to maintain her psychic connection with the animals. She hadn't been able to confirm Alex's claim that his horses were hurting, and that bothered her. Other than their momentary fear of an unknown driver, she had only detected a deep desire to return to work. Still, she had a nagging sensation something was amiss; she just didn't know what it was. And in hindsight, her nagging sensations usually proved to be right.

Bree walked back to where Alex stood waiting, wishing she had something more tangible to tell him. Judging by the scowl on his face, he needed something to perk him up. She figured it was best to start with the good news to put a positive spin on her reading.

"Your horses are strong, and from what I can see, they're willing to go to work." She tried to sound more optimistic than she felt, but his scowl only deepened.

"How can you say that? All you did was stand there for the last thirty minutes staring at them." He sounded as angry as he looked. She really couldn't blame him. From his point of view, it would look as though she hadn't made any progress, but sometimes knowing what wasn't wrong was as important as knowing what was.

"I told you it would take some time to evaluate them. I'd like to see them in the harness."

"Is that how you evaluate them? By standing in a field for an hour just staring at them? You didn't even touch them until a few minutes ago."

The dark feelings she had sensed from Alex earlier grew stronger, deeper. She rallied her defenses.

"If you'll just let me finish. I still need to see them in the harness."

"Yeah, you're finished all right. That damn McGregor got me good, getting me to chase all the way down to Diablo Valley to bring you up here. If he wanted to see his precious, little old granddaughter so badly, he should have just picked up the phone and called you. Or better yet, he could have driven there himself. But no, he sends me on a wild goose chase, wasting my time and making me look like a fool."

She couldn't believe what she was hearing. It felt as if she'd been slapped. She'd done nothing to provoke his anger. "You're not a fool. I just need to—"

"Oh, yes, I am. I'm a fool for falling for that horse whisperer crap. Come on, let's go. I'm taking you back to McGregor's."

Bree stood her ground, not willing to back down just because he was angry—because he didn't understand her gift. "What if I'm not ready to leave?"

"Well, I am. I've had enough." He stalked over to his bike and grabbed his helmet, shoving it on his head. He looked at Bree. "Are you coming?"

"No. I'm not ready to leave. I'm not done here." She crossed her arms in front of her chest and stood her ground.

"Suit yourself. You can walk back, for all I care." He climbed aboard his bike and took off down the road, leaving her behind.

~*~

Damn that woman. He wished it were true. He wished he didn't care. He had wanted to trust her, to believe in her ability to help his horses, but she'd done nothing but stand there for nearly an hour, hardly moving, and then she had the nerve to tell him there was nothing wrong with Malt and Barley. That they were anxious to get back to work? What the hell was that all about. He'd seen his horses nearly ruin a rig, trying to escape their harness. What kind of horseshit was that?

His dad was right. He was a fool for believing McGregor's claim she was a horse whisperer, the best he'd ever seen. What a crock. This foolhardy adventure had cost him two days away from the ranch, and now he was further behind than before. He'd let a pretty young face turn his head, and he only had himself to blame.

Distracted by his anger at his dad, Bree, and everything else, he sped toward home. When he came to a tight curve in the road, he was traveling much too fast. Leaning hard into the turn, he nearly laid down the bike. Suddenly, the rear tire lost traction on the slick asphalt. A fraction of a second later, the back tire regained traction, tightly gripping the pavement and nearly throwing him over the handlebars. A hot bolt of adrenaline shot though his body as every muscle fought to keep the bike upright. Only quick reactions and an ungodly amount of luck kept him from completely losing control.

Though frightfully close, thankfully, he was able to keep the bike off the blacktop and himself out of the hospital. He rolled over to the side of the road to recoup his composure and slumped over the handlebars, taking deep, calming breathes. Several moments passed before he could restart the bike and ride the rest of the way home.

Even after he slowed down, he felt the residue of adrenaline heating his skin. It was a real jolt to his senses.

Damn it. What was he thinking? He had nearly killed himself, letting his emotions get the better of him. It was time to let go of his dad's negative influence and do what he thought was best.

By the time Alex rode into his driveway, he knew exactly what he needed to do, and it didn't include abandoning Bree or blaming her for his problems. It didn't take an on-line chat session with Dr. Phil for him to realize his bad mood wasn't Bree's fault. Once again, he had let his dad jerk his chain, and he had no one but himself to blame. He had needed to kick a cat, and unfortunately, Bree had been too conveniently available. Now, it was time to take responsibility for his actions.

When he pulled into the driveway in front of the large carriage house at the edge of the property, he saw his Uncle Wayne getting the landau ready for use. Judging by the white decorations, he was prepping for a wedding. Alex banged the palm of his hand against his forehead. *Dang,* he had completely forgotten about the Smitherson wedding being on Friday, not Saturday. He should have known better, but he'd been too preoccupied with Bree to check the business schedule. Instead of heading to the office as he had planned, he walked over to where his uncle was working.

"It looks like you're getting ready for the Smitherson wedding," Alex said as he drew close, hoping he had remembered the customer's name correctly.

His uncle was polishing one of the brass lanterns that hung on each side of the carriage. "Aye, we need this down at the Valley View Hotel by noon to pick up the bride and take her to the chapel. I was just getting ready to send Howard over to pick up Malt and Barley. We've got the other four Clydesdales working in town with the big coach. The place is full of tourists. Fine paying customers, just what we need."

"Howard? Has he left yet?"

"No. He's still hitching up the horse trailer to the truck."

"Who's scheduled to drive the team?"

"I am. Howard needs to relieve Roy for the afternoon shift on the coach."

Alex had an idea. "Call Howard and tell him to stop. I'll go get the horses."

Wayne shot him a quizzical look. "You! You hate driving the horse trailer."

"No. I'm going to ride them over from the field. It's not that far, and the warm-up will do them good. We don't need the trailer. I'll go get the gear. Can you just call Howard and tell him we don't need the truck?"

Wayne rubbed the stubble of whiskers on his chin with the back of his hand. "Well, look who's giving orders around here now. Does Angus know?"

"Look, Uncle Wayne, can you just help me out here?" Alex didn't want his dad to get involved, and for his plan to work, he needed to keep the MacDonald truck out of sight.

"Sure, Alex, whatever you say. Are you going to drive the carriage, too?"

"Yes. Yes, I am," he confirmed. "I'll be right back." This was better than perfect; this was just what he needed.

Turning on his heel, he headed over to the office. On his way, he pulled out his cell phone and called Franklin McGregor.

"Hey, Frank. Is Bree there?" Alex asked.

"Alex? I thought Breanna was with you."

"She was, but I, um, I left her in the field with the horses, and well, I'm wondering if she headed back to your place."

"Hell no; she's not here. You want to tell me what happened? What excuse do you have for leaving my little girl out in the field with your horses?" Frank sounded mad, and rightfully so. He'd been a cad.

"Hey, she's only a couple of miles from your house. It's not like I left her out in the forest somewhere."

"Yeah, and you're not answering my question. What happened out there?"

Alex breathed a heavy sigh. Frank wasn't going to let him off easy. "Bree spent nearly an hour just staring at my horses, and then she started telling me they're ready to go back to work when I know they're not."

"So you drove off and left her? Didn't even have the courtesy to give her a ride back here? What kind of lowland hellion did yer dad raise?"

"Look, Frank. I got mad and took it out on Bree. It wasn't right, I know, and now I need to fix it. Will you help me or not?" Alex waited through a moment of dead silence.

McGregor finally spoke. "What do you need?" The old Scot still sounded less than happy, but at least he was willing to listen.

"If Bree shows up, keep her there. Tell her I heard what she said, and I'm coming to get the horses. We have a job for them to do. It's not the big passenger rig, so it'll just be the two of them, but Bree wanted to see them harnessed, and I'm willing to do what she wants." Besides, it wasn't as if he had a choice. The horses needed to go to work, and he'd feel a lot better if Bree were with him to help in case they acted up.

"Okay, I'll tell her. But she better be fine, or I'll—"

"Yeah, I know. You'll come looking for me and skin me like a rabbit." Alex clicked off his phone as he climbed the stairs to the office above the carriage house.

Originally, the upper floor had been built as an apartment for a caretaker, but now it was used as office space for the family business. A large, dark wood desk dominated the living room of the one-bedroom apartment. Two of the walls were lined with bookcases, filing cabinets, and neatly stacked storage boxes.

Over the years, his dad had become something of a pack rat, holding on to memorabilia and books about horses, history, science fiction, and anything else that caught his interest. He probably should sort through it all someday to see what they held, but he'd never had the time or energy. His dad's collection of books and stuff had been too long in the making, and he didn't even know where to start. As far as he knew, it was mostly ancient history. In other words, a useless time suck.

Alex stepped through the main room into the single bedroom. A small double bed that was rarely used rested against the wall next to more storage boxes. It seemed as though his dad never threw anything away. Ignoring the mess, he opened the closet doors and pulled out a hanging garment bag holding his vintage tuxedo then laid it on the bed. From the closet, he took out a white dress shirt, a couple of bow ties, and his classic top hat. Though he always felt a little pompous in the top hat, the paying customers seemed to like the look. Shuffling through the closet, he found a few other things he would need if his idea panned out. He pulled out another white button-down shirt, a tweed jacket, and a newsboy cap then stuffed them into the garment bag along with the other items. Once that was all done, he headed out the door and down the stairs.

Back outside, he draped the garment bag over the passenger seat of the ATV they used to haul around light equipment. Next, he jogged over to the tack house and grabbed a couple of bridles and horse blankets. He stowed them in the cargo box of the all-terrain vehicle and drove it the short distance to where Wayne was working.

"Did you get a hold of Howard?" he asked, climbing out of the ATV.

"Yeah. He hasn't left the shed yet," Wayne said, referring to the large garage where they stored the trucks and trailers.

"Good. Go ahead and finish dressing the carriage. I'll go get the Clydes and be back in a few minutes." Alex grabbed the garment bag and stashed it in the back of the landau.

"Sure thing, Boss," Wayne drawled, mocking him.

"Thanks, Uncle Wayne. I'll be back soon." After hopping back in the ATV, Alex pushed the accelerator pedal to the floor and buzzed off across the field.

CHAPTER 7

Bree watched Alex ride away, feeling more disappointed than angry. It was best to let him go. He obviously wasn't in the mood to talk.

She turned back to the horses, wishing she could have told Alex what was causing their problem, but horses didn't think like humans. They communicated with actions and emotions, not with words. It wasn't as though she could just ask them a question and they would give her an answer. Their mode of communication didn't work that way.

When she was working with the show poodles, she'd been able to pick up on their feelings of pride at having won the dog show. Bree had felt the emotional memory they carried as they went through their paces at practice. Both dogs knew they had performed well and had pleased their owner as well as the crowd of people watching. She had felt their memories and had understood their meaning.

With the horses, she'd been able to briefly tap into their feelings of fear, but she hadn't been able to figure out the cause. Now she wanted to spend more time with the Clydesdales. They were impressive beasts, and she enjoyed their presence. She didn't want to continue probing their minds; she just wanted to hang out with them. Intuitively, she sensed they trusted her, and she wanted to build on that emotion to strengthen their newly formed bond.

No matter what Alex had said, she wasn't ready to quit and walk away. Maybe after he cooled down, she could try talking to him again and explain what she had in mind. He'd been in a foul mood all morning, and she suspected his emotional outburst wasn't about her or the horses. Something, or someone, had triggered his defenses, and she had reaped the results. Being the brunt of his frustration might not be fair, but such was often the case between people. Emotions, like life, didn't play fair; they just played out.

A while later, she heard an unfamiliar humming sound coming across the field from the direction of the horse path. It took her a few minutes to realize it was Alex, driving a funny little motorized open carriage, a go-kart. He had returned. She stood near the horses, waiting for him to approach.

"Bree, I'm so glad you're still here." He stopped a few yards away and hopped out of the cart.

"Did you think I would leave?" Did he really have so little faith in her?

"I wouldn't blame you if you did. I wasn't very nice when I left." His eyes held hers, looking hopeful.

"No, you weren't," she agreed. It wasn't quite an apology, but it would do, for now. "So why did you come back?"

"You said you wanted to see the horses harnessed, and we have a job for them to do. It's not the big rig, so it'll just be the two of them. We need them to pull the landau."

"What's a landau?" she asked.

"It's an old-fashioned convertible carriage. We use it mostly for weddings. In fact, we've got a job scheduled for noon today. I was hoping you'd help me take the horses back to the carriage house and get them harnessed. But we don't have much time."

Bree almost rushed to say yes, but paused for a moment before speaking. She didn't want to sound too anxious, not after the way he had acted, but there was no use denying she was thrilled with the idea of seeing the Clydesdales harnessed to a carriage.

She eyed the gear in the cargo box. "Are you planning to ride them back or lead them with that cart?"

"Ride, bareback. We don't have time for a saddle. You don't mind riding bareback, do you?" Alex said as he reached for the horse blankets.

Bree laughed. "Of course not." She'd ridden bareback most of her life before she left Skye, but that was centuries ago. Grabbing the bridles, she set to work helping him ready the Clydes.

A few minutes later, they were mounted and trotting the horses across the field toward the carriage house on Alex's ranch. The experience was thrilling. Bree rode Barley, the smaller of the two Clydesdales by mere inches. She had needed a boost up from Alex to mount the large horse and then another minute more to adjust to Barley's size, but then she had felt right at home on the animal.

When they arrived at the carriage house, the landau was sitting out in the parkway, waiting for them. It was beautifully decorated with white silk roses and satin ribbons. With obvious pride, Alex explained that the white-and-black carriage was a restored rig from the early twentieth century, over one hundred years old. He hadn't been kidding when he claimed to appreciate the classics.

Together they harnessed the Clydesdales without any problems. Alex clearly knew what he was doing and went about the task in a brisk, professional manner. All through the process, Bree kept her mind tuned into the horses' emotions. Although they flinched once or twice, she didn't detect any noticeable fear. Alex was wrong. It wasn't the harness they were afraid of, and it certainly wasn't Alex. It must be something, or someone, else.

Alex pulled out his cell phone to check the time. "I've got to get changed, and then we've got to get going. Bree, I'm hoping you'll come with me. You can sit up on the driver's bench next to me. What do you say?"

She glanced down at her jeans and riding boots. "I can't go to a wedding dressed like this."

Alex stepped over to a garment bag sitting in the back of the landau. "I knew you'd say that, so I brought you something to wear." He unzipped the bag and began pulling out clothes. "You can go as my assistant. It'll give you more time to evaluate the horses, to see how they react around strangers."

He was obviously prepared and made a darn good argument. She was impressed.

"Here, you can put these on over your tee shirt." He handed her a man's white dress shirt and a tweed jacket. "See, I even have a newsboy cap to go with it. You'll look real cute."

His flattery made her smile. "What are you going to wear?"

"Since we're both wearing dark jeans, I'll just wear the jacket of my tux and a top hat. No one really cares what the carriage drivers wear, as long as they stay out of the pictures. It'll be fine."

"Okay, I'll go, but I want you to know, I'm only doing this so I can see more of the horses. As far as I'm concerned, this is all part of the job." For the most part, that was the truth. She didn't want to admit, even to herself, that she enjoyed spending time with Alex. Besides, this was all about the horses, not him.

"Agreed. What else would it be?" Alex replied in a rush. He started to change right in front of her, pulling his dark tee shirt up over his head.

Fascinated, Bree didn't look away. She watched Alex struggle for a brief moment when the tee shirt caught around his neck, using every precious second to gape at his muscular chest. *Holy crap,* she thought. *He's freaking buff.* She had heard the term "six-pack," but until now, she had never fully appreciated what it meant. When the shirt popped off over his head, she quickly looked away; she didn't want to get caught staring at his chest, tempting as it was.

Bree unbuttoned her plaid flannel shirt and replaced it with the dress shirt he'd given her. It was large on her, but not overly so. From the corner of her eye, she could still see Alex as he loosened his jeans to tuck in the tails of his white dress shirt. *Nice.*

Alex moved quickly as he buttoned up his shirt and fastened a black bow tie around his neck while she shrugged into the tweed jacket. Lastly, he pulled a top hat from the bottom of the bag and popped it on his head. *Damn.* He looked good.

~~~

After helping Bree into the driver's seat, Alex climbed aboard and took the reins in hand. To start them on their way, he gave the Clydesdales a "yee-haw." He was glad she had agreed to go with him; it felt good having her by his side. He hadn't been wrong. She looked darn cute in the oversized jacket and newsboy cap.

Directing the team, he drove the carriage out of the parkway and down the back road that led into town. Once they were safely on the graded road, headed away from the ranch, he began to relax.

"So, maybe you can try to explain to me again what happened out in the field," Alex said, breaking their silence.

Bree gave him a dour look.

"I know. I didn't listen too well the first time."

"I could tell something was bothering you. Was it something I did?" She looked at him expectantly.

"No. It wasn't you, not really. I'm just worried about the Clydes, and well, I really don't understand what happened out there. I mean, you just stood there and stared at my horses. By the time you were done, I was fit to be tied." He had also nearly killed himself on the way back to the ranch, but she didn't need to know about that.

Bree shook her head and sighed. "You didn't even give me a chance to explain."

"I know. I wasn't listening," Alex admitted again. "I'm listening now."

Bree hesitated, nervously fingering the edge of the tweed jacket, rolling it back and forth between her fingers. "Are you sure you want to know?" she asked, looking up at him from beneath lidded lashes.

"Yeah, I'm sure."

With an air of reluctance, Bree took a deep breath and looked off in the distance. "Have you heard of psychics? People who can read people's auras and emotions and such?"

Alex was uncomfortable with her question. He didn't believe in the paranormal, not really. Maybe there were a few honest people with true mystical talents, but he believed most were quacks or con-artists preying on gullible folks to rob them of their money.

"Yeah, of course, I've heard of them, but I don't know much about it. I've never had any experience with them personally."

"What if I told you I'm psychic?"

"Are you telling me you can read my mind?" That idea didn't sit well with him. He felt his comfort level drop toward his stomach.

"No, I can't read your mind. Not really. I don't read humans. Though I can pick up on your emotions, and I might be more sensitive than most, I can't read humans."

He felt a little better, but still not at ease. "Then what can you do? Why do you think you're psychic?"

"Actually, I read animals. For instance, I can read your horses. It's my gift. I'm able to tap into their thoughts and emotions."

"You think you can read animals?" He almost laughed, but choked it back.

"No," she said, sitting a little straighter and stiffening her spine. "I know I can."

As much as he wanted to dispute her claim, he thought it best to keep his thoughts to himself, at least until he heard her out. For the moment, he would give her the benefit of his doubt, but only for the moment.

He gave her a sideways glance. "Okay, go on. I'm still listening." *Listening, but not necessarily believing.*

"I know this sounds like new age stuff, but actually it's an old and established talent that goes back to ancient times. Since I was a little girl, I've been able to read animals, feel their thoughts and emotions, and sometimes I can project my thoughts into theirs. I was able to do that with your Clydesdales. They were very receptive to my reading."

She sounded so sure of herself, and yet he found it harder and harder to accept what she was saying. "You mean you can understand them, and they can understand you?" Alex looked at his horses pulling the landau and tried to imagine having a conversation with them. It wasn't working.

"In a way. It's more like a silent communication with pictures and feelings instead of words. Keep in mind, psychic connection does have its limitations, but in a way, yes, we can communicate. Animals don't speak with words; they think in concepts, images, and emotions. They're rather simple, you know, but not dumb. When they experience something, they react quickly and mostly on instinct.

It's often a question of should I be afraid? Is this person safe? That sort of thing. From what I could see, they're not afraid of the harness, and as you can see, we really had no problem hitching them up to the carriage. They're happy to be back at work. Can't you just feel it in the way they're pulling this rig?"

He watched as the long hair of their manes bounced, keeping pace with their lively trot. They did seem to have a spring to their step. "I don't know. I guess they seem happy, but something has them spooked. The last three times they were out with the big wagon they misbehaved, and the last time they bucked so hard they nearly flipped the wagon."

"Were you there? Can you tell me what happened?"

"I wasn't here the first two times. Both times Howard was the lone driver, but he's experienced and knows how to handle a team. But I was there the last time it happened. Howard and I were just getting ready to take on a new load of passengers when the horses went berserk. They started to buck and fight the harness. If I hadn't been there to help get them under control, they might have caused real damage to themselves or the rig. Thankfully, no one was hurt, but we had to stop for the day. We couldn't risk an accident."

"That's odd. The only time I was able to detect outright fear in the horses was before I introduced you as a driver."

Before he could speak, she answered his questioning look.

"Mentally, I took the horses through the process of being hitched up to a rig. I projected my thoughts and mental images to them. They were fine until I got ready to bring in a driver. For a brief moment, I felt extreme fear from both of the horses, like they were ready to bolt, but as soon as you appeared in the image, they quieted down. Then, I tried bringing in Franklin as a driver, wondering how they would react to someone they didn't know, but the fear never came back. It could be they were picking up on my own comfort with Franklin; it's

83

hard to be sure. Either way, I wasn't able to pinpoint what sparked their fear. Do you think your driver, Howard, could have done something to cause them to react so badly?"

"Howard? Maybe, but I doubt it. He's been around these horses too long. They know him well enough by now. No, he's not an unknown driver to them. It must be something else."

"Still, if we have the chance, I'd like to see how they react around Howard. Is he expected to work with the Clydesdales anytime soon?"

"Not today. He's working with the other rig in town, and I can't pull him off the job." Alex still wasn't sure he believed her, but for the moment, he was willing to at least consider her suggestions. Besides, for the moment, she was all he had. He wasn't ready to go back to his dad and tell him this had all been a waste of time.

He also didn't want Bree to discover his last name before he found out what she had against the MacDonalds.

"I guess we'll have to arrange a meeting with Howard some other time when he's not busy," Alex said.

"Do I get to keep working with your horses?" she asked, looking hopeful.

"Sure, if you're still interested."

"I can't stop now. I need to know what happened. You're right, though. Something or someone spooked them, but until we know what it was, I can't help them." She relaxed beside him with a happy smile. "So, if I'm supposed to be your assistant for this job, maybe you should tell me what to expect. What do I have to do?"

"Nothing, really. I'll handle it all. You just have to sit there and look cute."

"Not funny. I'm serious. How does this work?"

He almost laughed. Her pout was so adorable. "Okay, first, we're riding over to the bride's hotel. We'll pick up the bride and a couple of her bridesmaids. There's room for about four people in the landau, less if they're wearing those wide, poufy skirts. There'll be lots of posing and picture taking, and then we'll take the bride to the church where they're having the wedding. After the ceremony, there'll be more pictures with the bride and groom. Then we take them over to the reception back at the bride's hotel and drop them off. Once they take their final photos and disembark, we're done. Not a tough way to make a living, wouldn't you agree?"

"Sounds easy enough. Actually, it sounds like fun."

The horses made good time pulling the carriage, and they picked up the bride as scheduled. There was plenty of time for the excessive picture taking the bride wanted as she posed in the carriage with her bridesmaids. Now that they were on the clock, Alex could relax. For the rest of the afternoon, they were on the bride's dime, and she could take all the time she wanted.

"Where did you learn to drive a carriage?" Bree asked. They were sitting on the driver's bench, waiting while the photographer snapped pictures of the bride and her attendants.

"I've been driving rigs with my dad and uncle since I was thirteen, and I soloed for the first time when I was fifteen. Before that, I always had an adult with me. Driving a carriage is harder than it looks, handling the horses and maneuvering a rig through traffic. Most people in cars have no respect for me and my horses. It's a lot like when I'm riding my bike, except I know darn well they can see us."

"Have you always worked for the family business?"

"Not until recently. I moved away to go to college and lived on my own for a while, but a couple of years ago I had to move back home to help my dad. He's getting old and has a bum knee that's giving him problems. He can't get around as well as he used to." Alex didn't want to talk about all the other reasons he had for moving back home, like his excessive partying and overspending on cars, bikes, and women, or explain how he had lost his apartment because he ran out of money. Instead, he changed the subject. "You said you grew up on Skye?"

"Yeah, I moved to California when I was eighteen."

"How long ago was that?" he asked, thinking he could get her to confirm her age.

"Four years ago. I'm twenty-two, if that's what you're asking."

"I guessed as much. How was it over on Skye?"

"Um, different. It's a lot colder than here in California, that's for sure, and there's a lot more rain. How about you? Have you ever been to Scotland?"

"A couple of times—mostly Edinburg and Inverness. I've never made it to the Isle of Skye, but I'd love to go someday. How about you? Do you have any plans to return?"

"Maybe, someday." A momentary look of melancholy shadowed her face before she resumed a half smile. "I'd much rather go someplace warm, like Mexico or Hawaii. Have you ever been there?

"I've been to San Diego and Mexico, but never to Hawaii. It's on my list of places to go."

"Maybe someday we'll both—" Bree stopped talking and turned to stare at the horses.

Alex suddenly felt a tightening in his chest. Something was wrong. Bree had sensed it, and so could he. The horses were jerking their heads, fighting the bit, as if they were trying to avoid a swarm of bees or shake loose their harness.

"Hold the reins and speak to your horses, Alex," Bree said softly under her breath as she started to climb down to the curb. "Just talk normal. Let them know you're here."

She stepped down from the carriage and slowly walked to the front of the rig, keeping her eyes focused on the Clydesdales.

Alex began to speak softly. "Hey, Malt. Hey, Barley. Good day for a wedding, wouldn't you agree? I bet you're proud to be pulling these lovely ladies. Yeah, don't worry there, lads, you're looking mighty fine." He was speaking nonsense, but he didn't care. He didn't want his paying customer to know something was wrong, and like Bree said, he wanted his Clydes to know he was there.

Keeping his head down, he glanced around, trying to see what was disturbing his team. The bride and her maids seemed oblivious. They were too busy posing for the photographer. About a dozen people stood nearby watching the show, mostly friends and family of the bride. A few other spectators, probably people from the hotel, also lingered, some with small children. One little girl had a bright red balloon tied to her arm, and it bobbed in the air every time she moved her hand.

Nothing too unusual there; people always liked to watch the bride, and she liked being watched. After all, it was her day. But none of them seemed like a threat to his Clydesdales.

Farther down the street, a bunch of youths in dark jeans and hoodies were practicing with their skateboards. He hadn't really noticed them before; he'd been too busy talking to Bree. The sound of their skateboards rolling over the concrete and smacking the curbs as the boys attempted to get air under their jumps was annoying, but they were too far away to be an immediate problem and didn't appear to be threatening his horses. One of the taller boys caught his eye for a brief second then looked away as he rolled farther down the street, taking his gang of buddies with him. Alex was glad to see them move on. This was no place for loud and rowdy skateboarders.

His drew his eyes back to Bree standing in front of the rig with her hands suspended in midair just above the horses. She was obviously trying to draw their attention to her, but she had placed herself in a very dangerous situation. If the horses suddenly decided to buck or bolt, she could be knocked down and trampled. He knew she wasn't an idiot; he trusted she knew what she was doing. But still, this felt wrong. Sweat rolled down the ridge of his spine as he watched her do her thing. As a precaution, he wrapped the leather straps of the reins a bit firmer in his grasp, ready to restrain his team if they showed any signs of stirring.

Slowly she lowered her hands, bringing them down to stroke the horses. She took a moment to touch her forehead to each of the horses, first Malt and then Barley, reassuring them with tender, whispered words. Whatever had caused their fears was gone. The danger had passed. Alex felt his muscles relax and realized just how tense he had been.

She lingered a moment longer, as though hesitant to leave their side. A few minutes later, she climbed back up to the driver's bench.

"What was that all about?" Alex whispered under his breath as she sat down beside him.

"Something scared the horses. You felt it, too, didn't you?" Bree leaned in close, keeping her voice low.

"I don't know. Maybe I felt something. But why? What happened?"

"I'm…I'm not sure. By the time I felt their fear, I was too focused on keeping them calm to think about what caused it. I didn't think it was a good idea to probe their fears, not here with your carriage full of customers. It wasn't safe, and I thought it was more important to calm the horses than look for the source. Alex, I'm sorry. I know something spooked them, but I don't know what it was." From the way her shoulders slumped, she looked sad and tired.

Alex wrapped an arm around her, drawing her near. "No, Bree, you did good. You're right. The safety of those ladies back there was our first priority." He felt her lean into him, accepting his support. It felt good just to hold her. "Don't worry, Bree. We'll figure this out."

She looked up at him, her eyes brimming with tears, but she blinked them away. "Then you believe me?"

"Of course, I believe you." His arm tightened around her.

He heard her sigh. "I wasn't sure before."

"Neither was I," he confessed. "But I am now."

~~~

Bree's heart was still thumping hard in her chest, definitely faster than the clip-clop of the Clydesdales' hooves on the pavement as they started to trot down a side street on their way to the chapel. Back at the hotel, she had felt the horses' fear, and she'd known it was real. They had been ready to bolt. But she hadn't been able to see what had caused their anxiety. Hard as it was to admit, she'd been too distracted by Alex and had failed to focus on her job.

She also hadn't told Alex everything.

She hadn't wanted to sound paranoid or speak before she knew all the facts, but she had felt a malicious presence. Someone nearby had wanted to harm the horses. But why? Why would anyone want to harm the Clydesdales? They weren't a threat to anyone. The team had just been standing there, harnessed to a rig. It made no sense.

Several groups of bystanders had been milling around the carriage with the bride and her attendants. It seemed folks loved to spy on weddings. Since they had been parked near the gardens of the hotel for the picture taking, a fairly steady stream of people had been coming and going around them, but she didn't think the hostile feelings had come from the direction of the hotel.

When she was standing in front of the Clydesdales, she had sensed loathing and disgust coming from somewhere behind her, farther down the street. It had taken all her focus to mentally shield the horses and draw their attention away from the menace until, thankfully, it had passed. She didn't know what had caused their fear, but it was obvious someone did not like these horses.

Because she hadn't been able to detect the source of their fear, she hadn't wanted to speculate or make false accusations. She'd seen the spectators, the skateboarders, and a family with young children holding party balloons, but she hadn't noticed anyone posing a threat to the horses.

However, the Clydesdales had sensed something that had put them on alert. Perhaps it had been a noise coming from the crowd. Whatever the cause, they had been only seconds away from reacting when she had perceived their discomfort. If she had waited any longer, they might have bucked or bolted with the wedding party in the carriage. That would have been bad for everyone, especially Alex. Intuitively, she had known it was more important for her to focus on calming the horses than look for the source of their fear.

By the time she'd climbed back up to the driver's bench, she had been close to having a meltdown. Bree tried to shake off her regret for having missed something so important, but it stayed stuck in the back of her mind. She would have to deal with it later. There was nothing she could do right now. The source of their fear had disappeared, and she had missed her chance to find out what it was. Now as she struggled to compose herself, she didn't want Alex to know how badly she had failed.

She appreciated that he believed her; he had even admitted to feeling something himself. But knowing she'd had an opportunity to find the source of the horses' fears and had failed was more than she could handle. Still, she was grateful Alex hadn't shown signs of being disappointed with her. Instead, he had done his best to console her, much as she had done with the Clydesdales. He'd even gone so far as to give her a reassuring hug before setting off for the church with the bridal party finally settled. The embrace had been unexpected.

Even so, regardless of how kindly he had reacted, she couldn't shake the feeling she had let him down.

Seeking a diversion from her mental flogging, Bree looked over her shoulder to watch the bride. No wonder she had wanted to hire Alex and his carriage for her special day. She looked so pretty—sitting in the carriage, wearing her wedding gown, surrounded by her bridesmaids—she reminded Bree of a faerie princess going off to a ball in a magical coach.

Only a few days away from the spring equinox, the crepe myrtle trees were in full bloom with bursts of bright pink-and-white blossoms. Patches of daffodils dotted the roadside, and the hotel gardens were bursting with new spring growth. The bride had picked a lovely setting for her special day.

Sitting next to Alex, Bree felt special, too, as though she were part of the celebration.

When they arrived at the church, Alex handed her the reins and hopped down to help the bride and her attendants out of the carriage, once again stepping into his role as coachman.

"I don't believe I've ever had a finer looking bride in my carriage," Alex said as he handed the bride down to the curb. "I believe my horses are just bursting with pride to be pulling your coach."

Bree was amazed. Since leaving the hotel, the horses had felt proud and strong, but how did Alex know? He claimed he couldn't read them. Was it just his way of charming his customers, or could he really sense more than he was willing to acknowledge?

Either way, it worked. He put everyone at ease. The bride and her attendants loved the attention, and she had to admit, he made a great looking coachman in his top hat and cutaway coat.

As Alex helped the last woman down from the coach, she lost her balance and fell into his arms. Bree could have sworn she did it on purpose. The pretty, young bridesmaid apologized for being so clumsy, and claimed she was just excited about the wedding, but Bree was certain she had clung to Alex much longer than necessary to regain her footing.

Alex didn't seem to mind. Why should he? These were beautiful women dressed in beautiful gowns. What man wouldn't appreciate some extra attention from any one of them? He probably spent a good deal of time surrounded by fancy dressed bridesmaids; after all, weddings were a big part of his business. She took stock of her jeans and riding boots, and felt hopelessly out of place.

Eventually, everyone left the carriage and headed into the chapel. Alex climbed back onto the driver's bench and sat down next to Bree. It wasn't long before she heard the piano music from inside the church announcing the arrival of the bride. The wedding ceremony was about to begin.

"Now we sit and wait for them to come back out," Alex said. "The actual wedding doesn't take long, maybe fifteen or thirty minutes. It's all the sitting and waiting that eats up the time."

"So we wait." Bree closed her eyes and leaned back against the seat, soaking up the sun of the waning afternoon as a light spring breeze danced across her face. She couldn't imagine a finer way to spend the day than sitting outside in nature, feeling the warmth of the sun on her skin.

"You know, I have to stay here with the rig, but if you want, you can sneak into the back of the church and watch the ceremony. I know women like that sort of thing," Alex suggested to Bree.

She glanced over to the front doors of the church, but disregarded the notion. "I'll admit it would be nice to sneak a peek; I've never seen this kind of wedding before. But I don't know the bride and groom. It seems rather intrusive to crash their wedding, don't you think? Besides, I think I should stay here with you. I mean, you know, if the horses get spooked again, I want to be ready. Maybe if we're both here, we can figure out what's causing their fear." It sounded like a good enough reason to stay by his side; although, right now, the horses seemed perfectly at ease.

"You can't be serious. You've never been to a church wedding? Women live for this kind of thing."

"I don't know anyone who's gotten married, at least not here in California. I wasn't here for my Aunt Teressa and Uncle Robert's big wedding. They were married before I moved here. And the weddings I attended back home in Scotland were very different from this."

"How so?" Alex asked.

"Well, for one thing, the groom usually wore a kilt."

"Yeah, well, I'm not sure how good Steve in there would feel about wearing a kilt," Alex said, referring to the groom. "I can just imagine him trying to climb into the carriage." He shook his head as if to dislodge the image. "We're probably better off if he sticks with a tux."

They both laughed, but Bree could easily imagine how good Alex would look in a MacNicol plaid with a broadsword strapped to his hips, all handsome, strong, and warrior looking. She felt a slow pink blush rise up her cheeks as the image threatened to burn a hole in her brain and leak down to her lady parts. Not good, so not good.

She reminded herself that she had a job to do and this was strictly a business arrangement. However, being with Alex sure didn't feel that way. Being with Alex felt like so much more.

Then again, she hadn't met very many modern men. Franklin was right, she needed to get out more.

Still, there was something appealingly old-fashioned about Alex. He had the kind of warrior chivalry that appealed to every woman. Heck, it wasn't as though she were the only one who found him attractive; look at how the bridesmaids had fawned all over him.

Nevertheless, as long as they were working together, their relationship had to be strictly business, which meant he was strictly off-limits.

CHAPTER 8

The rest of the afternoon rolled along smoothly, just like clockwork, and thankfully, there were no other incidents with the horses. When the event was all over, Alex breathed a sigh of relief.

After the ceremony, and another long session of picture-taking with the bride and groom, Alex and Bree had delivered the newly married couple back to the hotel for their reception. At one point, Bree had told the bride how lovely she looked, comparing her to a faerie princess, which had delighted his customer. Other than that one brief encounter, she had seemed content to remain in the background, staying close to the horses to avoid the jubilation of the wedding party.

During the picture-taking session, Alex had noticed a couple of the groomsmen eyeing Bee, but he'd made sure they knew she was off-limits. A few pointed looks and some well-timed touches to Bree had been enough to convey his point. She wasn't part of the wedding party; she was with him.

Their day together had been a grand success, and he didn't want it to end, but he needed to get her back to McGregor's place. She still had a long ride back home to Over-Yonder, and it would be dark soon. He trusted her ability to ride, but she was a novice, and he didn't like the idea of her traveling alone at night. Motorcycle riders tended to be ignored by most car drivers, as if they were invisible.

Just before they reached the road leading to McGregor's farm, Alex saw his dad's truck heading their way—the one with *MacDonald's Clydesdales and Carriages* painted large across both sides. The last thing he wanted was to run into his dad and Uncle Wayne. Alex flipped the reins and shouted, "Ha," spurring the horses into a trot. He hoped to make the turnoff before they met up with the truck.

It didn't work.

They had almost reached McGregor's road when the truck pulled up alongside them, forcing him to bring the carriage to a stop. His Uncle Wayne was driving, and his dad sat, big as life, in the passenger seat.

He was so close. Why did this have to happen now?

His dad leaned out his open window. "Hey, Alex, how did the Smithersons' wedding go? Any problems with Malt and Barley?"

"No, everything was fine. The horses were fine." Alex gave a short reply, trying to shrug off his dad's inquiry. Maybe if he could keep their encounter short, he could control the outcome. Knowing his dad, it was unlikely, but it was worth a try.

"I knew those horses were fine. No need to keep them out in the field." His dad pounded the side of the truck with the flat of his hand in a show of bravado. "So, who's the little lady, Alex? Did you get lucky with one of the wedding guests?" his dad asked in a contrived whisper, loud enough for Bree to hear.

Alex rolled his eyes, knowing there was no saving this train wreck. Like it or not, his time of reckoning was upon him. Bree remained quiet by his side, her expression unreadable. "No, she's not a wedding guest. This is Breanna Ellers. She's Frank's granddaughter. I'm taking her back to his place right now." Taking a deep breath, he added, "Bree, this is Angus and Wayne MacDonald. My dad and uncle."

Alex heard Bree gasp.

His dad spoke louder. "Frank's granddaughter? Well, I'll be. It's a pleasure to meet you, Bree."

When Alex turned to face her, she looked like a deer caught in headlights, her eyes as big as a doe's. In not much more than a whisper, he heard her say, "Angus MacDonald?" It was as if she were seeing a ghost.

A sick feeling rose up from Alex's gut. His hopes were dashed. "Look, Dad, it's been a long day. If you don't mind, I've got to get Bree back to Frank's place."

"Sure, have it your way," his dad snorted.

"Uncle Wayne, can you take Dad home? I'll talk to you both later," Alex shouted past his dad through the truck's open window.

"Sure thing, Boss," his uncle drawled, making fun of him. Wayne put the truck in gear and pulled away.

Oh, shit. That had not gone well, and Alex was sure he hadn't heard the last of it. There would be hell to pay when he got home, but any grief he would get from his father could wait. Right now, he had to do some serious damage control with Bree.

Alex didn't have to be psychic to know something was bothering her. A few minutes ago, on the ride back from the wedding, she'd been animated and laughing, full of life. Now she was shut down tighter than the cinch belt on a horse's belly. Her whole body seemed to shrink away from him.

He drew a deep breath and ran a hand through his hair. Maybe he could try to ignore what had just happened, but that wouldn't

97

make it go away. They were nearly at Frank's farm. If he didn't try to fix this now, it would remain broken. This wasn't how he wanted their day to end, but he knew it was time to confront the issue.

"Are you going to tell me what's bothering you?" he asked.

The look in her eyes was one of seething anger. Her reaction was worse than he had expected. "Can you just take me home? Now?"

With a flip of the reins, he got the horses moving. "Look, Bree, I can explain if you'll just listen."

"Explain? You lied to me. You knowingly lied to me." She bit out each word. "You said your name is Alex Conner."

"My name is Alex Conner. Alex Conner MacDonald."

"Ashamed of being a MacDonald? I don't blame you."

"I'm not ashamed. What do you have against the MacDonalds anyway?" He didn't like being put on the defensive.

"Then why lie?"

"Stop saying that. I didn't lie. I just didn't tell you my last name."

"You lied about being a MacDonald."

"I was going to tell you, but Frank warned me not to. He said you don't like the MacDonald clan, which makes no sense to me. Why would a person dislike a whole clan? Now that you know, maybe you can explain why my last name is such a problem for you."

They had reached McGregor's driveway. Alex pulled the horses to a stop, but before the wheels had even stopped turning, Bree grabbed her jacket and climbed down from the carriage. As quick as he could, Alex set the brake and tied off the reins. He jumped down from the carriage, jogged around the horses, and caught up to her just as she was about to open the front door.

Alex reached out and grabbed Bree's elbow. "We're not done here."

~~~

Bree pulled away from him then shot through the front door of Franklin's house with Alex close behind. "Leave me alone."

"Not until you tell me what's wrong." He stormed in behind her, slamming the door.

She spun around to face him. "Why didn't you tell me you're a MacDonald?"

"Frank said you wouldn't help me if you knew."

"He's right. I won't."

"You'd refuse to help my horses because my last name's MacDonald? What kind of crap is that? Or are you just using that as an excuse? Is the job too big for you? Are you in over your head?"

For a second, his words hurt, a low blow to her gut, but she quickly shoved them aside. They were spoken by a MacDonald. They meant nothing to her.

"You know what your problem is?" Bree spat, shaking with fury. "You think you can have anything you want. You think you can just show up on my doorstep, snap your fingers, and I'll do your bidding. Ha! I bet you've never known a day of struggle your whole life."

"I've had my struggles," he shot back.

"Yeah, I'll bet."

"I've learned to put them behind me."

Bree felt blood rush through her head as her heart thumped painfully hard in her chest. Anger took control of her words, shutting out any chance for kindness or understanding. "No self-respecting MacNicol will ever help a MacDonald. Not after what they did to my clan."

"Your clan? What the hell does that mean?"

"My mother was a MacNicol. I'm of the MacNicol clan. From the Isle of Skye. At least I was until the MacDonalds drove us from our land. They destroyed our home and killed my mother. I lost everything and everyone I loved because of the MacDonalds. Vicious men led by Angus MacDonald, a man who betrayed his own sister."

She thought back to how cruelly Angus MacDonald had treated his sister Janet, all because she was married to Duncan, chief of the MacNicol clan. Her uncle had married Janet MacDonald to help secure an alliance with the large, aggressive clan, not that it had done a lot of good. Soon after the death of Hugh, Janet's father, Angus had conquered and destroyed the MacNicol clan after siding with the English. Angus MacDonald was the worst kind of traitor.

"What the hell are you talking about?" Alex yelled at her.

Franklin strode into the room, shaking the floor boards. "Breanna Ellers," he bellowed over their shouting. "Watch what you say."

She turned to look at the man she called Grandpa. "Do you think he shouldn't know? Would he even care?"

"This isn't about him, Breanna. This is about you."

"What the hell is she talking about, McGregor?" Alex asked.

Franklin remained silent, his eyes locked on Bree. She stood rooted to her spot, staring back at Frank. *Had he lied to her too*?

"Come with me, Breanna." He reached out an old, weathered hand, hardened with age and softened with love. "We need to talk. Ye need to calm down."

She tore her eyes from his commanding gaze and glanced at Alex. "What about *him*?"

"It'll sit. Let it be for now. Come with me."

Bree didn't move. She didn't accept Franklin's offered hand. To leave would be a retreat, akin to admitting defeat. Another defeat at the hands of a MacDonald. She couldn't do it; she wouldn't do it. She tore off the coat, hat, and shirt Alex had loaned her and threw them at Alex. She wanted nothing of his to touch her.

As Alex gathered up the clothes, Franklin gave him a no-questions look. "Maybe it's best if ye leave."

"Fine," he barked. "That's just fine with me. She's all yours."

Alex stomped out of the room, closing the door so fast and hard behind him, it shuddered in its frame.

Franklin reached for her again, but she jerked away. Bree didn't want his comfort. She wanted to stay mad. Being mad made it easier to blame Alex for her pain and the hurt she felt inside. Being mad dulled her senses and held back her tears. Being mad allowed her to forget how much she had enjoyed being with him.

"Breanna, you've got to stop. You're living in the past. What you're talking about, what you're hurting about, happened seven hundred years ago."

"Not to me." Tears threatened, burning at her eyes. She wiped them away with a quick swipe of her hand.

"Maybe not to you, but to everyone else. Is your past and anguish what you want to hold on to? You chose to follow your dad to the future, to a new life."

"That's not true. I didn't have a choice."

"Little lass, we always have a choice. It may not have looked that way at the moment, but you always had a choice."

"Ma was dead. Da was leaving. My brother and sisters were scattered, barely surviving. There was nowhere else for me to go."

"Bree, darling, you could have stayed and lived with one of your sisters, not that it would have been easy. Or gotten yourself married. Lord knows, a pretty young thing like you had plenty of men knocking on your door. 'Twas you who wanted to take the adventure. You wanted to see what was on the other side of tomorrow."

"But my dad—"

Franklin held up his hand, halting her words. "I'm sure your dad told you enough stories to sweeten the deal, but 'twas you who chose, and acted, with enough strength and determination to make the leap. I saw you when you first arrived. Skittish as a newborn foal and just as excited to test your legs. You had so much to learn and such grand desire you soaked it all up like a sponge."

"What good has it been? I should have stayed. I should have tried." Bree turned away, her eyes glazed over with regret, no longer seeing Franklin or the room around them. Her mind drifted to another time and place, making memories out of shadows on the wall.

The Scottish isle was often cold and wet, with nearly unending rain, but Scorrybreac had been her home—until the MacDonalds had attacked, destroying her life and everything she'd loved in one horrifically brutal battle.

She was the youngest daughter of Daniel Ellers and Kayla MacNicol, and the last one still living with her parents at Scorrybreac when the MacDonalds had shown up in force, led by Angus MacDonald. They had attacked with ruthless malice, cutting down everyone they found in the keep, including her mother, her sister Glenna with her unborn bairn, and William Gregory, the man Bree loved. Only by the good grace of God had she and her father had survived. They had been away from Scorrybreac on the day of the attack, visiting her two elder sisters, Lorene and Treasa. The third eldest, Glenna, had returned to Scorrybreac to deliver her second child, and Ma, their clan healer, had stayed behind to tend to her daughter. It had cost them their lives. She learned later William had died, trying to save her mother and sister when their clan was attacked. Though she'd been told Uncle Duncan and his warriors had done their best to fight off the ruthless MacDonalds, in the end, even the chief's wife, Angus McDonald's own sister, had been struck down, and Duncan's only daughter Amy had been forced to take refuge with a neighboring clan. So many had perished at the blades of the MacDonalds. So many of Bree's clansmen had died that day, and the few who had survived fled the MacNicol lands, taking refuge wherever they could, mostly with the MacLeods. Her brother and sisters were among those driven from their lands.

Franklin spoke, as though reading her thoughts. "I can't believe you're missing the cold, the wet, the mud, and the hunger of the past. Don't be telling me you'd give up your warm bed and hot showers to return to that terrible time. You came to the warmth of California and left the fighting behind. 'Twas the right thing to do."

Bree shook her head, but she didn't look up. "I often wonder if I should have stayed."

"And done what? Lived out a hard life like your brother Alan, who was off fighting with the Bruce? Or your sisters, routed from their homes? Yer staying wouldn't have saved them or changed their lives for the better. Don't try to romanticize something that happened seven hundred years ago. Life wasn't easy and was only destined to get worse, what with the way the English treated the Scots. What good is it to come all this way if you're just going to cling to the past?"

Her head jerked up. "I don't cling to the past. I've learned all about living in this modern world, all except computers. But I know how to talk and act. I'm no longer an old Scottish lass."

Since the day they had met, Franklin had called her his "old Scottish lass," and he had become the grandfather she'd never had. She had arrived in California nearly four years ago and liked to believe she had shed the identity of being an old Scottish lass.

But seeing the name MacDonald painted large across the side of that truck brought the horror, the rage, and the guilt all crashing back around her.

"It doesn't look that way to me," Franklin said with a firm shake of his head. "Seems to me you're hiding out on your father's ranch, staying there as much as you do. You need to move beyond tending to broken animals. You need to fix yourself."

"You don't know what you're talking about. I'm doing just fine. I'm getting the ranch running again. I'm taking on clients, and I'm giving riding lessons. I'm doing just fine."

"Yes, it's all good. You give riding lessons to children with special needs, just like your animals have special needs. You tend to them all beautifully. But do you tend to yourself? When was the last time you went to a party or hung out with other young people? It's great how much you love your new modern family, but you need to move beyond us old folks. You need to seek a life for yourself. That's not going to happen staying home on the ranch."

"I have Jenny and Jack."

"Your cousins are over thirty. Breanna, you're surrounded by people who love you. Your Aunt Teressa and Uncle Robert love you dearly. Jack and Jenny love you. I love you."

Bree finally looked him in the eye, a half smile creeping to her lips.

"If you'd let him, Alex will love you."

"Grandpa!" Bree was appalled. "How can you say such a thing? He's a MacDonald. And you know it."

"Hell, what's not to love about my little girl? You're as smart as the day is long and as pretty as a sunrise. He's an arrogant little bastard, but he's a charmer, and he's neither blind nor stupid. Alex knows a good little lass when he sees one. Don't be holding that against him."

"You set us up." The light bulb turning on in her head was so bright she wondered why she hadn't seen it before.

"Darn right, I did. I've waited long enough to see you climb out of that shell you've created, staying all warm and cozy at the ranch, and secluded. I figured Alex was just the man to rattle your cage."

"Grandpa, how could you?"

"Well, it worked, didn't it? He's got you wanting something more."

"I oughta—"

"You oughta thank me." Franklin softened his voice. "Breanna, if you don't take this job because he's a MacDonald, I have to ask, who are you trying to help, and who are you trying to hurt? Those horses need your love, your special gift, regardless of who owns them. If you turn down this job, Alex will find someone else, someone not as good as you. How will that make you feel? I'm guessing not so good. Kind of like taking poison and hoping the other guy gets sick. I've never seen it happen."

Bree sat there, silently stewing in her anger. Part of her knew Franklin was right, but it was more than she could accept, much less admit. It felt too much like defeat.

"Give yourself some time, sweet lass. Listen to your heart. If you can hear horses' thoughts, surely you can listen to your own heart. Sometimes it just takes getting quiet."

Bree spoke softly, "I'm sorry, Grandpa. I just can't do it. I can't help the MacDonalds. Not for you, and not for Alex."

"I'm not asking you to do this for Alex. I'm asking you to do it for yourself."

"I really don't see what good it would do." Bree picked up her bike pack and started to gather her things. It was getting late, and she needed to hit the road. She didn't like the idea of riding all the way home in the dark, but she had no other choice.

Franklin grabbed her helmet, holding it hostage. "Where do you think you're going?" he asked.

"Back home. I need to leave tonight. I have a riding class in the morning." She reached for the helmet, but he snatched it away.

"Oh, no, you don't. Your Aunt Teressa called; she said the riding class had to be canceled. Your students are going on a field trip with their school. Besides, little lady, I know you rode up here on your motorcycle, and Teressa told me this is the first time you've ridden this far from the ranch. Do you think I'd let you ride home in the dark? Not on my watch."

"You talked to Aunt Teressa?" Her aunt was her guardian, her mentor, and her tutor. When she had first arrived in California, in the twenty-first century, she had needed someone to lean on, someone to show her the way, and her aunt had done all that and more. She was like a second mother to her.

"Dang right I talked to your aunt. Didn't you just hear me say she called?"

Bree sat down hard on the sofa. She felt trapped. "Are you sure you didn't call her?"

"Now why would I go and do that? Unless there's something else you're not telling me?"

Franklin towered over her, making her feel uncomfortably small and childlike. For a moment, she did feel guilty, as if she had something else to confess. But there was nothing. Her conscience was clear.

"No, I've got no other secrets," she sulked. None she needed to discuss with him.

"And no place else you need to be. You might as well settle in. You're here for the night."

Bree folded her arms across her chest. "Okay, but I'm leaving first thing in the morning."

"By all means, get an early start. You'll be able to beat the traffic. But you're not going anywhere until the sun comes up. We'll see how you feel in the morning," Franklin said. When she remained silent, he added, "Agreed?"

"Agreed," Bree said, begrudgingly.

She watched Franklin turn and head to the kitchen to begin dinner. She knew he loved her and was only looking out for her, but still, it rubbed. Franklin had known Alex was a MacDonald, and yet, he had sent him to her doorstep to ask for her help. He had even told Alex to conceal his last name, knowing how much she hated the MacDonalds. And he claimed he had done it because he loved her.

How could he?

She couldn't think of anything worse than being lied to by her grandfather—except knowing he had done it out of love.

CHAPTER 9

Franklin stepped out to the back porch, wondering how he was going to fix this problem. He had known Breanna wasn't going to be happy when she learned Alex was a MacDonald, but her reaction had been worse than he had expected. They had sat through dinner in near silence. Bree had refused to discuss the matter. There was so much he wanted to tell her, but he couldn't. He'd been on this earth for too long and knew there were some things you just didn't mess with. Karma was one of them.

"This certainly isn't going as well as we had hoped, now, is it?" a voice spoke behind him.

Franklin turned to see Moezell sitting in one of the rockers. The faerie's long, pale, blond hair hung loose around her shoulders, falling to her waist. As always, she wore a silver-blue dress that matched the color of her eyes. The effect was startling.

"Don't ye worry. Breanna's a tough old lass. She'll pull through this." He took a seat in the empty rocker next to the faerie.

"That's not how it looks to me, Souyer," Moezell said.

"Franklin," he corrected her. "In this life, my name's Franklin."

"Yes, well, Franklin, we need to fix this. She's your goddaughter. Don't you want her to be happy?"

Again, he corrected the faerie. "Granddaughter. In this life, I'm her grandfather, more or less. At least I've brought them together. That's more than you can say."

"I'm the one who brought her to this century. Besides, we're not done yet. We know he's her soulmate, but the Fates have a wicked sense of humor. Having William Gregory reincarnate as a MacDonald is a bloody shame, but this is what we have to work with. If we can't mend this thing—"

"I know. I saw what happened to Rory," Franklin said, referring to the lonely years Rory MacNicol lived without his soulmate. Moezell had been honor bound to send Teressa Ellers back to the future where she had come from, even though it meant leaving Rory behind in the thirteenth century to live out his life alone. It had taken some time, but Teressa and Rory had finally been reunited when Rory reincarnated as Robert MacNicol in the twenty-first century.

"And you know how happy he is now, as Robert," Moezell said.

"At least he got to come back as a MacNicol. William's come back as a MacDonald."

"Yes, I know. Like I said, darn wicked sense of humor. To take a perfectly good Gregory and bring him back as a MacDonald. You must have been shocked when you found out." Moezell set the chair to rocking, looking a wee more smug than sympathetic.

"It's certainly not what I would wish for my nephew."

"You mean Souyer's grandnephew," she corrected him, flashing a grin of pure satisfaction.

Meddlesome old faerie. "Yes, my grandnephew. But the Fates have decided. Now he's a MacDonald, and I'm sure there's a reason. There's always a reason, even if we don't know what it is."

109

Moezell stopped rocking. "Oh, we know very well what it is. The Fates are intent on mending this centuries-old blood feud between the MacNicols and the MacDonalds, and Alex and Breanna have gotten caught up in the middle."

"I'll do what I can, but Alex and Breanna are the only ones who can make this right."

"I'm sure they will if I have any say in the matter. I have faith their relationship will come full circle before it's done."

Franklin gave the faerie a hard once-over. "Not to be insulting, but you're looking rather *human* today. What's up?"

"I plan to visit an ale house," she said, looking rather pleased.

"You mean a bar?" Franklin's brows shot up his forehead.

"Yes, I think that's what you call them." She shrugged off her error.

"Just what do you have planned?"

"Just a little information sharing."

"I don't like the sound of that. You know there are rules about what we can and cannot say." Franklin leaned forward in his chair, bringing his face closer to hers.

Moezell drew back in the rocker. "Don't worry. I know the rules. I won't say more than I'm allowed."

Her smile was sugar sweet, but he wasn't buying it. "Yeah, right. Like I believe that."

"Believe whatever you want; you humans always do. Now, if you will excuse me, I have work to do."

Before he could argue, Moezell stood and stepped away, fading from his sight.

Yeah, right, he thought. *Never trust a faerie.* Maybe it was time he did a little information sharing of his own.

~*~

Alex had just parked his bike and was headed toward the Old Hangman's Saloon when his cell phone rang. Frank McGregor's name showed on the caller ID. He thought about ignoring it, but didn't. He wanted to know about Bree.

"What do you want, McGregor?"

"Alex, let me ask you one thing. Are you a man, or are you an idiot?"

"What the hell are you talking about?" He was right; he shouldn't have answered the phone. In fact, he should probably hang up right now before McGregor could say anything else.

"If you screw things up with Breanna, you'll never get your horses healed. You may get them to work again, but you'll never get them healed. Breanna's got gifts you can't even begin to understand."

"You're right, McGregor. I don't understand any of this. I'm not going to risk losing my business over a woman who can't do the job or doesn't like my last name."

"Breanna can do the job all right. The question is can she work with you?"

"I'm not the one who went stomping off as soon as she learned I'm a MacDonald. I still don't understand what she has against us, but I can't change the family name to suit her needs." Alex paced back and forth outside the bar. Though he was tempted to hang up on the old man, he knew he couldn't. He had too much respect for McGregor. Somewhere, deep in his soul, he knew the old man had his best interests at heart.

"I'm not asking you to. I am asking you to try and understand."

"Okay, so try me. Try telling me what this is all about."

"Ye don't know what it's like to lose both your parents within a few months. Ye don't know what it's like to be an eighteen-year-old lass taking on a new life, a new family, hell, a whole new world. She

111

lost everyone she knew, everything she held dear, and came to this country. It's not been easy for her, but she's done it all; she's faced more than ye could ever know."

Alex stopped pacing and drew a deep breath. "You're right, McGregor. I don't know. How could I? She won't talk about it."

"Of course not. She doesn't sit there and babble on about her past, but it's there if you'd take the time to look beyond her pretty face."

"So, what are you suggesting? Now that she knows I'm a MacDonald, she doesn't want anything to do with me or my horses."

"All I'm asking is to give her some time. She's going to be here until tomorrow. Can you wait until then?"

Alex stared at the ground in front of him for a long moment, shaking his head. He wondered what the hell he was getting himself into. Finally he spoke. "Sure, I can wait. My horses aren't going anywhere."

"Thanks. That's all I'm asking. I'll call you in the morning."

Alex clicked off his phone and shoved it back in his pocket. From the way he spoke, it almost sounded like McGregor was the one who needed his help. He didn't know why, and it made no sense. Whatever it was, he figured it could wait. Right now, he was headed into his favorite bar with every intention of getting too drunk to drive home. If he were successful, it wouldn't be the first time he camped out in the back room of Randy's saloon.

Once inside, he took the seat nearest the bartender. Alex had just been handed an ice-cold bottle of beer when he noticed the long-legged blonde enter the bar. Her platinum blond hair hung loose to her waist, and her iridescent silver-blue dress hugged her curves better than lingerie on a Victoria Secret's model. She was a real looker.

Alex watched her as she moved through the room. Hell, every man in the place and a few of the women were watching her, too. She had that exotic, I'm-not-from-here kind of look about her. She also looked like the kind of woman who once she set her sights on a man would get exactly what she wanted, and he wouldn't even know what hit him.

In other words, definitely not his type.

The last thing he needed was a manipulative woman in his life. He didn't need an obstinate redhead like Bree, and he certainly didn't need a hot, flashy blonde fresh from the city.

He turned his head, focusing on the mirror behind the bar. The bottom half was lined with glass shelves holding a variety of liquor bottles. Though he tried to stay focused on Randy's whisky selection, his eyes were drawn to the blonde's reflection. It must have been a trick of the lighting, but suddenly she appeared as a simple, innocent, country girl, looking lost in her surroundings. His heart went out to her. He was even more surprised when she made a beeline for the empty barstool next to him. Alex was sure someone had been sitting there only a moment ago, but now it was vacant, and he hadn't noticed when his fellow bar-fly had left.

The blonde slid onto the barstool, hooking her heels over the chair's lower rungs as she wiggled around on the black padded seat. "They're not very comfortable, are they?" she said to him.

Alex resisted the temptation to look around to see if she was talking to someone else. "No, they're not," he muttered before taking a long, deep draw on his beer; that first swallow was always the best. He figured that would be the extent of their conversation. He was wrong.

The blonde tapped him lightly on the shoulder. He turned to face her.

"I said, these bar stools are not very comfortable, are they?"

"No, they're not," he repeated, looking right at her.

Actually, he stared. She had the most mesmerizing blue eyes he had ever seen. So blue, they looked surreal, as though not of this world. He blinked several times and looked away, focusing again on his beer.

"Why are you sitting here when there are empty chairs at the tables?" she asked.

Was she really that naïve? He glanced sideways at her, trying to avoid eye contact. "Maybe it's because this is closer to the alcohol. Or because this is where people sit when they're drinking alone. Or maybe it's because it's the thing to do. Take your pick."

"Oh, my," she said. Her hand came up to her chin as if seriously considering the choices. "I'll pick 'because it's the thing to do.'"

"Whatever. Why do you even care?" He wasn't angry, just irritated. Alex couldn't figure out if she was flirting with him or just desperate. Either way, it didn't matter; he wasn't interested. He had come here to drink alone, by himself.

"I was just asking. You're Alex MacDonald, aren't you?"

That surprised him. He was sure he'd never seen her before. His memory was darn good when a beautiful woman was involved. "How did you know?"

"I'm Moezell," she said, as though that should mean something to him. When he drew a blank, she added, "I saw you at the Smithersons' wedding, driving the carriage. You were with a woman, a tall redhead. What's her name?"

"Bree. Breanna Ellers. She's my assistant, or at least she was for the day."

"Is she no longer with you?"

"You don't see her here, do you?" He gestured to the seats around them.

"I mean, is she no longer your assistant?" Moezell looked miffed, observably frustrated by his lack of cooperation.

"Nope, I'm pretty sure we've reached a dead end." She probably figured he was at the bar looking to pick up a woman. She was wrong.

He was too preoccupied, thinking about Bree, but this little filly didn't need to know about that. Maybe it wasn't such a bad idea to leave the barn door open for Miss Moezell.

"What a shame. You two looked so good together." The woman looked genuinely concerned.

Alex looked her over at her, trying to figure her out. If she were trying to flirt with him, she had a strange way of going about it. He found himself staring again. *Damn those blue eyes.*

Seemingly unfazed by his stare, she continued talking. "You know, MacDonald is an old, established Scottish name. Have ye ever researched your clan's history?" she asked.

He took another deep drink of beer, considering her question. "Can't say I have. I know my father and uncle moved here from Scotland, and I know my grandfather was a hard-core Scottish loyalist, but that's as far back as my knowledge goes."

"Have ye no interest?" she asked. Her voice had taken on a distinctly Scottish accent.

"No, actually, I don't. Why should I care what my ancestors did back in Scotland long before I was born? We're Americans now."

She smiled brightly. "I have a great fondness for Scottish history. Ye could say I'm a bit of an expert. I can tell ye all about the history of yer clan, if you'd like." She definitely spoke with a Scottish accent.

"No, thanks. If I want to know more, I'll just use Wikipedia or Google."

Moezell continued speaking, completely ignoring his response. "There's an interesting old story about how the MacDonalds battled with the MacNicols of Scorrybreac back in the early thirteen-hundreds."

Alex's ears perked up.

"The MacDonalds attacked without provocation, just because they could—because they were bigger and stronger. They eventually drove the MacNicols from their home, forcing them to become tenant farmers, virtual slaves, on their own lands. Can you imagine that? Those old MacDonalds were rather ruthless. I'm sure yer nothing like that." She gave him a critical eye, as if she weren't entirely sure.

Bree had said she was from the MacNicol clan, and now this Moezell woman was spouting facts about their history. She definitely had his attention. After taking another swig of his beer, he gave a nod, asking her to continue. "Go on."

"Their battle nearly destroyed the MacNicols; so many were killed. It broke the clan apart. Amy MacNicol, the only daughter of Duncan, the MacNicol chief, married Torquil MacLeod, hoping to align the two clans to fight against the MacDonalds, but after that one fateful battle, the MacNicols were never able to regain their previous position of power. It was truly a difficult time for them."

"This is all very interesting, more than you can know, but why are you telling me?" He couldn't help but wonder at the freaky coincidence of learning Bree was descended from the MacNicol clan and then, from out of the blue, having this strange woman give him a lesson on their ancient history.

"You were born into the MacDonald clan. This is vital information, part of their history I think ye should know."

Now he got it. She was a nerd, a regular history geek. A beautiful history geek with amazing blue eyes, but still a geek, nonetheless. "Do you always go around spouting clan history to the men you meet?"

Moezell drew back. "Of course not. Why would I do that?"

"That's good to hear. I can't imagine you get a lot of dates with that routine."

She blinked several times. "Dates? Do you think I'm flirting with you?"

"Well, aren't you?"

"No, I'm telling you about your clan's history—about the MacNicols and the MacDonalds. The MacNicols suffered horribly at the hands of the MacDonalds. Don't you care?"

"Why should I? It's ancient history. It doesn't concern me."

"Oh, yes, it does. Everything that happens in our past affects our present. You may not remember, but you bring it all back with you."

What the hell did she mean, "You bring it all back with you?" Back from where? She wasn't making any sense, and it was starting to freak him out.

He finished his beer and stood. "Sorry, don't mean to be rude or anything, but I've got to get going. You know, a big day ahead of me and all."

"As ye wish, but mark my words. Remember what I've told you." There was that Scottish accent again. It was just plain weird.

Alex turned to pay his bill. When he looked back at the bar stool next to him, she was gone. She must have slipped into the crowd, looking for another victim to assault with her ancient history lessons. That was fine with him.

He couldn't get home fast enough. All he wanted was for this day to be over. As soon as he got in the door, he picked up the TV's remote control, hoping to find some mindless entertainment to help him unwind, and began flipping through the channels. When he came upon a reenactment scene on the History Channel, he stopped. What caught his interest was ancient Scotland, by the look of it.

Listening to the announcer. he sat down to watch. "Early in the fourteenth century, the MacDonalds rose up in battle against the

MacNicols, a neighboring clan on the Isle of Skye, nearly wiping out the once-prosperous clan."

Holy crap, he thought. *This day just keeps getting weirder and weirder.*

Wasn't it enough that his horses were misbehaving? Why were these strange things happening to him? Why did he find a crazy, cute, MacDonald-hating, psychic horse whisperer so darn attractive? Was it coincidence some wacky, strange, Scottish history buff had insisted on telling him all about the MacDonalds and the MacNicols two minutes after she'd met him? And what the hell was a frigging documentary about that very subject doing playing on his TV right now?

As much as he wanted to flip the channel, he couldn't; he was too enthralled. Alex put down the remote and settled back in his chair to watch. A half hour later, he'd learned everything there was to know about the battle between the MacDonalds and the MacNicols—and none of it was pretty.

CHAPTER 10

The fact she hadn't slept well didn't surprise Bree. Her brain was too busy trying to sort out her feelings. No matter how hard she tried to put Alex and his horses out of her mind, the thoughts kept looping back in, stealing her rest. After several hours of debating with herself, she knew she couldn't turn her back on those innocent horses. It wasn't their fault they were being terrorized, and it darn sure wasn't their fault they were owned by Alex and Angus MacDonald. That was just their bad luck.

Times like these were when she hated how her logical mind battled with her emotional heart, knowing full well no matter how painful the outcome, her emotional heart would be the winner. It was disconcerting to admit she cared about Alex because he cared about his horses, even though he had lied to her. She knew he had his reasons, including the fact that Franklin had warned him about her contempt for his family name. Mostly, she hated knowing the real issue wasn't her contempt for the MacDonalds, although that was a big one. The real issue was her attraction to Alex, and even more compelling was her desire to help heal his horses. If she could figure out what was causing their anxiety, maybe she could prevent it from happening again.

Too restless to wait for the sun, Bree got dressed and quietly slipped out the front door of Franklin's house while it was still dark. She thought about riding off on her bike, but she didn't want the sound of the motor to wake Franklin. Instead, she zipped up her riding jacket and started walking down the road. The Clydesdales were boarded nearby, and the stroll would help relieve her pent-up restlessness. Setting off at a brisk pace, she braced herself against the chilly morning mist hugging the countryside. Within minutes, the soft glow of the rising sun began to make its appearance, warming the air and lighting her way.

When she rounded the final curve in the road, she stopped to catch her breath and take in the sight. The lush green pasture spread out before her was dotted with tiny purple and yellow wild flowers creating a vivid springtime tapestry. Standing not far off were the Clydesdales, looking magnificent in the golden rays of the morning sun.

She climbed over the fence and walked a few paces toward Malt and Barley then stood there for several minutes, allowing the horses to become comfortable with her presence. As she had done the day before, she reached out to create a psychic connection with them. The horses seemed much more accepting of her after their previous day together.

Her connection to Barley was stronger than Malt, so she focused her attention on the younger gelding. Barley seemed more open to her psychic probe, showing less resistance. Once the connection was made, she slowly began searching his thoughts, quietly observing and listening. Unless an animal was in a heightened sense of awareness, usually brought on by a threatening event, their thoughts were fairly benign. Since the Clydesdales were safely ensconced in their familiar pasture, Barley's comfort level was quite high.

Cautiously, she searched his memories from the previous day, looking for the event that had triggered his fear. This required slow, careful probing. If she accessed the images too quickly or with too much force, the horse was likely to think he was in danger again, causing him to flee the perceived threat, real or not.

It took some effort, but Bree was eventually able to access the memory she was looking for. She started with a moment prior to the hotel street scene and gradually walked him through the memory, all the while sending reassuring messages that Barley was safe, standing in his pasture, away from any danger. It didn't take long for her to find the moment when Barley's fear was first sparked. Doing her best to keep him calm, she searched for similar situations. Soon, she found more of the same, and she had to admit, it scared her, too.

Bree slowly withdrew from Barley's thoughts, leaving him with pleasant thoughts of hay and sunshine. As she started to walk away, her legs wobbled, too weak to support her, so she sat down in the field and wrapped her arms around her. Only then did she allow herself to cry. She hadn't wanted Barley to feel her tears. The idea someone could be so hateful to another living being was beyond her ability to comprehend.

When she finally felt strong enough to move away, she quickly rose and scrambled out of the pasture then pulled out her cell phone. "Aunt Teressa, this is Bree. I think I need your help."

As she walked back to Franklin's house, she told her aunt everything that had happened. She had already told her about meeting Alex back at the ranch in a previous phone call; now she told her about the Clydesdales.

Without going into too much detail, she told her aunt about connecting with the horses and working with Alex at the wedding. She gave her a quick rundown on how she had agreed to go on the job with him as his assistant and how the horses had gotten spooked while they were at the hotel. What she didn't tell her aunt was about Alex being a MacDonald. Bree wasn't ready to deal with that issue, and knowing her aunt, she'd want to talk about it, considering she was a relationship coach.

"I felt really bad I wasn't able to figure out the reason for their fear, but my first priority was to keep them calm," Bree said, referring to the Clydesdales.

"You did the right thing, Bree. I'm sure Alex understands," Teressa said.

"I know; he said as much. But I still feel bad." Bree recalled how Alex had been more concerned about comforting her than worried about what had spooked his horses. At the time, she'd been too focused on her disappointment over not being able to locate the source of their fear. She hadn't fully appreciated his actions.

"So, anyway, I went out to see the horses this morning, alone. I wanted to see if I could probe their memories to find out what sparked their fear." She had no problem discussing her talents with Teressa. Her aunt knew all about the fae bloodline of the women in the MacNicol clan. She never questioned Bree's unique abilities.

"What did you find?" Teressa asked.

"There was a group of skateboarders near the hotel where the bride was getting her pictures taken before the wedding. They weren't bothering the horses, at least, it didn't look like they were, but apparently one of the boys in the group has been mean to them before. When the horses saw the boys, or maybe they just heard the skateboards—those things make a lot of noise—it reignited their earlier fears, and they became skittish. That's why I wasn't able to figure out what had set them off. It was too much of an instinctive reaction to a previously bad experience. Do you know what I mean?"

"Oh, yes, I follow you exactly. It's the same with people. When something bad happens and we're put into a similar situation, we tend to relive that emotion, even if we don't understand why. Kinda like a grown-up being afraid of playgrounds and not knowing why. It might be because they fell off the swing set and broke a leg when they were a child. Or maybe they associate playgrounds with the school bully. The memory of the past experience is so strong, it's carried forward to the present, even if the person no longer knows what caused it. I'm sure it's the same with Alex's horses."

"Exactly. I'm worried that every time the horses hear that noise or encounter a group of skateboarders, they'll remember this fear and want to bolt. It makes it kind of hard for them to work out in public. These days, skateboarders can be anywhere."

"I agree. It's not as though Alex can always avoid them. It's bound to happen again, like it did at the wedding, only you won't be there to help, and he'll have a bigger problem on his hands."

It was interesting to Bree that her aunt was thinking about how this would affect Alex. Bree had only been focused on helping the horses, ignoring the problem this created for him. It wasn't his fault someone held a grudge against his horses, and yet his company was feeling the effects.

Right. His company, the family business, *MacDonald's Clydesdales and Carriages*, was counting on her to heal their Clydesdales and as a result, help fix their financial problems. Bree told herself she didn't care what happened to them; her only interest was helping the horses. Well, she tried to convince herself the horses were her only concern, but she knew she couldn't separate Alex from the problem. If she had any hope of helping these horses, sooner or later, she was going to have to deal with Alex—probably best if it was sooner. *Darn it.*

"If we could just find the boy who's been hurting the Clydes, maybe we could get him to stop. That's where I need your help. I don't think I can do this alone. I doubt I could get the boy to listen to me. You're a relationship coach. Surely you'd have better luck than me."

"Maybe, Bree, but first you'll have to find the boy who did this. Even if you do find him, and we're able to get him to stop hurting the horses, which is already asking a lot, that might not solve the problem. It won't erase their fear of skateboarders. From what you've told me, just being around the skateboarders was enough to spook them even though the boys weren't bothering them."

Aunt Teressa was right. This wasn't going to be easy. Life rarely was. Placerville wasn't that big of a place, but there could be dozens of young boys who used skateboards around town. It would take a good bit of luck to find the one boy who was causing their fear. Even if they could find him, could they convince him to stop hurting the horses? She believed her aunt was good at her job, but could she really defuse the malicious grudge the boy held against the Clydesdales?

Bree wondered what had happened to turn him so mean to the horses. She hadn't been able to find anything in Barley's memory to explain his wrath. Maybe she would learn more if she probed Malt's memory, but she was too spent right now to make an attempt. That would have to wait for another day.

Even if they could find the boy and get him to stop—already some mighty big *IFs*—she still needed to find a way to eliminate Malt and Barley's fears if they were going to continue to work around town. The best way would be to have the boy interact with the horses so they could restore their confidence. If she could get the boy to make peace with the Clydesdales, it might do the trick, but that again was a pretty big stretch. To get the boy to admit his guilt was one thing; to get him to play nice might be more than she could pull off. It felt as if she were in over her head.

"What do you think I should do? Should I just go home and forget about this?" Bree asked her aunt. She was getting close to Franklin's house and figured he was up by now. She wouldn't be able to leave without speaking with him.

Teressa was quiet for a moment before she asked, "Is that what you want, Bree? To leave this undone?"

"Maybe Alex can find someone else to take over. I'll tell Franklin what I know, and he can pass the info on to Alex. You know, they're not my horses. They're not my problem."

Bree walked up to the front porch of the old farmhouse and sat down to finish her call with her aunt. She wasn't ready to go inside, not while she was talking to Teressa, and she certainly wasn't ready to speak with Franklin. She still wasn't sure what she would tell him.

"Is that how you really feel? Then why not tell Alex yourself? It'll make more sense coming from you. Why do you need Frank to act as your messenger?"

Dang, why did her aunt have to ask so many questions? "You don't understand," Bree said, starting to feel defensive.

"Why don't you try me?"

"Okay, Aunt Teressa, maybe you would understand." Anger fused with grit hardened her heart, and her need to vent erupted in a rush of words. "You more than anyone would understand. Alex lied to me. He didn't tell me he's a MacDonald. He tried to hide it from me. He told me his name is Alex Conner, but it's not. It's really Alex Conner MacDonald." She spat out his last name as though it were a nasty, bitter taste in her mouth. "It was Franklin's idea for him to hide his name. Can you believe it? Franklin told Alex to lie to me."

"Yes, I know," Teressa said, sounding unbelievably calm.

Bree couldn't believe her ears. "What? You know? Are you in on this, too?"

"Breanna, calm down. I've talked to Franklin. I know he's worried about you. He told me everything."

"How could you?" How could her aunt betray her? How could Franklin betray her? She trusted them both.

"I only found out yesterday, when I called about the canceled riding classes. I understand you're upset."

"Upset? Upset? You're darn right I'm upset!" How could everyone she loved and trusted have plotted against her? She felt so all alone. It seemed no matter how hard she tried to fit in, she always ended up feeling like an ancient relic in a modern technological world that didn't care one wit about her or have the time for things like honor, honesty, and integrity. Too many people seemed content to sit and stare at a computer screen all day while all she wanted to do was live at the ranch and work with her animals. She was the quintessential square peg in a round hole.

"Look, Bree, I'm sure you're right. Franklin asking Alex to not mention he's a MacDonald wasn't a good idea. I'm also sure Franklin had good intentions. You know how he is. He sees someone in need, and he has to help. Even if it was a little misguided, he was only trying to help Alex. If you don't want to help . . . if you don't think you can do this, for whatever reason, then just come home. No one's going to make you stay if you don't want to."

"Franklin did. Last night he wouldn't let me leave."

"He didn't want you to ride home in the dark. You know what he always says."

"Yeah, I know." Bree recited Franklin's mantra, "'There are only two kinds of motorcycle riders: the ones who have fallen and the ones who will.' But I've never taken a spill." However, Franklin was right. It was usually only a matter of time before a rider went down. Nevertheless, like any confident young rider, Bree hoped she would be the exception to the rule.

"Bree, darling, I know he's a bit old fashioned, but you can't fault him for that. You know he loves you. He would do anything for you. All of us would."

As fast as it had ballooned, Bree felt her anger deflate. She couldn't fault the man she loved as a grandfather for looking out for her. And he was right, it would have been scary to ride home, alone, in the dark.

When Alex had come to him, seeking his advice on how to help his horses, Franklin had done the only thing he could. He had recommended the best person he knew for the job. Her.

If she could stay focused on helping the horses and not on the fact that Alex was a MacDonald, she knew she could help, and she wanted to help. Bree had told Franklin she wouldn't take the job, but that wasn't true. She had come too far and was in too deep to simply turn her back on Malt and Barley and walk away, even if it meant seeing Alex again.

"Bree, are you still there?" her aunt's voice broke into her thoughts.

"Yeah, I'm still here."

"So what are you going to do? Are you coming home?"

"No, not yet. I have some things I need to do."

"Bree, honey, if you'd like, I can drive up . . . if you need any help. I wouldn't mind seeing Franklin again, and I could be there by noon. We could have lunch together."

"You don't have to do that. I don't want you going out of your way."

"It's not a problem. I'd like to help. Isn't that why you called?"

Yes, it was. She knew she'd feel better if her aunt were here. Aunt Teressa had a way of understanding things better than anyone she knew. "Okay, Auntie, if you're sure it's not a problem."

"Are you kidding? There's nothing I want more right now than to help you figure this out. We'll get to play detective together."

"You make it sound like fun." Bree almost laughed. She felt herself being lifted by her aunt's spirit.

"Of course, it'll be fun, if I'm there. I'll see you around noon."

Her aunt was right. Together, it would be fun. Alone, it would have been work.

As if hearing her thoughts, her aunt continued, "Remember, Bree, you're never alone."

"Thanks, Auntie. I needed to hear that."

Bree glanced over her shoulder at the front door. Franklin, the man she called Grandfather, was on the other side, awake, and waiting for her. It was time to go inside and tell him her plan.

She walked through the living room to the back of the house and found Franklin sitting in the breakfast nook next to the kitchen drinking his morning tea.

"Morning, Grandpa," she addressed him affectionately.

"Morning, Breanna. You're up early." Franklin looked up from the book he was reading, setting it aside. Judging the book by its cover, it was probably one of those New Age philosophy books Franklin was so fond of.

"Yeah, I couldn't sleep. I took a walk to clear my head."

"Ready for breakfast? I've got some farm fresh eggs. You like them over easy, right?"

"Sounds great. Need any help?"

"No. I've got it covered." He went into the kitchen and pulled a carton of eggs from the refrigerator. A frying pan sat waiting on the stove top. "Did you have a good walk?" he asked nonchalantly. He was probably itching to ask her what she'd been thinking about, but he'd wait until she was ready to talk. Patience was one of his many virtues.

"Yeah, I think so. I talked to Aunt Teressa. She's going to drive up here and meet me for lunch."

"Really? Now, isn't that interesting? Last night you were so anxious to ride back home. Now you're staying to have lunch. What changed?"

"I had time to think," she shrugged.

"Always a good idea." He nodded, looking slightly pleased. Instead of pursuing the subject, he continued making breakfast.

Unable to sit and do nothing, Bree manned the toaster and made herself a cup of tea.

As they were setting their breakfast on the table she asked, "I was wondering, Grandpa, how did you know?"

"Know what?" he asked as they sat down at the table.

"How did you know what I needed? You sent Alex down to get me, to bring me here to see his horses even though you knew I wouldn't come if he told me he's a MacDonald. So you warned him not to. You knew I'd be mad when I found out, and yet you did it anyway. Why? What made you think it would work?"

"Breanna, my sweet lass, sometimes you have to take a chance. Besides, I know you much better than you may think." Franklin paused and rubbed his chin, as if considering what to say before he continued. "You call me Grandpa, and I couldn't be more proud to carry the name, but back on Skye, I was your godfather."

Bree's jaw dropped. "You've got to be kidding. That's not possible." Her mind whirled, trying to figure out what he meant.

"Your father knew me as Souyer."

"The wizard?" Her eyes opened wide. She had heard numerous stories about the beloved old wizard from both of her parents, but

Souyer had died while she was still young. Her one vague memory of him was that of a kindly white-haired old man wearing a long gray robe, sitting on the high north tower and looking out over the ocean.

Bewildered, she stared at the man sitting across the table from her.

Franklin chuckled lightly. "Daniel liked to say I was a wizard. It was an old family joke. Really, I was only a druid, and sometimes a sage. I was a counselor to Daniel when he first arrived on Skye. He honored me by naming me your godfather, a tradition he brought with him from the future."

"You were Souyer?"

"Yes, in another life . . . like your Uncle Robert was once Rory."

"You know about Uncle Robert?" Bree knew her uncle was the reincarnation of her mother's brother, an ancient Scottish warrior named Rory, who had died before she'd been born. Her dad and Aunt Teressa had told her the story soon after she had arrived in the future, but as far as she knew, this was a family secret.

Teressa had met Rory during her time travel adventure to thirteenth-century Skye—courtesy of the faerie Moezell—and had fallen in love with the gregarious and charming warrior. Since Teressa was obligated to return to her own time, and Rory had to stay in his, Rory's soul had chosen to reincarnate as Robert. Moezell had arranged for his past life memories to remain intact, a magical gift from the winsome faerie who watched over the MacNicol clan.

No matter how many times she heard the story—she must have heard her Aunt Teressa tell it a dozen times, usually at her bidding—she always sighed and cried when she heard how Teressa and Rory, now Robert, had been reunited in the present.

"There's not much about your family I don't know," Franklin said. "I know about you and Teressa and Daniel's time travel. I know about Robert being Rory. I even know about William."

Bree glared at her grandfather, dumbfounded and slightly worried, her stomach suddenly churning. "William? What do you mean, you know about William?" She had never spoken to anyone about William. Her brief love affair with him was one secret from her past she kept private and totally hidden.

Franklin cocked his head. "William Gregory, the lad who died trying to save your mother's life. Surely you remember William."

Bree didn't trust that look. "Of course, I remember him," she said, looking away. "How could I ever forget any of them? They were all so dear to me." This was one story she wasn't ready to share. No one knew she had lost her innocence to William, or that they had planned to marry, at least no one still alive.

She'd only been eighteen years old, but back on Skye in the fourteenth century, she'd been of marriageable age, and William had been the man she wanted to marry. They had been waiting for the right opportunity for him to approach her father, but William had died before their betrothal could be arranged. After William's death, she had agreed to accompany her father into the future. There was no one left to keep her in the past.

"So, are you going to do it?" Franklin asked, bringing her thoughts back to the present.

"Do what? Forgive you and Alex for the dirty rotten trick you pulled on me?" Bree did her best to sound angry, but doubted she was fooling him. And she was glad they were changing the subject.

Franklin reached out and gave her hand a squeeze. "Are you going to work with the horses?"

Bree sighed, giving Franklin a weak smile. "Yeah, I'm going to do it. In fact, I was out with the horses early this morning. I know they need me; I can feel it. I'm just not ready to tell Alex. I thought I'd let him wait a while . . . if you know what I mean."

"Trying to drive up the price?" He looked impressed, and maybe a little proud.

Bree laughed. "No, nothing like that; besides, I don't think he has any money. I just don't want to appear too eager, especially after the way I acted yesterday. Shouldn't a woman take a wee bit of time to change her mind?"

Franklin's eyes softened, taking on a loving glow. "I think he cares for you, lass."

Again, she laughed off his comment. "I think he wants me to heal his horses."

"Oh, I'm sure he wants that, too. He knows how much progress you've made with Sunnyside. A month ago, no one could get near that horse. Soon you'll be using him to work with your students, those kids with special needs. That never would have happened without your love."

"Yeah, and I'd never be here without yours. Thanks, Grandpa. Or should I call you Godfather?"

"You best keep calling me Grandpa; I kinda like it. No need to change now." Franklin gave her a wide smile that crinkled the lines around his eyes, making him appear loving and wise at the same time. "So, do you know what you're going to do?"

"Well . . ." Since she was going to tell him about her plans sooner or later, she might as well not make him wait. "You see, I have an idea."

CHAPTER 11

B ree gave Franklin a rundown on everything she had learned that morning about Malt and Barley and their fear of skateboarders. She told him about her phone call with her aunt and informed him Teressa was coming to help. By the time she had finished filling him in, Teressa arrived.

After a short visit with Franklin, Bree rode with Teressa over to Big Guy's Burgers in old town Placerville for some lunch and to discuss strategy. Her aunt had a way of looking elegant, even in jeans and a tee shirt. Teressa's long blond hair, pulled back from her face, was done up in a fancy French braid that hung to the middle of her back. She wore very little makeup, and her stunning green eyes stood out against her fresh peaches-and-cream complexion. At thirty-two years old, she looked much younger than her age.

Beautiful and elegant as she appeared, Bree knew her aunt's good looks were deceiving. Teressa MacNicol could pitch hay and muck stalls just as easily as she coached her clients through their relationship problems. When it came to running the family ranch, there wasn't much her aunt couldn't do, and Bree admired her all the more for her versatility.

Her aunt began speaking as soon as they slid into the booth. "I thought about how to solve the Clydesdales' problem on the drive up here. We don't need to focus on finding the boy who hurt the horses; what's done is done. Besides, I doubt we could find an eyewitness who was there when it happened, and we can't very well make accusations based on your psychic connection with Barley. No one's going to believe you can read horses. Instead, I suggest we approach the first skateboarders we can find and ask for their help working with the horses. We'll tell them the horses have been acting skittish around skateboarders, which is true, and we need their help to get the horses comfortable around them."

"Do you really think they'll agree to help just because we ask?" Bree asked.

"Of course I do. You'd be surprised how often people are willing to help if you only ask."

"Why would they do that? What's in it for them?"

"Nothing, but it's only human nature to want to help. When Alex came to you asking for help, that's what you did. You wanted to help."

"Yeah, but I also thought I'd be getting paid." Although, if she were being honest, she'd acknowledge her real reason for taking the job had been her curiosity about working with the Clydesdales and their Scottish heritage, as well as their apparent emotional distress. Of course, it didn't hurt that she was attracted to Alex. Getting paid, if that ever happened, would only be a bonus for a job well done.

"Are you still helping because you think you'll get paid?" Teressa asked.

"No. I'm helping because the horses need me."

"Exactly. All we need to do is convince those boys that we need them."

A waitress came over to take their order. After a quick glance at the menu, Teressa asked for a tuna melt with Swiss cheese on wheat toast, and Bree decided on a veggie burger with everything.

Getting back to their conversation, Bree said, "I sure hope you know what you're doing."

"Of course, I do." Teressa answered without hesitation.

"Because I sure as hell don't."

"Well, Bree, honey, that's why I'm here." Looking far more confident than Bree felt, her aunt shined a smile that stretched from ear to ear.

~*~

It was Saturday morning, a beautiful spring day, the town of Placerville was full of tourists, and Alex was counting on them to part with some of their money for the right to be pulled around town in the back of a fancy landau driven by their own personal tour guide.

His Uncle Wayne and Howard were running a job down in Old Town Sacramento with the surrey and the four other Clydesdales. That left Malt and Barley to pull the landau. With money to be made, he didn't have the luxury of leaving them out in the field, lazing the day away.

He knew he was taking a risk, especially after what happened yesterday. If his horses misbehaved, he could lose his business license and the right to use his horses in town. Nonetheless, he needed to maximize his income if he had any hopes of paying off his dad's debt.

With all that in mind, Alex had hitched Malt and Barley to the landau and was heading into town, looking for his first fare of the day.

Earlier, he had called Frank to ask about Bree and had been told she was in town having lunch with her aunt. Though he knew it was a long shot, he was hoping he could get her to ride with him again, at least for a few trips around town. He needed her to help keep an eye on his horses. While he knew she wouldn't do it for him, he hoped she would do it for Malt and Barley. Alex knew she cared about his horses, and he counted on her caring nature to exceed her loathing of him.

Also, since he was armed with a little more insight into her hatred for the MacDonald name, he felt better prepared to do battle. If her grudge really were based on how the MacDonalds had treated the MacNicols, it was a centuries-old argument that needed to be put to rest. Hopefully, he could convince her there was nothing he could do about the past, and he shouldn't be held accountable. Not only did he feel no responsibility for the past deeds of relatives he'd never even known, he agreed with her. They were despicable acts perpetrated by despicable men. He felt no allegiance to his long dead ancestors.

As he drove past Big Guy's Burgers, he spotted a bright red MINI Cooper parked outside, the same type of car McGregor had said Bree's aunt drove. He pulled the rig over to the side of the road, wondering what he should do next.

While there was a good chance Bree was inside, and he wanted to speak with her, Alex couldn't leave the horses unattended. He also couldn't sit there and wait. There was no way to know how long it would be before she came out of the restaurant, and even then, his chances of catching her before she rode off with her aunt were pretty slim.

Hell, who was he fooling? This was never going to work. He was pegging his hopes on a woman who hated him because of his last name. How lame was that? So what if his horses got spooked for no good reason? He'd just have to keep a tight rein on them and hope for the best.

The problem was if his horses got a reputation for being disorderly, he risked losing his license to drive them in town. That license was much more valuable than a day's worth of fares. Maybe it was best if he turned the landau around and went back home.

He was just getting ready to pull the rig back into traffic when he saw Bree come out of the diner with another woman. It was obvious they had seen him and were headed his way, so he set the brake on the landau and climbed down from the carriage to greet them.

"Hello, Alex," Bree said, sounding stiff and formal.

"Hello, Bree," he said, equally reserved.

"This is my Aunt Teressa." Bree had barely finished making the introduction before she stepped over to give his horses a loving pat. "Hi, fellas, how ya doing?"

"Pleased to meet you." Alex extended his hand to Teressa, half expecting her to swat it away. There was no telling what kind of stories Bree had told her aunt.

Teressa reached out her hand to shake his. "The pleasure's all mine," she said. "I've heard a lot about you and your horses." He wished Bree had greeted him so warmly.

"So, what brings you into town?" Alex asked.

The two women exchanged a knowing glance. "She's come to help," Bree said, finally freeing a shy smile.

Hope bounced in his chest, but he played it cool. "Really? What did you have in mind?"

Bree shifted her weight from one side to the other. "First, I should start by telling you I went to see Malt and Barley this morning. I wanted to see if I could access their memories from yesterday."

"Access their memories?" This sounded like more of her psychic mumbo jumbo.

"Yeah, I wanted to see if I could find out what sparked their fear. And I did."

Alex waited, holding his skepticism and his tongue, while Bree paused. He was tempted to ask just how she was able to access a horse's memories, but he figured it was best to let that one ride for now. It didn't matter if she could really do such a thing or how it was even possible. What really mattered was she was still interested in working with his horses.

"Do you remember seeing any skateboarders hanging around the hotel?" Bree asked.

"Yeah. There was a group of guys practicing a ways down the street, but they weren't close enough to the Clydes to pose a threat."

"I know what you mean. That's probably why I didn't notice them. But apparently, one of the skateboarders has been terrorizing your horses. Now, just the presence of those skateboarders is enough to make your horses skittish."

Alex's temper flared. "How the hell could that have happened? The horses are never left unattended, not when they're in town."

"I can only guess it happened when your driver wasn't paying attention. Maybe he was busy with customers. I'm sure it wasn't you." She shrugged, looking a little nervous. "But someone was able to get too close to your horses and tried to do them harm. I was able to read Barley the best, maybe because he's younger. Keep in mind, what I saw were only images, flashes of memory, but there were at least two and possibly three times when a young man did some mean and spiteful things to your Clydesdales. In one memory, the boy spooked them with fire by flicking a lighter with an oversized flame in front of their faces. In another, I got the impression he had created some type of loud popping noises, maybe from bursting a balloon or by throwing pop-caps on the ground. I can't be sure, but he definitely spooked them.

"It was bad enough he picked on these innocent horses, but he seemed to know exactly how to prey on their most basic fears—fire and loud noises. Now the horses associate the skateboarders with an instinctual need to flee. Unfortunately, he's made a lasting impression, which we need to undo."

Everything she told him made Alex sick with anger, except when she said "we." That made him hopeful. It sounded as if she were taking the job, despite hating his family name. After what he had learned last night, he couldn't say her feelings were without cause. Maybe they were a little outdated, even stuck in the past—the far distant past—but some people were irrational about family ties and loyalties, regardless of how ancient the incident was. Once they got a thorn in their side, they couldn't pull it out, no matter how badly it festered.

Running with her use of "we," Alex asked, "Okay, so what do you suggest *we* do?"

Bree looked at her aunt. "You tell him, Aunt Teressa."

Alex detected excited energy in Teressa's eyes. This was obviously her area of expertise.

"Rather than focus on finding the one boy, or maybe it was a group of boys—we don't really know for sure—I suggest we try to find a group of skateboarders willing to work with Malt and Barley to overcome their fears and increase their confidence around them. It's called familiarity training. They're less likely to be afraid of something they're familiar with. You must have done something similar to get them comfortable working in town."

Her idea had merit. Alex almost allowed himself to become excited. "Yeah, we had to get them used to working in traffic, you know, like being around cars and strange people. Things that would normally make a horse skittish."

"Right. Since the horses have developed a fear of skateboarders, the best way to overcome their fear is to get them to make friends," Teressa said.

Alex shook his head. It sounded reasonable, but not necessarily easy. "So you're saying, all we have to do is find some skateboarders who are willing to help, and everything will be hunky-dory?" He didn't know if he should feel hopeful or helpless. He wasn't at all confident they could pull this off.

"Exactly," Teressa said with a broad smile, sounding much more confident than he felt.

"Well, good luck with that." Alex rolled his eyes.

"Why?" Bree asked.

"In my experience, those skateboarders are not all that accommodating," he said.

"Really? Have you had a lot of experience with them?" Teressa asked.

"Not really. But I've seen how they try to take over a park or shopping center so they can practice their tricks. Now you tell me they've been terrorizing my team. Doesn't sound very friendly to me."

"Not all of them have been mean to your horses, just one or two. I agree with Aunt Teressa. It's worth a try. Besides, when it comes to talking with strangers, my aunt has a special talent," Bree said, defending her aunt.

"Okay, I guess it's worth a try." He had nothing to lose and a whole lot to gain. Besides, he trusted Bree. Alex knew she wouldn't do anything to hurt his horses. If nothing else, it gave him more time with Bree. Besides, if there were a chance Teressa's idea might work, he was interested enough to see them put their plan into action.

It was also worth it to see the smile light up Bree's face as she quickly took charge.

"Great. Here's what I think we should do. Aunt Teressa, you get in and ride in the back. I'll sit up front with Alex."

Her aunt gave her a questioning look as Bree began to climb up to the driver's seat.

"So I can be closer to Malt and Barley, you know, in case anything happens," she explained.

"Of course," Teressa said as she climbed into the passenger section of the carriage. Alex noticed she was sporting one of those funny little "yeah, right" grins, but he wasn't about to complain. He climbed onto the driver's seat next to Bree.

"Let's make a run through the town following your normal route. If we encounter any skateboarders, I'll be here to help calm Malt and Barley," Bree said. She turned to speak over her shoulder to her aunt. "If we do, you can get out and talk to them. Right?"

"Right," Teressa agreed. She settled into the back of the landau, looking like one of his regular customers, happy to enjoy the ride.

"Good. I think we have a plan. Go ahead. Drive on," Bree said with a wave of her hand.

Alex contained his smile to avoid slipping into a bold-faced grin. She looked too darn cute with her take-charge attitude, and he liked it. He liked seeing her happy and confident. She was in her element, and it showed.

Casting a shielded glance toward Bree, Alex was hoping he could take advantage of their limited privacy as they drove through town. From experience, he knew if they kept their voices low, they couldn't be heard over the noise of the carriage and the surrounding traffic.

Somewhat apprehensive about this whole endeavor, Alex fumbled through his mind, searching for something to say. Should he ignore what happened the day before, or should he address the elephant sitting on his back? He could merely ask Bree about her aunt, and their plan to help the horses, and pretend he wasn't curious as hell to know what she was thinking about him and his family, but he knew that wouldn't give him any satisfaction. He needed to know where her head was before they went much further.

Before he could think of the right thing to say, Bree spoke softly, as though she, too, wanted to keep their conversation private. "I just want you to know, I'm only doing this to help your horses."

Well, that answered his question. "Yeah, I get it," he said. "After yesterday, I pretty much figured we were through. You looked pretty mad."

"I was," she confirmed with a hiss. She paused, taking a deep breath. "But Franklin calmed me down. He also refused to let me drive home alone in the dark. He held my helmet hostage." She shot a quick glance over her shoulder, and continued, "He found out from my aunt it was my first long ride on the bike."

"Smart man. I'm glad he did." Deciding to take a risk, he added, "I would've been worried about you."

Bree shrugged off his comment. "It gave me time to think. I don't agree with what you did, but I know why you did it. If my horses were hurting, I'd do whatever was needed to get them help."

"I knew you'd find out, sooner or later," he said, referring to his sin of omission.

"Yeah, that's exactly what I mean. That was pretty damn arrogant of you to decide I was better off not knowing."

"I was trying to buy time. Frank said you wouldn't help me if you knew I'm a MacDonald." As soon as the words left his mouth he regretted them. They sounded lame and childishly defensive.

"I know. He told me. But that doesn't make it right. You could have told me. You could have trusted me."

For a brief second, he saw the hurt in her eyes. She was right, of course. He could have trusted she would care enough about his horses to look beyond his last name, but he hadn't. Admittedly, he'd been too afraid she wouldn't agree to help, and after meeting her, he hadn't wanted to take the risk. It might have been a dickhead decision, but at the time, getting to know her had been a whole lot more appealing than telling her the truth and risk being sent away before he had a chance to win her over.

Lot of good that did him. He hadn't considered the long-term consequences of his choice. At the time, he had only wanted to spend more time with her. He'd hoped he could charm her into looking past his family ties, but he had failed.

Now the lie was coming back to bite him on the ass, and he had only himself to blame. Regardless of Franklin's advice, he could have told her the truth right from the beginning. If she refused to help him because he was a MacDonald, then so be it.

"About that. I think I know why you hate the MacDonalds," he said.

"Ha!" she huffed. "What would you know?" She gave him a sideways glance. "It's not like you were there."

"I happened upon a documentary on the History Channel about the MacDonalds and the MacNicols. You did say you were part of the old MacNicol clan, didn't you?"

"Yes," she nodded.

He was glad he had the documentary to use as his source of information because he darn sure wasn't going to tell her about the strange blonde in the bar. Besides being a really bad idea to tell her about another woman hitting on him, the coincidence was simply too weird to believe.

"What did it say?" she asked, referring to the documentary.

"The show was about how the MacDonalds nearly wiped out the MacNicols in the early thirteen hundreds. It looked pretty brutal." Given all that had happened, he hadn't been at all surprised when he woke dreaming of ancient Scottish battles. What surprised him was how real his dream had seemed.

"It was," she adamantly assured him.

Alex gave her a questioning look.

"Trust me, I know my clan's history."

Alex wondered what it was about ancient Scottish history that appealed so strongly to women like Bree and that woman at the bar. *What was her name? Mosey, or Moezell, or something like that.* He hadn't cracked a history book since high school, and he darn sure never felt a need to explore his family's history. Even if he had, he doubted he would have gotten so worked up about something that happened almost seven hundred years ago. Then again, his family had been the victors, not the victims.

Still, it had happened so very long ago. He wondered why Bree cared so much. It wasn't as though their families were still fighting. At least, not that he knew of.

"Do you really hate the MacDonalds because of something that happened hundreds of years ago?"

"I'm not saying anything. I don't want to talk about it. Besides, it doesn't change the fact you lied to me."

Dang. They were back to that old thing. Alex decided to let it all go. Apparently, nothing he could say would make a difference.

CHAPTER 12

Alex turned away to watch the cars, minivans, and SUVs filled with weekend tourists drive slowly past them. The expressions on the occupants' faces were often split between half-hidden curiosity and frustrated annoyance. Half seemed to welcome their quirky presence as part of the ambience of old Placerville, while the other half resented having to share the public roadway with such an antiquated mode of transportation.

They made the first trip through town without any problems, passing shops selling everything from Western crafts and clothes to books stores and thrift shops. Many sported the frontier Western theme that characterized the old Hangtown section. When they reached the end of old town, Alex circled the block to turn the rig around. Teressa asked to be let out so she could have a look around.

Within minutes of her vacating the passenger seat they had a paying fare, a young couple dressed all in black with an excess of silver jewelry, including a nose ring on the woman. The pair looked out of place in the old Western town in their matching Goth fashions, but as long as they were able to pay the fare, they were able to ride.

Alex opened a small cubby under the driver's bench and pulled out a headset with an attached microphone, which he slipped on his head. Then, he handed the couple a pair of earphones and pointed out the two small speaker inserts discreetly installed in the back of the landau. He explained how the setup allowed him to give his passengers a guided tour of the old town without having to shout over traffic.

The youthful passengers expressed their delight. "Cool, man. Totally mod."

"I'm impressed," Bree said. "Modern electronics in the old-fashioned carriage. What a great idea."

"Thanks," Alex said. "I didn't use it for the wedding because the bride and groom don't need my running commentary; they usually prefer their privacy. But for the old town tours, the tourists love it. It helps bring in more business. I got the idea from those big tourist buses they have in San Francisco. This speaker system has more than paid for itself since I installed it a few years back."

"Every little bit helps, right?"

"Right," he nodded with pride. Besides being a horse whisperer, Bree was a business woman; she understood how it worked.

After their second trip through town with paying tourists, they found Teressa waiting for them back at the town square. A young man sat beside her. Alex guessed him to be about Bree's age or younger. His mop of brown hair hung just shy of his shoulders, and he wore oversized jeans and a tee shirt advertising an indie rock band Alex was unfamiliar with. He also noticed a skateboard resting at his feet. Teressa stepped forward with the young man to perform the introductions.

As the skateboarder approached, Alex's brain went into high alert, but he did his best to hide his anger. He'd already made enough mistakes with Bree; he didn't want to add overreacting idiot to the mix.

"Alex, this is Jeremy Bench. He tells me he's one of the best skateboarders this side of Lake Tahoe. Jeremy, this is Alex MacDonald. His family owns these Clydesdales," Teressa said.

Alex acknowledged Jeremy with a curt nod. After Bree poked him in the ribs, he added, "Hey Jeremy, glad to meet you."

"Same," was all Jeremy said.

Great, a real conversationalist, Alex thought.

"And this is my niece, Bree Ellers," Teressa continued.

Being closer to the curb, Bree reached out to offer her hand, which Jeremy politely shook.

"Hi, Jeremy. Are you going to help us work with the horses?" Bree asked cheerfully.

"He's going to do better than that." Teressa beamed. "Jeremy thinks he knows who's been harassing the horses."

Alex fought his impulse to jump down from the carriage and grab the boy by the scruff of his neck. Like swallowing bile, he got his temper under control, reminding himself Jeremy wasn't the problem, he was part of the solution.

"Really? How did you find him?" Bree sounded ecstatic.

"I made a few inquiries. It wasn't too hard to find skateboarders taking advantage of this beautiful spring day. After watching them for a while, I picked out the best of the bunch and asked if he could help."

Jeremy reacted with puffed-up pride to Teressa's praise. "Yeah, right. Like I'm going to turn down a pretty woman." The boy sounded a bit too cocky, in Alex's opinion. He hoped Teressa knew what she was doing.

"Thank you, Jeremy," Teressa said, acknowledging the skateboarder's compliment. "Would you mind telling Alex what you told me?"

"Sure thing. Anyway, like I was telling Teressa," Jeremy looked at the older woman and flashed her a big, toothy grin.

Keep dreaming, Alex thought. *You don't have a chance.*

"There's this guy, Benny. I think his last name is Taybac, or something like that. Anyway, he's not one of us; he's a fringe."

"What's a fringe?" Bree asked.

"You know, a guy who's not really in the gang; he just hangs around the fringe. Anyway, I've seen him messing with your horses. For some reason, he seems to like messing with this brown pair. He leaves the other ones alone."

"You mean the dark ones with white markings?" Alex asked, referring to his four other Clydesdales.

"Yeah, the ones that pull that tourist trap."

"Tourist trap?" Bree asked.

"You know, the funny looking wagon that holds about a gazillion tourists," Jeremy told her.

"It's a surrey, and it only holds nine, besides the driver," Alex informed the skateboarder.

"Yeah, whatever. Anyways, a few weeks ago, Benny had this little accident. He was skating behind your carriage there, trying to impress one of the girls sitting in the back, when one of your horses took a dump right in the street. Usually, that shit bag you have hanging off their ass does the trick, but not this time. Your driver must have missed it or something, cuz he just kept going, and Benny ran right into that shit, fresh and hot from the oven. He took a gnarly spill, ate some ground, and came up pissed. Anyways, I think he's been messing with those brown horses whenever he gets a chance."

"Have you actually seen him hurting my Clydes?" Alex asked, doing his best to mask his anger. It wasn't easy.

Jeremy shrugged his shoulders, looking a bit nervous. "I ain't no snitch. Teressa said I didn't have to snitch."

"Jeremy, we really appreciate your help. We're not asking you to snitch. We just want to know what happened so we can help the horses," Teressa assured him.

"Because of Benny, these horses have a fear of all skateboarders, and that's not right. I'm sure all skateboarders aren't mean," Bree said. The look in her eyes could have melted butter, she looked so earnest and concerned. Alex had no doubt her sincerity was anything less than genuine. He believed she honestly cared.

"We're always getting a bad rap. One guy does something wrong, and everyone assumes we're all bad. It's a crock, I tell you."

"I'm sure you're right," Teressa said, agreeing with Jeremy. "So, Bree, now that we have a skateboarder to help us, one of the best around," Teressa flashed Jeremy a glowing smile, and he ate it up like a starving man at a free food buffet, "what do you suggest?"

Bree turned to Alex. "Can we do this now? Or do you need to keep working? I know you've had a steady stream of customers. Is it okay if we take a break?" It surprised Alex when Bree addressed him. Until now, all her attention had been focused on the skateboarder.

"Yeah, sure, if Jeremy's ready to work," he said. Alex tried to set aside his initial dislike for the skateboarder and give him the benefit of the doubt. After all, the young man was willing to help, even though he had no stake in the matter.

"I've got the time," Jeremy said.

"I saw a small city park over by Big Guy's Burgers. Do you think we could use that for our practice?" Bree asked.

"Maybe. What do you have in mind?" Alex asked.

149

Once again, Bree's face transformed with glowing confidence as she laid out her plan. "I'm thinking we can take the horses over to the park and drive around it. Jeremy can be there, practicing with his board. We'll start off with him kinda far away, like at the wedding. Close enough for Malt and Barley to be aware of him, but not close enough to be an immediate threat. I'll monitor the horses and reassure them they're safe. If they seem to be handling it okay, we'll signal Jeremy to move closer and closer until the horses start to scare. Then we'll back off and try again."

"Do I have to pet them or something like that, so they'll know who I am?" Jeremy asked, looking a bit worried.

"No, you better not. You should be a stranger, like the other skateboarders in town," Bree said.

"I agree," Teressa seconded. "We might be creating a controlled environment, but we want to keep it as close to real life as possible."

Teressa and Jeremy climbed into the back of the landau. Once they were settled, Alex set off for the park. When they were about a block away, Alex stopped to let Teressa and Jeremy get out so they could get into position.

While they waited for Jeremy to start doing his thing, Alex turned to observe Bree. She sat forward on the driver's bench, anxiously watching Jeremy. He wondered if it was anticipation or admiration he saw in her eyes. Bree seemed completely enthralled with the skateboarder. Alex hated to admit it, but the young man had a lot going in his favor. Jeremy was closer to her age, he was agile, athletic, and full of self-confidence, and Bree obviously appreciated his willingness to help. Even though Bree was there because she wanted to help his horses, he felt his chances with her falling lower and lower, while Jeremy's seemed to be rising.

Bitter acceptance seeped in. He had to let her go. Any hopes he had of moving forward with her were pretty much smashed. Why should he care? She had made it clear she wanted nothing to do with him; she was only here for Malt and Barley. That was fine with him. At least he was getting his horses fixed. Once this problem was solved, they could go their separate ways. No big deal.

When this was over, she could return to her beloved ranch down in Diablo Valley, and he would continue to run his dad's business here in Placerville, putting two hours and a long stretch of highway between them. At least Jeremy shared the same long stretch of highway. Considering Bree's attachment to Over-Yonder, Jeremy's chances of dating Bree weren't much better than his.

"Do you really think this is going to work?" he asked, drawing her attention from Teressa and Jeremy.

Her eyes met his. "I'm hoping it will. In theory, it sounds right, but until we try, we just don't know." As she spoke, he saw her self-confidence fade. "I want this to work for you, Alex. Really, I do." She reached out to place her hand upon his.

Dang. How could she go from being aloof and totally in charge to looking as if she had just lost her best friend? He gave her hand a reassuring squeeze.

"I'm hoping it'll work, too. But regardless, you've already earned your pay."

"Is that why you think I'm here? For the money?" She pulled her hand back as her spine stiffened, becoming ramrod straight.

Alex felt himself backpedaling. "No. I know you're here because you care about Malt and Barley. I just want you to know, regardless of how this goes, I'll pay you for your time."

"Never mind. I don't want your money." She dismissed him with a wave of her hand.

"What, are you too good to take money from a MacDonald? I have every intention of paying for your services. Remember, this all started as a business proposition, no more, no less. I assure you, I'll make good on our deal."

"Do whatever makes you happy," Bree said, turning away.

"You've already made it clear that's not possible," he snapped.

"What does that mean?" She turned back to glare at him.

"Never mind. It doesn't matter," he said. But it did.

Alex wanted to know if there was any possibility of them seeing each other again, but he dared not ask. He figured he already knew the answer.

He didn't understand why he was so darn attracted to Bree, but he was. Of course, she was an attractive woman. Her pretty face, bright eyes, cute smile, and happy laugh were all very appealing. And when packaged up with a great body, it was a no-brainer he'd have the hots for her, no matter how ill-advised or illogical it might be. But he also knew his feelings went above and beyond simple physical attraction. There was no good reason he could pin-point, and yet he wanted to protect her, body and soul.

Seeing Jeremy roll into the park, he said, "Look, your skateboarder's ready for us. We should go." He flipped the reins, spurring the horses down the road surrounding the park.

~~~

Bree wondered what Alex was talking about, and why she had such a hard time understanding him, but she didn't have time to question him further. She needed to focus on the horses. As soon as Malt and Barley heard the sound of Jeremy's skateboard rolling and smacking against the pavement, Bree sensed their rising fear. Interestingly, the two geldings seemed uncannily in tune with each other. She tried to make a connection to one and then the other to reassure them they were safe, but they kept shutting her out, apparently choosing instead to focus on their fear of the skateboarder.

As they drove around the park, moving closer to Jeremy, she felt Malt and Barley's desire to bolt increase. They were fighting the reins, trying to shake off the harness in an effort to flee. These were big, powerful horses; if they wanted to bolt, it would take a lot to stop them.

Bree felt herself beginning to panic. It was all happening so fast.

"Move away," she shouted at Jeremy.

He was so engrossed in performing his stunts for Teressa, he didn't hear her.

"Pull back," she shouted at Alex, though he was sitting right next to her. He was straining with the reins, struggling to control Malt and Barley. "Jeremy, stop. Move away," she shouted again.

Teressa heard her shouts and rushed to intercept Jeremy. Alex continued to fight for control of his horses, cursing as he pulled on the reins. "Settle down boys, goddamn it. Settle down."

Bree hung on to the edge of her seat as the carriage rocked and jerked with the bucking horses.

Alex finally got the team under control and pulled over to the far side of the street while Jeremy retreated to the other corner of the park. They looked like horribly mismatched contenders squared off in an oversized boxing ring.

Her idea had failed. Disappointment threatened to overwhelm her, but she refused to give in to self-pity. She would not cry. She was stronger than that.

"Uh, that didn't go so well," Alex said.

That was an understatement. They hadn't even gotten near Jeremy before the horses had spooked. If there'd been passengers in the landau, it would have been a disaster. She'd been seriously afraid, and she thought she knew what she was doing.

"I think we should give them a rest before we try again," Alex said, sounding far more reasonable than she expected.

"You're not mad? You're willing to try again?" She had expected him to kick her out of the landau and send her packing.

"Of course. Aren't you?" He gave her a half-hearted smile. It was like rain in the desert.

"I am if you are." She felt so relieved, she wanted to hug him, but she didn't. They needed to get back to work.

"Here, hold the reins," Alex said, handing them off to her. She grasped the straps and felt the leather, damp from the sweat of his palms.

Alex climbed down from the driver's seat then went to Malt and Barley, stroking them while whispering words of encouragement. "Hey, boys, calm down now. There's nothing to be afraid of. I'm here. Nothing can hurt you. It's just a guy with a skateboard making loud noises. You can handle more than that, right guys?"

Bree wished she could be down there with him, soothing the animals, but that was his duty, his prerogative. After all, they were his horses, his responsibility, not hers. So she waited and watched, taking in the scene as Alex bestowed his loving care on the Clydesdales. Her seed of envy grew, along with her admiration. He really was a caring man.

After a few minutes, he looked up at her. "They seem better now. Would you agree?"

"Let me check." Bree made a quick connection to the horses, trying to read their feelings. They seemed jittery but trusting. "You're right. They're better. They trust you." Her admiration for him continued to grow. "You make them feel better."

"Are they ready to try again?" he asked.

"Yeah, I think they are." She gave him a watery smile, pleased he had asked for her opinion.

She signaled to her aunt they were ready to try again. Alex maneuvered the horses back into the street, and Jeremy began doing his thing. As they drew closer, she felt Malt and Barley's anxiety grow, but interestingly, they didn't let it get out of control. Bree sensed they were fighting their deep-seated fear of the skateboarder against their trust Alex would protect them from harm. Thankfully, their trust won out.

They successfully made a pass near to where Jeremy was practicing without Malt and Barley fighting their harness. Although Bree still sensed their nervousness, they didn't demonstrate a need to bolt.

At the end of the route, Alex climbed down again to reassure his horses all was well and he wouldn't let anything bad happen to them. Again, he checked with Bree to confirm they were all right.

Before they started their third attempt, Alex stepped to the back of the carriage and pulled a couple of treats out of the boot of the landau to feed to Malt and Barley. They made two more passes around the small park. Each time, Jeremy moved closer to the street as they passed, and each time, they got similar results. It seemed the horses weren't completely at ease around the skateboarder, but they were much better at overcoming their fear.

Alex and Bree were discussing whether they should give it another try when she noticed Jeremy had stopped skateboarding and was rushing over to Teressa. A moment later, Teressa hurried over to speak with them.

"Hey, Alex, Bree, do you see that guy over there, walking past Big Guy's Burgers?" Teressa asked in a hushed voice.

Bree looked where Teressa was pointing. A young man wearing dark, ragged jeans and a black hoodie was rolling down the sidewalk on a skateboard. He had a sour look on his face that seemed to get darker the closer he came to the carriage.

"Yes, I see him," Bree whispered back. "He's not very friendly looking. I don't think we should ask him to help."

"No, that's Benny—the guy Jeremy says has been hurting these horses."

"Really?" Bree and Alex responded as one.

Bree focused on the boy. Though he was simply rolling down the street, as if planning to pass on by, it was obvious he was watching them.

When it looked as though he was going to roll on by without stopping, Teressa spoke up. "I'm going to go speak with him."

"Teressa, you can't. What are you going to say?" Bree asked.

Her aunt was already walking away. With an impish smile, she called over her shoulder. "I'm going to ask for his help."

Alex turned to Bree. "She can't be serious."

"I think she is."

Teressa rushed over to catch up with Benny. The skateboarder looked as though he wanted to ignore her, anxious to get away, but Teressa made that nearly impossible, flagging him down as if it were some kind of emergency. She got the boy to stop and began speaking with him.

Knowing her aunt, Bree suspected Teressa was talking to Benny as though she had no clue who he was. Besides, Teressa would never accuse or pass judgment on the boy. That wasn't how she worked. Instead, she would turn on her charm, saying exactly what the young man needed to hear to get him to help.

At first, Benny shook his head, looking down at the sidewalk and not at Teressa. Eventually, he looked up and nodded, sporting an expression of hard-ass pride. Teressa glanced over to Bree and motioned for her to join them. Bree didn't need to be asked twice. She was anxious to know what was going on. She scrambled down from the carriage and jogged over to her aunt.

"Hey, Bree. This is Benny," Teressa said.

"Hello, Benny," Bree said with a friendly smile, hoping to make a good impression.

"Hey," was all he said. He was tall and lanky, with overgrown limbs that looked as if they threatened to take over his body. His dark hair, black and thick, was cut short except for a long hank of bangs that hung down his forehead, partially covering his dark brown eyes.

"I told Benny about us working with the horses to get them comfortable with skateboarders. Jeremy's been a big help, but Benny tells me he's as good, maybe better than Jeremy, at doing his stunts."

Judging by the look on Benny's face, Bree figured it was her aunt who had made that suggestion.

Teressa continued, "I'm thinking the more noise they can make together, the better it will be. I understand it isn't unusual for skateboarders to hang out together. Isn't that right?" Teressa looked at Benny, as though hoping for his approval.

Benny nodded once. "Right."

"Bree, if you wouldn't mind explaining to Benny what we've been doing, I'll go tell Jeremy our plan."

In other words, Teressa wanted Bree to keep an eye on him while she went to clue in Jeremy. "Sure. It'll be my pleasure."

Teressa flashed another bright smile at Benny, but he didn't seem to notice.

She described their routine of driving the horses around the park while Jeremy practiced nearby with his skateboard. As she talked, she tried to read his aura. Bree couldn't read his thoughts or emotions like she could the animals', but she hoped she could get a better understanding of his feelings. It seemed rather strange for him to agree to help the horses if he really was the one who had been terrorizing them. No doubt, her aunt was thinking the best way to lose an enemy was to make him your friend.

Benny was hard to read; he was so closed and withdrawn. His aura was dark and jagged, releasing very little light—a sure sign of a troubled individual.

Bree stopped what she was saying mid sentence, struck by a sudden urge to follow her intuition.

"Can I ask you something?" she said.

"What?" Benny said.

"Why did you agree to help?"

"Why?"

"Well, excuse me for noticing, but you don't seem very excited to be here." She was taking a big risk asking him this, but she needed to know if he could be trusted.

"Because she asked," Benny said with a jerking nod toward Teressa. He was obviously a man of few words.

Bree wondered if her aunt had taken on more than she could handle. She shifted her weight, shuffling her feet. "That's it? Because she asked?"

"Would you rather I said no? You know, I don't have to do this."

She felt his anger grow. Worried she had blown it and he was about to walk away, Bree went into a mini-panic. "No. No. Please stay. I'm thrilled you're here. We need your help." For a split second, she wanted to reach out and grab him, but everything about him said, "Hands off." He didn't seem like a touchy-feely kind of guy.

"You sure?" He looked tough, but his eyes suddenly told a different tale. Behind his tough guy exterior, she saw a boy loaded with insecurities.

"Yeah. I'm real sure. I'm so grateful you're here. We've been trying all day to help these horses overcome their fear of skateboarders. Did Teressa tell you what happened?"

A spark of pure panic sprinted across his eyes. "Tell me what?"

Following her instincts, Bree decided to share what she knew. "The horses have been getting spooked whenever they're around skateboarders. We think someone may have tried to harm them, but we have no way of knowing for sure."

She watched him closely, knowing there was a chance he would leave if he were afraid of being caught because he had hurt these horses. His eyes darted around, as though looking for a way out. Teressa and Jeremy were heading their way. If Benny were going to flee, now would be the time. Sending up a little prayer for help, she hoped he would stay.

Overcoming her earlier hesitation, she reached out and touched his arm. "Will you help us, Benny? Will you stay and help the horses?" she asked.

Benny jerked his eyes back to her. "What are you going to do?"

Bree felt herself relax a small degree. "Like I said, we're trying to get them used to being around skateboarders, you know, because of the noise those things make."

"No. I mean to the guy who did it. I mean, if you find out who did it?" His tough guy persona was slipping, replaced by uneasy apprehension.

"We'd talk to him," she said, speaking in the same soft, soothing voice she used on her horses. "We'd ask him what happened so we could hear his side of the story. In my experience, people don't usually lash out unless they have a reason. Maybe something bad happened, and well, maybe he just got mad."

"Wouldn't he be in trouble? Don't you want to kick his ass?"

She felt his fear. Her heart went out to him. "What good would that do? Enough damage has already been done. We're just trying to fix it."

"Aren't you mad someone tried to hurt your horses?"

159

Bree looked past Benny for a moment, her eyes focusing on Alex, alone, sitting with the carriage. He looked anxious, but she knew he wouldn't leave his horses unattended. She looked back at Benny. "A little, I'm sure, but we're more concerned about why. Why would someone want to hurt innocent horses? What could they possibly have done to deserve such torture?"

Like a volcano with hot lava flowing just below the surface, Benny exploded. "They dump shit everywhere," he blurted. "It's a fucking mess. No one likes us skateboarders, but at least we don't shit in the street. These horses leave a fucking mess. They shouldn't be allowed in town."

Wowzier! Bree had tapped into the cavernous well of his distress, and now she had a gusher on her hands. She resisted the urge to take a step back. Gathering all her self-control, she focused on remaining calm. "The drivers are required to clean it up," she said. "They have poop bags to catch it, but if the horses take a dump on the street, the drivers are supposed to stop and clean it up."

"What if they don't?" Benny spat.

"They could get a ticket, like a dog owner who lets their dog poop in public and doesn't clean it up, only worse."

"Then one of your drivers should get a ticket." Benny was nearly shouting.

Teressa had jogged ahead of Jeremy and was running to Benny's side. Apparently, she had heard at least part of their conversation and wanted to get involved. "Did you see one of them leave a mess? Do you know who it was?" Teressa asked.

Benny's eyes zipped between Bree and Teressa, his anger evident. "Damn right I did."

Feeling her fear clench inside, Bree pointed to Alex. "Was it that guy over there?"

"No. It was that older guy, the one with short black hair. The one who always wears that fucking ugly tractor hat."

Bree let out the breath she'd been holding. "Would you mind telling this to Alex? He's one of the owners."

"No way, man," Benny snapped, and started to turn away.

Teressa latched on to Benny's arm. "Please, wait."

Benny said nothing, but at least he wasn't leaving.

Teressa continued. "Bree, why don't you go talk to Alex? I'd like to stay and talk to Benny." She turned to address Jeremy, who had joined them. "Jeremy, we really appreciate your help, but I think we're done for today."

In his lighthearted manner, Jeremy shrugged. "No problem, man. It was rad." He reached out to give Benny a fist bump. "Hey, dude. See ya."

"Yeah, see ya." Benny returned Jeremy's fist bump.

While Jeremy headed down the street on his board, Bree returned to Alex and the carriage. When she looked back over her shoulder, she saw Teressa and Benny sitting down on a nearby bench. It was time to let Teressa do her thing.

It occurred to her Benny was a boy who wanted love and acceptance and had no understanding of how to ask or receive because that type of support had never been given to him. Jeremy had said he'd been trying to impress someone special when he fell—one of the young women riding in the carriage—making his humiliation so much worse. It would explain why the wound cut so deep. Besides suffering a devastating public embarrassment, he would have felt like the world's biggest fool in front of his love interest when he ran into the horse manure. It was understandable he still carried a grudge.

She also knew his holding onto the anger served no purpose other than to create more bad feelings, feelings so strong he wanted

161

to lash out and harm innocent horses that had done nothing more than answer nature's call at an inopportune time and place. The boy blamed the horses for something that was out their control. They hadn't intentionally taken a dump where he was skateboarding, but because a poop bag hadn't been setup properly by the driver, they had suffered his wrath.

Interestingly, she felt a deep vein of empathy for Benny. His experience was all too similar to how she resented and blamed every MacDonald, including Alex, for the pain she had once encountered at the hands of their ancestors.

~*~

Alex anxiously waited for Bree to return to the carriage, curious to hear what had happened out in the park.

Bree walked up to the carriage but didn't climb up, as he expected.

"Everything okay?" he asked, trying to sound nonchalant.

"Mind if I join you?"

"Sure, climb on up." She didn't even need to ask. He wanted her by his side. Bree scrambled up to the driver's seat as if she were an old pro, rather than the novice she'd been only a day before. As soon as she took a seat beside him, he asked, "So, how did it go?"

"It looks like Jeremy was right. I think Benny is the one who's been harassing your horses. He says one of your drivers didn't stop to clean up after the horses, and I think Benny got the worst of it. Do you have a driver with short dark hair and wears a tractor hat?"

"That sounds like Howard."

"Well, I think you better talk to him. He needs a reminder on public safety and sanitation. Your company could be fined big bucks for leaving horse droppings in the street."

"I'll take care of it as soon as I get back to the ranch." Maybe this was the excuse he needed to fire Howard's ass. He had never liked the older driver, and as far as he was concerned, Howard had never pulled his weight. Howard was always looking for ways to slough off work, and Alex didn't like the way the surrey driver flirted with the young female tourists. It wasn't good for business to have the old guy chasing after their customers, and it was just plain creepy.

Bree turned her head to look back in the direction of the park where her aunt and the skateboarder were sitting. Alex followed her gaze, taking a moment to watch them.

"What do you think they're talking about?" he asked, motioning with his chin toward Teressa and Benny. From what he could see, it seemed Teressa was doing most of the talking. "What do you think she's saying?"

"I think she's saying he shouldn't blame the horses. That it wasn't their fault. That it happened in the past and he should let it go. That what's done is done, and the best thing, the only thing, is to let it go and move on. That holding on to his grudge is only hurting himself."

Alex was impressed. "Really? You think she's saying all that?"

"Oh, yeah. I'm sure of it," Bree said, still watching her aunt.

"How do you know?"

She turned back to look at him. "Because that's what she said to me about the MacDonalds."

Alex's heart dropped down to his stomach and leaped back up into his chest, twisting as it bounced around. "What did you say?"

"That I came here to help your Clydesdales. Now it's time for me to go home."

Alex's heart dropped back down to his stomach and stayed there. It took him a moment to speak. "Do you want me to take you back to Frank's?"

"Not yet. If you don't mind, I'd like to wait for Teressa and see what she has to say."

"Sure, what the hell, I'll wait." Lately, he was doing a lot of waiting.

A short while later, Teressa approached the carriage. "Bree, honey, I'm going to give Benny a ride home."

Bree nodded, "Okay. I kinda figured as much."

"Would you mind taking Bree back to Frank's place, Alex?" Teressa added.

"Sure. No problem."

Bree looked a little uncertain. "I'll wait for you at Franklin's. You know he's expecting us for dinner," she said. Sounding a bit nervous, she added, "Both of us."

"Don't worry, sweetie. I won't be long," Teressa said with confidence. She reached up and patted Bree's leg then turned and walked back to where Benny waited. When she reached him, she linked her arm in his as if they were comfortable old friends. Benny seemed to accept the gesture, looking quite a bit more at ease than he'd been before.

Bree was right, when it came to talking with strangers, her aunt had talents.

Alex urged the horses back into the street, directing them down the road toward Frank's place. He waited until they had turned onto the two lane country road leading out of town, where they'd have fewer cars and distractions, before speaking to Bree.

"It was pretty amazing what you and your aunt were able to do today. I'm really grateful for all your help." He didn't say anything about paying her, but he would make sure there would be a check in the mail.

Sitting quietly beside him, Bree looked reluctant to speak. "I'm glad we could help. For a while there, I wasn't sure."

"Really? You could've fooled me. It looked like you had everything under control."

"That first pass we made around the park, when Jeremy had just started doing his thing, I thought the horses were going to bolt. It felt like we were losing control."

Alex understood her concern. He had felt it, too. "But they didn't. Between the two of us, we were able to settle them down."

"It was you, Alex. You're the one they trust."

He appreciated her endorsement, but for some reason, it seemed less than enthusiastic. Though he believed she was happy with the results of their efforts, he could tell something else was bothering her. "Don't sell yourself short. I couldn't have done it without you."

"Thanks. I'm glad I could help." Bree gave him a weary smile, but it seemed her heart wasn't in it. She was probably only being polite. Then she added, "It's what I would do for any of my clients."

Ouch, that hurt. Damn it. Alex didn't want to be just another one of her clients. He'd hoped for so much more. But for every step forward he made, she took another step back, always maintaining the gap between them. No way was he going to give up so easily. Regardless of what she said, he knew there was something between them.

By the time they reached the turnoff for Frank's road, his mind was churning. He couldn't let her go without making one last try. As they pulled up to Frank's house, he spoke. "Bree, I'd like to see you again. I don't think we're done here."

"I'm sure your horses are going to be all right. You can handle it now."

"This isn't about my horses, Bree. I want to see you." He tamped down his frustration. Why couldn't she be reasonable?

She drew back and blinked. "I live two hours away."

Was *that* what was bothering her? Alex drew the horses to a stop and set the brake. "Some things are worth the ride." He reached for her hand, grateful when she didn't resist or pull away. "I think this is one of them."

Bree looked down at her hand nestled warm and small in his before meeting his gaze. "Are you sure that's what you want?"

His chest swelled with hope. He might have been knocked down, but he wasn't out for the count, at least not yet. Maybe, with a little bit of luck, he still had a chance to charm her. "I'm sure. Can I call you?"

Bree smiled, but her eyes remained shuttered. "Do you still have my card?"

"You bet your sweet ass—I mean—of course I do," he said.

Bree laughed. "Then I guess you can call."

Gently pulling her hand free from his grasp, she turned to hop down from the carriage. Before she could leave, he reached out and pulled her back. "Wait," he said.

Twisting back around, she locked her eyes on his with a questioning look.

He wrapped an arm around her, drawing her near. With his other hand he caressed her cheek, brushing his fingers across her incredibly smooth skin.

"I've wanted to do this all day," he whispered. Lowering his head, he covered her lips with his. She responded to him with sweet surrender, warm, full, and too lush for words. Passion. By God, he felt her passion, contained, but simmering hot just below the surface of her fierce composure. He was tempted to push her limits, but it was a fool's risk to take too much, too soon. Instead, hard as it was, he reined in his desires.

When their kiss ended, he continued to hold her close, wrapping his arms around her, unwilling to let her go. "My dear, sweet, Bree," he whispered into her hair. "Can you ever forgive me?"

Bree didn't answer. She didn't even move. For one brief moment, she simply accepted his embrace.

When he felt her pull back, he let her go. It wasn't good to hold on too tight, not with Bree. She was too unpredictable, confident one minute and skittish the next.

"I've gotta go," she said. With a final brush of her lips upon his, she climbed down from the carriage and hurried off to Frank's front porch. As she opened the door, she turned to wave good-bye, gracing him with a warm, sweet smile.

Alex's heart soared. There was hope. He planned to grab this second chance for all it was worth and hold on tight.

CHAPTER 13

B ree closed the door behind her and reached for the nearest chair, not trusting her legs to carry her any farther. What had she been thinking? Why she had let Alex MacDonald kiss her good-bye? How could she have agreed to let him call?

When he'd reached for her, her body had reacted before her mind had a chance to refuse. Even when she'd pulled back—tough as it had been—her traitorous body had yearned for more. She had wanted more of his kisses, more of his taste, and more of his arms holding her close. It would have been easy to sink into his arms and surrender to the passion he offered—so easy and so wrong.

She felt like a windup toy with a spring that had been frozen tight for too long and was now being released. Her world was twirling and whirling out of control while her pent-up needs sought release with a willing and available playmate. But Alex was not a child, and she was not a toy. He was a MacDonald.

Yes, he was one hot-looking dude. Yes, he was a great kisser. Yes, he made her blood boil. But none of that made him any less of a MacDonald.

Maybe she could just have a fling, lead him along with no strings attached, and move on when it was over. She had seen it done in the movies, but she knew better. Bree couldn't be dishonest with him about her feelings. There wasn't a dishonest bone in her body. Well, maybe one or two in her little toes. But to be really dishonest required a whole different bone structure from the one she had. To be really successful, deceitfulness required a backbone as hard as nails and just as brittle, not the soft and pliable one she owned.

No matter how good he looked, or how well he kissed, or how much her body yearned for more, nothing would change his heritage or what his clan had done to hers. Any relationship between them was doomed to failure.

After taking a moment to regain her composure, she walked through the house, looking for Franklin. She found him in the kitchen, cutting up bright red peppers and freshly washed tomatoes, prepping for dinner. Whatever he had planned, it looked good.

He stopped what he was doing and turned from the cutting board to face her. "Hey, Breanna. How did it go with the horses?" he asked, reaching for a kitchen towel to wipe off his hands before he greeted her with a hug.

"Good, I'd say. In fact, better than I had expected." She tried to sound upbeat, but wondered if her less than genuine smile gave her away. Franklin had a way of knowing what she was thinking without her saying a word.

"Good. You'll have to tell me all about it over dinner." He looked over her shoulder toward the front door. "Where's Teressa? I thought you were together."

"Oh, she stayed in town to give a boy a ride home. He seemed to need her help."

"How did you get home?"

"Umm, Alex dropped me off on his way back to his ranch." *Darn.* She should have seen that coming. Bree looked around for a distraction. "Hey, would you like some tea?" A cup of soothing English tea with a dash of cream suddenly sounded good. Without waiting for his answer, Bree turned to the stove and set the kettle on the burner. She needed something to do—something to keep her hands busy and her thoughts away from Alex. Franklin's scrutiny was way too close for comfort.

"None for me. Not while I'm cooking. I'll wait for Teressa and dinner. Then you two can tell me all about what happened in town. I'm sure it'll be interesting." He turned back to his cutting board and picked up his knife then began slicing through the vegetables with finely tuned strokes.

"Sounds like a good idea to me." She pulled a packet of fragrant tea from a canister on the counter, grateful Franklin hadn't asked her about Alex. It'd be a whole lot easier to field his questions when Teressa was there. "Do you need any help?" she offered.

"Nope," Franklin answered over his shoulder. He turned to reach for something in the refrigerator. "I've got it covered. Just sit and relax while I finish up here."

Bree nodded, welcoming the break. Right now, a few minutes of meaningless small talk was about all she could handle. She reached for a ceramic mug up in the cupboard and proceeded to brew her tea. After her beverage had steeped long enough, she found a comfortable seat at the kitchen counter to watch the chef at work and compliment his artistry.

Less than an hour later, Teressa had arrived and Franklin was ready to serve them a meal as pretty as it was tasty. Along with the crunchy salad made from farm fresh vegetables, he had prepared bowtie pasta covered with pesto sauce and accompanied with lightly toasted sourdough bread. The smell of it alone was bliss. They ate outside on his back deck to take advantage of the warm spring evening and the soft light of the late afternoon sun fading in the west.

As soon as they were all seated and served, Franklin pelted them with questions regarding their day. Thankfully, Teressa did most of the talking, allowing Bree to avoid saying more about Alex than she wanted.

Interestingly, though Bree had planned to drive home while it was light out, they were still sitting with Franklin long after the sun had set and dusk had turned to dark. Franklin managed to con Bree and Teressa into staying the night before heading back to Diablo Valley in the morning. He even took it upon himself to call Robert to let Teressa's husband know his wife wouldn't be coming home. Bree knew Franklin's idea of social networking was sitting around a table drinking strong tea laced with Scottish whisky while catching up on the latest family news, or reminiscing over stories from their past. It was only natural he hadn't let this treasured opportunity simply slip away.

He finally let them retire for the night when they had answered all his questions and exhausted him of all his stories. After making sure they had everything they needed, he gave them each good-night hugs and headed off to his room.

The minute they were alone in the guest bedroom, Bree asked Teressa how things had gone with Benny. Not surprisingly, Teressa refused to disclose the details of what she had discussed with Benny, honoring her commitment to client confidentiality as part of her coaching profession. However, she did reveal, once he started talking, it had been like opening a release valve on a reservoir of pent-up feelings. He'd been hungry for someone who would listen to him with understanding and without judgment. Respecting her aunt's desire to honor Benny's privacy, Bree didn't press further.

Knowing she could trust her, Bree was anxious to tell Teressa about the ride back to Franklin's with Alex, everything except the kiss. Bree talked while her aunt changed out of her jeans and tee shirt, replacing them with the oversized tee shirt Franklin had given her to use as a night shirt.

"Alex said he wanted to see me again," Bree said. "When I pointed out I live two hours away, he said some things are worth the ride. He said he would call. Do you think he will?" Bree pulled her pajamas out of her traveling bag and began to change, letting her jeans drop to the floor in a pool of denim around her ankles.

"If he said he will, then I think he will. I get the impression Alex is a man of his word," Teressa pulled out the rubber band holding her long blond braid and began brushing out her hair, letting it fall free around her shoulders.

Bree picked up her jeans and shook them out before folding them over the railing at the foot of the bed. She had thought their physical distance would have been enough of a deterrent to prevent Alex from considering the possibility of a relationship with her.

Even with the convenience of modern transportation, her visits with Franklin were usually reserved for special occasions. Back on the Isle of Skye, she had rarely, if ever, traveled this far from her home at Scorrybreac just to visit a friend. Though she had flown nearly halfway around the world with her Aunt Teressa and Uncle Robert to live in California, once she settled in at Over-Yonder, she seldom traveled far from the comfort and familiarity of the ranch. Over-Yonder had become her refuge.

"What about you, Bree? Do you want to see him again?"

"I'm not really sure. Besides, what's the point? We live so far apart."

"Do you like him?" Teressa began folding her clothes into a neat little bundle. She set them on the only chair in the room while she waited for Bree to answer.

"What does it matter? He's a MacDonald. That's not going to change. I can't see me getting involved with a MacDonald."

Teressa stopped what she was doing to stare at Bree. "Would you really refuse to see Alex because he's a MacDonald? Because of his last name?"

"You know what his family did to my clan. How can I ever forget?" Turning her back on Teressa, Bree pulled on her flannel pajama bottoms, yanking the draw stings tight.

"Bree, sweetie, those people lived seven hundred years ago. They have nothing to do with Alex, and he has nothing to do with them. Is it really fair to judge Alex for something his ancestors did?"

"I'm not judging Alex." She turned to face her aunt.

"But you admit to being prejudiced against the MacDonald name."

"Yes, against the clan, but not against Alex. You have to understand, I can't see me ever being loyal to a MacDonald or trusting they would be loyal to me."

"So, you are prejudging him. That's what prejudice means. It's not something I would expect from you."

"Auntie Teressa, I can't be with Alex." Why couldn't her aunt understand? Wasn't it obvious?

"Why not, Bree? Explain it to me. Because I don't think I understand you at all right now." Teressa looked as frustrated as Bree felt.

Bree spoke in a rush of emotion. "I can't be with a MacDonald. They killed William, and everyone else I loved. It would be too much of a betrayal."

"William? Who's William?"

173

Bree wished she could put a clamp over her mouth, or pull the words back, but it was too late for that now. She sat down on the bed, tears burning her eyes. "He was the young man I loved, back on Skye. He died defending Ma, fighting the MacDonalds."

"You've never said anything. In all these years, you've never told me." Teressa shook her head, sounding hurt, probably wondering why Bree hadn't confided in her sooner.

"I never told anyone. It was my secret." *My personal pain.* "When I came here with Da, he was old and dying, and there were so many other things to worry about. So many other things to deal with. Crying over William wasn't something I wanted to share with anyone. Especially people I'd just met. I'm sorry, but I didn't know you, and you didn't know him. He was my private loss. I didn't want to share him with anyone."

"Oh, Bree." Teressa sank down on the bed next to her. "If you don't talk about it, you can't let it go. Look what happened to Benny. He held on to his pain, and he turned it against those horses. You need to let it go, Bree. It's only hurting you."

"I can't let it go. And I can't stop loving William. Most of all, I can't betray him." Tears fell from her eyes, flowing down her cheeks before she could wipe them away.

Teressa gave her a hug. "Bree, honey, William's dead. Loving another is not betraying him."

Bree blinked hard and stepped away. How could her aunt talk about her loving another, so easily, so soon?

She grabbed her toiletry kit and headed into the bathroom. Though she had traveled across time and moved halfway around the world, opening her heart to a MacDonald was one bridge she didn't believe she had the strength to cross.

CHAPTER 14

Alex was looking forward to raising hell and firing Howard when he got back to the ranch, but by the time he walked through the front door, the need for retaliation had passed, thanks to his uncle.

Wayne had been out in the barnyard, waiting for him. He had helped Alex unharness the horses and stow the landau, and they had talked. They had agreed Howard needed to clean up his act if he wanted to continue to work as their driver, but for now, he still had a job. Besides, with their busy summer season coming up fast, they couldn't afford to lose an experienced driver. The arrangement seemed fair, and hopefully, it would put Howard on his best behavior.

They also had agreed Howard would do more work at the ranch and Wayne would take over as driver of the surrey. In exchange, Alex would have full responsibility for driving the landau, replacing Wayne and Howard as its primary driver. Alex knew this was a step up in his role in the company, and he appreciated his uncle's confidence in him.

In addition, Wayne had told him he had talked his dad into making Alex a full third owner of MacDonald's Clydesdales and Carriages, saying it would give him a stronger stake in the family business. He had always appreciated his uncle's support, and now he respected his advice.

Having finished his conversation with Wayne, Alex entered the house eager to complete his next task. He went right to the spare room they used as a home office and pulled out the business checkbook. Intent on staying true to his word, he planned to send Bree a check for her services. Alex wouldn't take advantage of her kindness or her dislike of the MacDonald name. She could do what she liked with the check, cash it or tear it up; it didn't matter to him, but he wouldn't renege on his debt.

Alex was running some figures through an Excel spread sheet when he heard his dad walk down the hall and stop at the open office door. He finished what he was doing before looking up from the computer.

"How did it go in town? Horses give you any problems?" Angus asked.

"We made a lot of progress. They may still need a little work, but Bree figured out what they needed to get over their fears."

"Ha, horses with fears. What a lot of mumbo jumbo. Sounds like a con to me." His dad ambled over to the upholstered arm chair and sat down, stretching out his bad leg in front of him.

"Say what you will, but it turns out some skateboarders were giving the Clydes a bad time," Alex began, expecting to explain everything that had happened to his dad.

"I'll kick their asses," Angus interrupted.

Yeah, right. Alex rolled his eyes. His dad seemed to forget he was an old man with a bum knee. There was no use going into details with him. His dad wouldn't listen, and even if he did, it was doubtful he would understand or even care how Bree had used her psychic skills to help heal their horses. Besides, with the help of his uncle, he felt he had the situation under control. "Let's just say Bree and her aunt figured out what was wrong with our horses and helped fix them."

"What are you doing now?" His dad's eyes roamed over the desk top, taking in the open check register and computer spread sheet.

"I need to write Breanna Ellers a check for her services." Alex picked up her business card and slipped it into the back pocket of his jeans.

"Her services? Let me see her invoice. How much is she going to charge us?" Angus sat forward, leaning on his cane, and stretched out his hand. "Come on, let me see her invoice. I'll tell you if it's fair."

"She didn't give me a bill, but she helped heal our horses, and I'm going to pay her."

"I say take the freebie." Angus sat back in his chair and started massaging his bad knee.

"Yeah, and my conscience says to pay her." Alex turned back to the computer to save his work and close down the file.

"How do you know how much she charges?"

"I know what my time is worth, and I'll pay her no less." He picked up a pen and began writing out the check based on his calculations.

"You'll go broke listening to your conscience."

"I'd rather be broke than dishonest. I said I'd pay her, and I will." Alex kept his head down, speaking over his shoulder. He had run their numbers and knew their income was down. They weren't broke, but for the past few weeks, Malt and Barley had cost more than they had earned. Their down time was starting to hit the bottom line. It would take some belt-tightening to make the numbers balance, but he was willing to eat peanut butter and jelly sandwiches for a week if it meant being able to pay their bills.

"It'll come out of your pay."

Alex finished signing his name before turning to look at his dad. "You don't need to worry. I'll make this work. I'm a third owner of MacDonald's Clydesdales and Carriages, and I say this company honors its commitments. That's my decision, and this discussion is closed." He slammed the checkbook closed.

"Well, I'll be damned. You're going to man up, after all." Adding injury to insult, his dad laughed, chuckling under his breath, as though he were in on some grand joke and the joke was on Alex.

"Excuse me?" He glared at his dad. Angus had a way of pissing him off, but this was stepping over the line.

"I had my doubts when Wayne suggested we make you a third owner. I didn't think you were ready."

"Oh, really? What a surprise! As if I never knew."

"Alex, my son, I think you just might make me proud."

"Save your praise. I don't need it. I've been running this company for the past year without any help from you. Wayne and I are doing just fine while you sit around on your ass, so don't bother."

His dad's face hardened, growing serious. "Now you listen to me. I've invested millions of dollars in this business. We own everything, free and clear. And I've got another half million sitting in a reserve account. Did you think I was going to just hand all that over to you without knowing if you could manage? Hell, no. I've talked to Wayne. I know how well you're doing."

Alex stared at his dad, unbelieving, digesting what Angus had just said. It took him a moment to speak. "You mean, we're not in debt? We're not broke?"

"Nope, never have been. Not in your lifetime."

"But you had me believing . . . I've had to scrounge for every dime to make ends meet."

"Yeah, I cooked the books to make it look that way. Those hefty mortgage payments you've been making have been going right into our reserve account." His dad laughed again, obviously pleased with his little scheme.

"Why, you bastard." Alex rose from his chair.

Angus cut him off with a stern look. "You best mind your manners. I'm still your Dad."

Alex bit his tongue and settled back down, his anger seething just below the surface. His dad had played him for a fool. And fool he was to have fallen for it.

"Look, Alex, I grew up poor, and it taught me I'd rather be rich. I wanted you to have the same kind of experience, but your mother, God bless her soul, was always too soft on you. Some people are okay with being poor. Some people will take what life gives them and then give up. Those people will never be rich. I wanted to know what you were made of. I was worried about you. You thought money came too easily. But money comes with responsibility, and until recently, it didn't look as though you knew that. I might be a hard-ass, but you're a charmer, a damn party boy with enough good looks to make that work. I needed to know if you could be dedicated enough to be responsible."

"So you never gave me an inch?" Alex was incredulous.

"Nope. Now I know I can give you the farm, someday, and rest easy it'll be in good hands."

The blink of an eye was slow compared to how quickly his mind and emotions assessed his dad's actions. As much as it bruised his pride, as much as he wanted to be mad, the exquisitely simple logic of his dad's plan was too effective to ignore. The old man had played him, that was true, but the gambit had been for his own good, and darn if it hadn't worked. He had gone from being a lazy partygoer to a knowledgeable businessman through his dad's school of hard knocks.

In the blink of an eye he hated him, resented him, and respected everything his father had done to make him grow up. Not that he would admit this to his dad, at least not yet. Alex couldn't deny the truth, but he could damn well pick his timing.

~*~

Bree woke early the next morning with too many thoughts whirling through her head, all vying for her attention. While Teressa slept, she quietly slipped out of bed and gathered her clothes then moved into the bathroom to change. She needed time and space to think, and she knew the perfect place to find some peaceful solitude.

The sun was barely peeking over the crest of the distant hills when she stepped lightly through the front door of Franklin's farmhouse. She recalled how her mother had often said she preferred sunrises to sunsets because with each new dawn came a new day to live, to learn, and to love. Today she felt a greater understanding of her mother's words than ever before.

With that thought in her mind, she walked down the back country lane to where Malt and Barley were pastured. Bree wanted to sit with them and absorb their presence. They had been her reason for coming to Placerville with Alex, and they had been her reason for staying. She wrapped herself in the thick wool blanket she had taken from the living room sofa and sat down, cross-legged, on the dewy grass with her back propped against a tree. Relaxed, she let her mind wander as the morning sun spread its golden rays across the field where Malt and Barley lazily chomped the fresh sprouted grass carpeting their pasture.

Twisting together two blades of grass in her hands, she thought about how much her family had wanted peace between the

MacNicol and the MacDonald clans and how elusive that peace had been. She knew her grandmother, Lady Lydia, had tried to arrange a betrothal between her mother and Arlin, Angus MacDonald's younger brother, but Daniel Ellers had appeared out of nowhere and had swept Kayla off her feet. Her dad had fallen madly in love with her mother while defending her honor.

She also knew Lady Lydia, with the help of Aunt Teressa, had been successful in bringing together in marriage her Uncle Duncan, chief of the MacNicol clan, and Janet MacDonald in hopes of bringing peace to the feuding clans. Next to her parents, Uncle Duncan and Aunt Janet had had the best marriage of anyone she knew. Everyone knew Aunt Janet had willingly pledged her love and loyalty to Duncan and would rather disavow her family than do anything to lose his trust. Bree always believed her aunt had made the right choice, choosing the MacNicols over the MacDonalds.

Bree wondered what she would have done if the roles had been reversed? Could she have turned her back on her family to be with the one she loved, if the one she loved had been a MacDonald?

In this century, it was highly unlikely she would ever encounter such a choice. Modern families weren't divided against each other as they had been centuries ago. Bonds of clan loyalty were no longer as strong or as important.

The more she thought about it, the more absurd it seemed that any two people should fight because of their last names. Wasn't that the whole point of Romeo and Juliet? That two young lovers had been pushed to the point of death over their family's feud? How stupid was that?

She had already lost one good man to the hatred of a clan war. It didn't make a lick of sense to let it happen again. The battle between the MacDonalds and the MacNicols happened over seven hundred years ago, and if there were one thing her mother would have wished for, it would be for their clans to live in peace. Kayla MacNicol had hated all the fighting and wanted nothing to do with it. Her mother was a healer by nature; violence was abhorrent to her.

Though her mother had tried to teach her the virtue of forgiveness, apparently, Bree had failed to take her mother's lessons to heart. Now she was presented with an unmistakable, golden opportunity to set things right, and she couldn't let it pass her by. She couldn't let the darkness of her past hold her back from creating a bright new day.

Alex was a good man. She saw it in the way he cared for his horses and the way he treated her with respect. Especially when he had listened to her talk about being an animal psychic even though he didn't understand the concept and wasn't sure he believed it possible. He was so like William; strong, dependable, and loyal. When they had needed him most, he had been loyal to his family's business and his horses. Yes, he had lied to her, but she'd been a stranger, and he'd been in need of her services. At the time, it wasn't personal; it was strictly business.

He also had those stunning hazel-green eyes, just like William. But he wasn't William; he was Alex MacDonald, a modern-day warrior, willing to fight for what he wanted, including her. She knew he cared for her, and she couldn't deny she had feelings for him. All she needed to do was open her heart to what might be and let go of what no longer was. It might be easier said than done, but at least she could try.

As she sat in the pasture with Malt and Barley, contemplating her past, present, and future, she felt something hard inside her heart melt away, leaving a soft place to land. The cold, ice-hard pain of past hurts and hatreds began to thaw as exciting new warmth spread through her body, lifting her spirit ever higher as it continued to grow. It was scary, but it was also freeing.

Impulsively, she stood and dropped the wool blanket, letting it fall to the ground as she raised her arms to the sky and twirled about. She felt light and happy, as though a heavy mantle had been dropped from her shoulders. As the chains of the past dropped away, she felt free and open to love again.

Bree would always love William. Those feelings would never change. Though William was gone, no matter what happened, she knew love remained. Once she let go of her anger and grief, there was room in her heart for more. More laughter, more life, and more love.

She picked up the blanket and headed back to Franklin's with a smile on her face and a secret in her heart. Of course, it was too soon to know how Alex really felt about her, but for the first time in four years, she felt willing and ready to love again. Perhaps it was a bit old-fashioned, but she felt it was important for him to properly win her hand. Besides, she didn't want to appear too eager. Bree believed a woman should take a wee bit of time to change her mind.

CHAPTER 15

It was nearly an hour after she had returned to Over-Yonder when Bree finally got around to checking her phone. Alex had sent her a text and a phone message asking her to call to let him know she had arrived home safe. She felt awful knowing he'd been waiting to hear from her, but her heart thrilled to know how much he cared. Bree called him immediately.

"I was looking at my schedule after you left. Since I'm busy most weekends, I'd like to come down to see you on Wednesday, if that's okay with you," Alex said. She heard a mixture of confidence and longing in his voice.

Okay? She was delighted. She hadn't expected him to want to see her again so soon. "Yeah, I'm okay with that," she said, trying not to sound too enthusiastic.

"Would it be all right if I spend the night again, like last time? I'm hoping I don't have to ride home the same day." There was a note of hopeful expectation in his voice.

Bree waited one, two, three heart beats before answering. "As long as you're okay with staying in the guest bedroom again, like last time."

Alex's laughter sang through the phone. "Yeah, I'm okay with that . . . for now."

She smiled, secretly elated by his innuendo, and wondered if it were their distance that allowed her to feel so bold. Soon he would be back at her home, sleeping under her roof, and she wondered if she would still be so bold when he was so close.

As it drew closer to Wednesday, whenever she thought of Alex coming to Over-Yonder, her stomach flipped, and then flopped, as if unsure whether she was delightfully happy or dreadfully nervous to see him again without the excuse of his horses in need of healing drawing them together. Whichever it was, for the first time in years, she felt as though she really had something to look forward to.

Jenny was excited for her. Claiming she only wanted to contribute, not control, Jenny suggested they organize a family barbeque for Wednesday evening. Bree loved the idea of introducing Alex to her family and invited Teressa and her husband Robert to join them. By Wednesday morning, Jenny's plan was confirmed and set into motion.

When Bree heard the distinctive, rumbling purr of Alex's motorcycle coming up the road, her heart did a little happy dance, sending electrifying sparks shooting through her nervous system, confirming it was joy, not fear she felt.

"He's here," she said to Sunnyside as she finished brushing his coat. "He's here, and this time it isn't strictly business." Although, to be honest, it never had been strictly business. She had known from the moment she met him there would be more. The only question had been more what?

She stepped out of the stables and watched Alex ride his Ducati into the driveway and dismount. Still standing in the shadow of the doorway, she watched as he set the helmet on the seat of his bike and ran his fingers through his dark, thick hair. It was nice to think he was primping for her.

With his dark jeans and leather riding jacket, once again, he reminded her of a dark warrior prepared to do battle. Only this time, she believed he was one of the good guys, and even better, he was on her side.

Alex quickly closed the distance between them and scooped her into his arms. He paused hardly a heartbeat before he dropped his lips to hers, kissing her like a hungry man seeking a feast. She had no choice but to respond. Her body was too revved up to put the brakes on now. Bree closed her eyes and let the passion flow through her, all warm and hot and buttery. *Dang.* This man knew how to kiss. And her body, acting totally on its own behalf, knew exactly how to respond. *Double dang.*

When Alex broke off the kiss and took a step back, it left her breathlessly dizzy, weak-kneed, and wishing for more. Her body's reaction was shocking and exciting and totally wrong. This took desire to a whole new level. This felt dangerous.

Whatever this was, it needed to be controlled, or it would control her. She took a step back and wrapped her arms around her waist like a straitjacket, hoping to get a grip on her racing hormones.

Then Alex surprised her by holding out his right hand with business-like manners. "Allow me to properly introduce myself. I'm Alex Connor MacDonald, of MacDonald's Clydesdales and Carriages. I've come to offer my services."

Bree wasn't sure where he was going with his act, but she figured it wouldn't hurt to play along. She accepted his formal greeting, shaking his hand with a confident smile. "Breanna Ellers. Pleased to meet you."

"Miss Ellers," he began.

"You may call me Bree."

"I'm here to offer you my services," Alex repeated.

Bree held back the giggle threatening to bubble forth. "Really? Now, why would a MacNicol be hiring a MacDonald?"

He stepped near, speaking softly. "I can't believe someone like you would be holding my family name against me. Not someone who can talk to horses and tame their fears. Not someone with a gentle and strong spirit like yours." The serious tone of his voice was offset by his beautiful smiling eyes. He had the kind of look that could melt her brain all the way to her toes and still leave her asking for more. In other words, the man was dangerous.

"What kind of services would ye be offering?" she asked, trying hard not to be distracted by his sensual look.

He straightened and looked around. "I noticed there's a fair amount of work that needs to be done around here. I'm thinking you could benefit from a handyman's touch, and I'm hoping you'll let me have a room for the night in exchange for a few hours of good hard labor. I'm real good with my hands." A mischievous grin played at the edge of his lips.

Considering his initial greeting, Bree could only imagine what he meant by all that. She tried to relax, despite the tingling sparks still shooting through her nerves. "Since you're here early, maybe you can help me get the back deck cleaned and ready for dinner. Jack and Jenny are planning a good old-fashioned family barbeque, and they want us to eat outside on the deck. My Aunt Teressa and Uncle Robert will be joining us."

Alex's grin wilted into a weak smile. "Oh, a family barbeque. How nice."

He didn't look nearly as pleased as she had expected. Didn't he know how important it was for him to be accepted by her family? When she had told Jenny about his visit, it had been her suggestion and they had immediately begun planning the dinner party. After the way she had treated Alex—rejecting him for being a MacDonald—she believed it was important for him to feel welcomed. For her, there was no better way to show her change of heart than to invite him into her home to spend time with the people she loved most.

"You seem disappointed. Aren't you happy about meeting my family?"

"No, no, it's nothing like that. I was just thinking I'd have some time alone with you, like last time. But, hey, a family dinner sounds good to me." The wattage on his smile brightened again.

"I planned on cleaning the deck myself, but right now, I have Edna and Otis coming over for their obedience class."

Alex's smile grew even brighter. "Really, Bree, I'm happy to help. Did I mention I'm good with my hands?"

His comment drew a nervous laugh. "Let's just hope you're good with a broom. The deck needs sweeping. We'll have to rearrange the patio furniture and clean off the grill." Bree began to tick off the list of chores she had hoped to finish before Alex arrived, but since he was here, she had to admit she welcomed his assistance.

"Well, then, you better go get ready for your clients, and I better get cracking on that deck."

"Are you sure?" She bit her lower lip, pulling it between her teeth.

He pulled her close, running his hands up and down her arms. "I'm sure, Bree. I'm here to help you, the way you helped me."

~*~

This wasn't exactly what Alex had in mind as he drove the two hours to see her. Then again, knowing Bree, he shouldn't be surprised. It wasn't as though she were just going to fall into bed with him on their first real date. He wondered if she even considered this a date, or if he were just another guest at her family's little dinner party.

That didn't seem to be the case, not after the way she had responded to his kiss. It had taken a hefty dose of control to stick to his game plan, but he was glad he did. He had wanted to set things right, give himself a fresh start with a clean slate, as Alex Conner MacDonald. And either she accepted him for who he was, or she wouldn't accept him at all. With him and Bree, it needed to be all or nothing. Alex didn't want it to be some kind of lukewarm something in between. Lukewarm wasn't worth having, and he was real sure Bree was worth having.

Bree was the kind of woman who liked to take things slow; she needed to maintain her image of control. Too many times, he'd seen her slip back into her shell whenever she felt her control slipping.

Frustrating as it was, Alex was determined to make the most of his time with her, even if it meant grabbing a broom and sweeping down her deck. He'd rather be sweeping her off her feet, but it looked as though that would have to wait until later. Hopefully, not too much later. In another week, he'd be heading out to work the county fairs for the summer, and it was hard to know when he would see her again.

He watched Bree conduct her obedience class with Edna and Otis as he cleaned and organized the deck. Using Laddy as her role model, he could see she was making progress with Otis. Alex doubted the rambunctious little pup would ever completely lose his desire to wander, but it looked as though Bree was helping Edna learn to control the little rascal better than before. At their last lesson, the dog had wandered off every chance he got, but now he seemed to be listening to Edna's commands, responding more often than not.

Bree had a way of crouching down at the dog's level to look him right in his eyes while speaking as if he understood everything she said. Maybe, at some level, he could. Maybe not word for word, but it sure looked as though he were listening.

Alex shrugged and returned to sweeping leaves and debris from the wooden deck. Did it really matter whether or not she could commune with animals? The bigger question was did she get good results, and from what he could see, the answer was yes. She'd certainly been able to tap into his horses to find the root of their fears. She'd also been able to find a way to cure them of those fears. Thanks to Bree, he knew what to do if the problem happened again.

After he finished sweeping, he wiped down the patio furniture and arranged the chairs around the large wooden table. Next, he went to work on the grill. As soon as Bree was done with her training session with Otis and Edna, she joined him. They had just finished scraping down the grill and were cleaning off the tools when he heard a truck pull into the parking yard next to the house.

"That'll be Jack and Jenny," Bree said, setting aside her work.

Jack and Jenny got out and began pulling bags of groceries from the back of the truck. Alex walked over to see if they needed any help.

"Hey Alex, I hope you brought your appetite," Jenny called in greeting. "Jack bought enough steaks to feed a small army."

In lieu of a greeting, Jack just nodded at Alex. "Hey, we've got three men to feed. I don't want them going to bed hungry, myself included." He picked up his bags and headed toward the back door.

Alex stepped over to Jenny. "Here, let me help," he said, reaching for tote bags bulging with groceries.

"Sure thing," she said, handing off both bags to him. "There's just one more in the cab. I had my students make the best apple crisp ever, and one of the perks of being the teacher is getting to bring home the samples."

"I hope there's vanilla ice cream to go with that," Bree commented, joining them as they headed up the deck and into the back of the house. She held the door open for Jenny and Alex as they stepped through.

"Duh, of course," Jack said from inside the house. He was busy unloading his groceries. "Alex, if you don't mind getting the charcoals started, I can start prepping these steaks."

Alex watched Jack stack six man-sized steaks on the kitchen counter. Jenny was right. He'd have to be pretty darn hungry to finish off one of those little monsters.

In next to no time, an organized frenzy was taking place as Jenny directed their efforts to get dinner on the table. Jenny worked mostly in the kitchen, preparing salads and boiled fresh corn on the cob. Bree moved in and out as she set the table and helped Jenny in the kitchen. Once the coals got hot, Jack took charge of grilling the steaks and handing out the beer, leaving Alex to relax with his drink as he watched from the sidelines.

Not much later, Teressa arrived with her husband, Robert MacNicol. Within minutes, it was obvious Robert was the head of this little clan. When they were introduced, Robert shook Alex's hand with the confidence of one who knew his place in the world, his grip firm and strong. It also said you're welcome here.

When he spoke, his Scottish brogue was nearly as strong as Bree's, reaffirming he had once lived on Scotland. Alex remembered Bree telling him Teressa had met Robert while on vacation on the Isle of Skye and he had accompanied her back to California. He had to give the guy credit; it was a long way to go to start a new life with a woman he had just met. Apparently, the gamble had paid off. Teressa stayed close to Robert's side as his hand rested protectively at the small of her back. From the way they interacted, it was plain to see they were deeply in love.

Alex could only hope someday he'd be blessed with that kind of loving relationship. Instinctively, his eyes sought out Bree as she spoke with her aunt and uncle. He wondered if she were the kind of woman he would cross an ocean to be with. Sometimes, it certainly felt that way.

~*~

Robert and Jack took their places at each end of the table while Teressa and Jenny sat across from Bree and Alex. Bree was grateful when Jenny offered to split one of the steaks with her; she could never eat one by herself. Jack was happy knowing there would be leftovers. He was already planning on having steak and eggs for breakfast. Bree also managed to slip a few good-sized chucks of meat to Laddy as he sat patiently next to her chair waiting for his usual share. From experience, Laddy had learned not to beg, he just waited.

They were catching up on small talk when Jack announced he was getting laid off as project manager at the college at the end of the school year. "It's all about budgets and cut-backs. They're not sure they can afford to pay me next year, so they have to lay me off now and hope they can hire me back when next year's budget gets approved."

"What about you, Jenny?" Bree asked. "Are you getting laid off, too?"

"No, I've got enough tenure to keep me safe. But Jack's right. I pity the young teachers who get their notices every spring and hope to get rehired in the fall. It's a tough way to run your life."

"I can't believe they treat you that way," Bree said, shaking her head. "Is there no regard for loyalty?"

"Not where school budgets are concerned," Jack said.

"What are your plans for the summer, if you don't have a job?" Robert asked, setting down his beer. Uncle Robert was Jack's older cousin, and Bree understood his concern.

"Guess I'll do more work around here. Get some of the projects done I've been putting off. I also want to do more work with the horses. I've been checking online, and there's a lot of money to be had if we turn this ranch into a fully operating horse sanctuary. It's good we're rescuing unwanted horses, but there are lots of people who will pay to give their kids riding lessons if we have the right resources," Jack said to Robert. Then he turned to address Bree. "Of course, I'm hoping I can work with you. I'm thinking we can expand the riding lessons to the public, maybe open a summer kids' camp for daycare, and offer overnight sleep outs. I've got a number of ideas, and now that I'm going to have some time on my hands, maybe we can put some of them to good use. You've been carrying too much of the load around here, Bree. I want to do more to help."

"Oh, Jack, you and Jenny have always been a big help. I couldn't do it without you. It'll be great having you here this summer. I like your idea about the kids' camp, but I always thought we were too remote for parents to bring their children all the way out here."

"I know, but I thought about that. We could have a bus stop near the college and run a shuttle service to pick up the kids. All we need is a van to run the kids back and forth. It'll be great for the parents."

"What a great idea," Bree said, excited by the ideas forming in her head. "We could still give lessons for the special needs children, but maybe with a regular kids' camp, we can find a way to introduce the special needs students to the mainstream kids in a way that would benefit them both." She was so excited, she could hardly eat. "We can call it 'Away to Over-Yonder, a sanctuary for horses and kids.'" She started waving her fork in the air, gesturing toward Jack.

"We need to talk. We need to get started, like now. School will be out soon, and we'll need to be set up as soon as possible."

Bree and Jack were still discussing ideas about the summer camp when she felt Alex's hand covering hers. Leaning close, he said, "I'm happy for you, Bree. You look so excited."

She turned to him, happy he was there. She hadn't meant to ignore him. "What about you? What are your plans for the summer?"

"Remember how I told you about our stage coach?" he asked.

Bree nodded, vaguely remembering him saying something about owning an old, rebuilt coach when they first met.

"After next weekend, I'll be busy working at some of the California county fairs. We have a contract to supply our stage coach and horses to about half a dozen fairs this year. We start in Sacramento on Memorial Day weekend and keep going from there." From the way he spoke, she could tell this was important to him.

"Wow, how exciting for you. So, you'll be leaving? Going out on the road?" she asked, trying to sound excited. She knew she should be happy for him, but she wasn't. Instead, she felt as though a plug had been pulled from her spirit, draining the energy right out of her.

"Only for the summer. Wayne and I will be working the circuit until mid-October. Our last gig is in San Diego then it's a straight shot back home for the winter. This is where we take in most of our income."

"What about the weddings?" Bree asked, thinking of the carriage ride they had provided for the bride and groom in Placerville.

"What about them?"

"Your Clydesdales and carriages. Don't a lot of people get married in the summer?"

"People get married all year long. That's a good thing. Wayne has a couple of sons in college who work for us every summer.

They've been doing it for years. Even his youngest daughter likes to help out. My cousins enjoy working the weddings, and during our summer season, it's an all-hands-on-deck sort of thing. It's our busiest time of the year."

Robert leaned forward to join the conversation. "Teressa told me about your business. She says your carriage is pretty impressive. It's even wired for sound."

"Yeah, I put that in myself. It really draws the tourists. I like knowing they can hear my guided tour without having to yell."

"What are you doing with a stage coach? Is it a real one?" Jack asked, setting down his beer.

"Oh, yeah, it's real all right. It's a classic from the late 1800s. We had to rebuild a good chunk of it, but it still looks rustic and rides like hell. Not a great way to travel, but people love the novelty. Mostly, we hire it out to county fairs for their Western shows. It's even been used in a few movies. We still have the invoice from when my granddaddy bought it over ninety years ago. He got it at an auction when the Denver stage went out of business. Proved to be one his best investments ever."

"What do you use to pull a thing like that?" Jack asked.

"Our Clydesdales. It takes a team of four. Years ago, my dad bought a moving van to store the coach and haul it around. When it's not in use, it sits in the padded truck parked on our land."

Bree sat and listened with half an ear as Alex fielded questions from Jack and Uncle Robert and told stories about working at fairs. They were interesting stories, and she was happy for the attention he was getting from the rest of her family, but she couldn't bring herself to be excited. It was wrong of her, she knew, to be so disappointed. What had she been expecting? They led separate lives, in separate towns, separated by miles of road.

She looked down at her plate and began to stir her mashed potatoes, moving them from one side of the plate to the other, no longer hungry. After a while, she speared her last piece of steak and fed it to Laddy then went back to playing with her food.

Thinking she'd been a fool to get excited about his visit—after all, he was a modern man with a business to run, and he didn't have time to court an old-fashioned lass like her—she told herself it was just as well. She had no business getting involved with him in the first place, since he was a MacDonald.

As soon as the thought hit her brain, she wanted to kick herself. Alex being a MacDonald had nothing to do with her disappointment. Her real problem was she had allowed herself to hope for something more with Alex when in reality he had a family business to run, and so did she.

When Jenny started to clear away the dinner plates, Bree jumped up to help her. As soon as they were in the kitchen, Jenny stopped her. "Bree, what happened out there? One minute you were flying high as a hot air balloon, and the next you were playing with your food. I saw you feed your steak to Laddy. Didn't you know about Alex's summer schedule?"

"Oh, no, I knew. He told me all about his stage coach. It's an impressive operation. I was just thinking about everything Jack and I need to do if we want to open a kids' camp this summer, and well, I guess I was feeling a little overwhelmed." Seeing the look of concern on Jenny's face, she added, "Don't worry about me. I'm fine. There's just a lot to think about."

"You won't be doing this alone. Jack will be there, and I'll do anything I can to help."

"Yeah, I know I can always rely on you. I don't know what I would do without my family." Impulsively, she reached out and gave Jenny a hug, needing to feel her cousin's support.

Jenny hugged her back. "Well, God willing and the creek don't rise, you'll never have to find out. Come on, girlfriend, help me finish clearing the dinner dishes so we can serve the dessert. Hot apple crisp ala mode." Jenny stepped back and wiggled her eyebrows in anticipation. It was enough to make Bree laugh.

"None for me," Bree patted her stomach. "I'll have to save mine for later."

CHAPTER 16

Bree paused for a moment with her toothbrush suspended in midair, wondering if there was any apple crisp left over from dinner. She decided it really didn't matter and proceeded to brush her teeth. It was already late, and she wasn't hungry enough to go looking for dessert. What she needed was to get to bed.

With Jack and Jenny's help, and without them even knowing it, she had managed to avoid being alone with Alex for more than two minutes since Teressa and Robert left after dinner. Thankfully, she'd been able to shuffle him off to the spare bedroom at the same time Jack and Jenny headed for bed. Then she had gone to her room, changed into her pajamas, and waited until the house was completely quiet before she slipped back down to the bathroom at the end of the hall.

The last thing she wanted right now was to risk finding herself alone with Alex.

She had allowed him to glimpse a moment of her passion when he arrived at Over-Yonder, but since he was leaving for the summer, she didn't want to start something that would be over as soon as it began. Once he left to go out on the road, there was nothing to say he would return.

With these thoughts rumbling in her head, she proceeded to run through her nighttime ritual of brushing her teeth, washing her face, and brushing out her hair. When she stepped out of the darkened bathroom to return to her bedroom, the hallway light clicked on, nearly startling her out of her skin. She clamped her hand over her mouth to keep from screaming.

Alex was there, waiting for her. Wearing only pajama bottoms, he leaned against the opposite wall with his arms folded across his chest—his very impressive, rock hard, muscular, naked chest. *Darn him.*

"Do you trust me?" he asked. His question surprised her.

She stopped staring at his chest long enough to look him in the eyes. "Um, sure I trust you." She glanced up and down the hall, considering her options. Her door was far away at the other end of the hall while his was too close, just next to him.

He stood away from the wall, filling the hallway and effectively blocking her escape. "Because you've been avoiding me all evening. What did I do, Bree, to scare you away?"

"You didn't do anything. You've been a perfect guest. I think my family really likes you," she said, trying to sound perky. Maybe she could slip back into the bathroom. Cowardly, but it would work.

"I'm glad. I like your family. But what about you, Bree? I thought *you* liked me." He wasn't moving, he stood there and watched her. She saw longing in his eyes, those darn mesmerizing green eyes of his, and felt her defenses slipping away like water down a drain. Once again, her body sent signals to her brain that were in direct conflict with her intention to remain uninvolved with Alex.

"I do like you, Alex, maybe more than I should."

He cocked his head. "I doubt that."

"I…It's just… You're going away." Bree looked down at her hands. She'd been fidgeting with the hem of her tee shirt, which barely reached the top of the thin cotton shorts she used as pajamas. Maybe not the best possible choice for tonight. Why couldn't she have worn something long and flannel with lots of fabric?

"But I'll be back. It's only for a few months. It's not like I'm going far. I'll still be in California."

"California is a big state. It's bigger than all of Scotland."

"Can we at least talk about this?" He reached for her hand, as if to lead her into his bedroom.

She commanded her body not to move, but she got the feeling it wasn't listening. Captured by his stunning, hazel-green eyes, she seemed unable to move. The mysterious effect they had on her was beyond reasoning.

"Do you trust me?" he asked again.

Sure, she trusted him. She trusted him to act like a man filled with needs and desire. And she trusted herself to act like a woman who hadn't been alone with a man in over four years. Not only that, he was too darn attractive for her own good, and his eyes had a way of looking into her soul. So, yes, she trusted them both to act accordingly, which meant her control was fading faster than snow during a hot, spring thaw.

When she continued to hesitate, he asked, "Would you prefer to sit in the living room?"

No, that wasn't a good idea. Though Jack and Jenny were sound sleepers, the last thing she needed was for one of them to come out and find them. Loosening the straps on her inhibitions, she allowed him to lead her into his room.

One step at a time, she told herself. That's all this is. It was still much too soon to know Alex's intentions toward her. Maybe he just wanted to talk, like he said. She certainly didn't want to roll into bed with him, only to be sorry in the morning when he rode off and left her.

He sat her down on his bed then sat beside her.

"It's true, I'm going away for the summer, but I'm not going far, and when I come back, I hope to see you again. Why do you think I drove down here today?"

"I don't know. To tell me you're leaving, I guess." She shrugged.

"And ask if you'll be waiting for me when I come back." He placed his hands over hers as they lay in her lap.

"Of course, I will. I'm not going anywhere." Her answer seemed to please him.

Alex moved his hands up her arms. "Can I just hold you, Bree? Since the moment I met you, all I've wanted to do is hold you. It's been the strangest thing. Like, if I could just hold you long enough..." His voice trailed off.

"What?" she asked. "If you could just hold me long enough, what?"

"I don't know. It's like I would remember something I'm missing."

"You mean like being with other women?" Oh, this was great. He was a love 'em and leave 'em kind of guy, which meant he wasn't the right guy for her. Maybe it was time for her to leave.

"No, Bree. I mean like being with you."

She blinked, wondering if she'd heard right. "That's impossible. We hardly know each other."

"Is that how you feel? Like you barely know me?"

She shook her head. Strangely enough, that wasn't true. Those hazel-green eyes of his were so darn hauntingly familiar. It also didn't help that every cell in her body wanted to be with this man, right here, right now.

This wasn't like the old days back on Skye when being intimate with a man meant you either got married or were ruined for life. In this modern era, sex between two consenting adults was considered an acceptable pleasure. It didn't require a marriage ceremony or even a commitment. And it wasn't as though she had to spend the rest of her life with Alex just because they spent the night together, but she hoped they would.

Where had that thought come from?

She wondered when he had gone from being a dreaded MacDonald to being the lust of her life. When had she let down her defenses long enough for him to touch her heart?

It must have been when they worked together to heal his horses. He had such a soft, sweet touch, it took her unaware and lingered still, gently drawing her into his loving embrace.

He pulled her close and wrapped his arms around her. She took a deep sighing breath and melted against him while her body kicked her brain to the curb. He felt so good, so strong, and so powerful. This was where she wanted to be.

And then he kissed her. He kissed her eyes, her cheeks, and her lips. And she let him, her resistance melting away, drop by sweet molten drop.

"Is this what you want, Bree?" he whispered into her hair. "Tell me now, because I won't take you where you don't want to go."

It was time, she acknowledged. This was the step that would take her out of the past and into the present. She was no longer at Scorrybreac with a fortress surrounding her and guards at the gate. Instead, she was in a semi-secluded farmhouse at the end of a long country lane, surrounded by open land and people she loved and trusted. Bree had come as close as she could to recreating the security of the clan she'd left behind. Now it was time to step out from behind the guarded gate.

She wanted him, and she knew he wanted her, and she couldn't very well hold it against him. Not when she was holding her body against his. She pulled back, searching his face.

"Maybe I should leave?" she whispered, voicing her earlier thoughts yet knowing perfectly well that was no longer an option.

She felt him go rigid beside her. "I'm hoping you won't, but if that's what you want, I won't stop you," he replied.

Apparently, he was leaving it up to her. She brought her hands up to touch his bare chest and felt his muscles grow taut beneath her slender fingers. He shuddered ever so slightly as she wove a path of discovery across his broad shoulders. Her eyes roamed freely over his body, drinking in the sight of his exposed chest.

Bree smiled, embolden by her feminine power. Lazily, her fingers snaked a slow, sensual path across his chest and down toward his stomach.

"Should I take that as a yes?" Alex asked, his voice deep and sensual against her ear.

"Yes," she said, noticing how her heart cheered for her body while her brain stood back and watched.

"I want you to know, this isn't about sex. This is about making love." He leaned down to touch his lips to her neck, his fingers brushing against her breast.

"Oh, my goodness," she gasped. He was so bold, and she hoped he was right. Back on Skye, this wasn't how a man courted a woman, at least it wasn't how William had courted her, but that was four years and seven centuries ago.

When he pulled her down to lie beside him, she didn't resist. She snuggled against him, feeling the heat of his arms surround her.

Her fingers crept down the firm, hard muscles of his back, absorbing the feel of his skin and the heat radiating from his body. Bree wanted to feel him, every inch of him. She felt brazenly bold, and she liked it. So this was what it was like to be a modern woman. How nice.

Alex kissed her again, softly at first, then with greater passion, teasing her senses into heightened awareness. He pushed his hands up under her shirt, splaying his fingers across her back, warming her skin. Grabbing the hem of her shirt, he pulled it up and off over her head. When he pulled her back into his arms, she could actually feel her breasts swell and harden against his bare chest with sensual pleasure. It felt as though every inch of her skin tingled with the anticipation of desire. She moaned and squirmed when he cupped her breasts in his large, strong hands, teasing the hardened buds with his thumbs. Soon, the tingling feeling moved from her skin to places deeper within, filling her with melted goodness.

He reached for her shorts, but paused for a moment, awaiting her approval. Bree nodded, yes. Quick as a whip, he pulled them off then leaned back to look at her. His eyes roamed over her body with naked appreciation. She was glad.

Not wanting to be naked alone, she began to untie the drawstrings of his pajamas with unsteady fingers. He smiled happily as she relieved him of his pants. Holy stars above, the man was well endowed. Again, she was glad.

Suddenly, he rolled away, reached into his bag, and pulled out a condom.

Protection, she thought. How considerate of him, and so prepared.

"Pretty sure of yourself," she said, raising her brows. She'd never been able to manage that one brow thing like him.

Alex tore the wrapper off the condom. "Just hopeful." He sheathed himself in one practiced move.

"You're pretty good at that," she observed.

"I went to college," he replied with a grin, as though that explained it all. And in a way, it did. She'd seen enough modern movies to have a pretty good idea of what happened on college campuses, even if some of it were exaggerated.

He lay down beside her, wrapping her in his arms. "I've waited so long for this."

"What—a week? A week is a long time for you?" *Dang.* He was a love 'em and leave 'em kind of guy.

"No, a lifetime. I've had sex before, but this isn't about sex. I think you know, this is something more."

"Well, of course, I'd like to believe . . . I think any woman would."

It surprised her how close to her heart his words hit. Regardless of the outcome, she was leaving her past behind and embracing her future, and it all pivoted on this moment.

"Trust me, Bree. I didn't ride here from Placerville for a one-night stand. I'm not going away. Not this time."

The look on his face told her he was just as surprised by his comment as she was. "What do you mean, not this time?"

"I'm not sure. It just came out. But I know I mean it with all my heart, if not my soul."

He started kissing her again, and the time for words was over. It was time for their bodies to do the talking, and right now, they were speaking loud and clear.

Alex resumed his attack on her senses, moving his hands slowly and methodically along the length of her, touching every curve of her body. His meticulous exploration became a form of ruthless, sensual torture as it blazed a trail across her body. He moved his hands along her long, slender legs and up her abdomen. When he seized the fullness of her breasts and began kissing and suckling her nipples, her body strained for release.

"Alex," she called. "Please, Alex, more."

"Good lord, Breanna, you're amazing," he breathed, his voice low and ardent.

She snaked her arms around his back and bound him to her with a steely grip. "Oh. My. Goodness," she cried, seeking their connection. It had been too long, and now that they were together, taking it slow was no longer an option. In her opinion, taking it slow was highly over rated.

"My sweet, darling, Bree," Alex moaned. He continued his exploration, touching her intimately, relentlessly savoring the wet readiness he encountered.

When she felt she could wait no longer, her body cried out for him and he moved to position himself between her thighs, pausing one moment longer in sweet anticipation before he sank himself deep inside her. Her muscles clenched around him, and she felt the oneness of their bodies joined together in sweet, blessed passion. Their union was beyond amazing.

She pulled her legs up to wrap around him, fully welcoming and embracing his body with her own. This was what she yearned for, this soulful connection with another, as their two bodies strived to become one, locked in an intimate lovers' embrace.

He started to move, slowly at first but then quickly gaining momentum to create a rhythmic thrust and pull that stirred her senses. She matched his rhythm, moving in sync, building a mounting force of pleasure. Together they moved in spellbinding bliss until their bodies reached the peak of sensory delight.

Thank God, the man had been true to his word. That was more than just sex. That was lovemaking at its finest.

Breathing in the warm, musky scent of him, Bree lay snuggled in his arms, feeling satiated and spent. It was grand. "Oh, my goodness, that was awesome."

Alex responded with a smile. "My thoughts exactly."

Bree laughed, slightly amazed at how comfortable she felt lying naked in his arms. She had expected her inhibitions to kick in somewhere along the way, but they never did, as if she had abandoned them, along with her pajamas, somewhere on the bedroom floor.

Suddenly curious, she asked, "How long has it been for you?"

Alex pulled back far enough to look at her. "Like this? Never before. Since sex? Over a year, maybe two." He pulled her back into his arms. "Funny, right now, I can't remember the last woman I was with. I can only think of you."

"Good answer." Oh, yes, he was definitely a charmer.

"How about you?" He looked down into her eyes and brushed stray strands of wayward curls from her face as he trailed warm fingerprints across her skin.

Interestingly, she knew this was important to him. "Over four years. Since before I left Skye." She felt the tears of remembrance filling her eyes, and she blinked them away.

His voice was gentle. "You were pretty young."

"It didn't feel that way. At the time, I felt like I was old enough to know my mind." She had planned to marry William, if only he hadn't been taken from her. Accepting the past for what it was, she forced the pain away, knowing it no longer served her.

"I'm sure you did. But why so long between then and now? You must have loved him very much to have waited so long."

How could he know? It was if he could look into her soul and know what she was thinking. All she could do was nod, not trusting herself to speak.

"I'm honored. I want you to know how much I value what you've given me. I don't take this lightly."

He was right. She hadn't waited four years between lovers only to take the first man who came along. She wanted to believe Alex was special, that he would give her the same care and attention he gave his horses, his job, and his family. Bree didn't necessarily believe this was the start of happily ever after, but she hoped he'd be around for more than a short-term affair.

Feeling her confidence wane, she looked away, worried she wanted too much, too soon. She was setting herself up for disappointment.

Alex turned her head gently back to face him. "I'm serious about this. I care for you, Bree. I wouldn't do anything to hurt you."

It was exactly what she needed to hear. "Are you sure you're not psychic?" she asked.

"I've never been before, but I kind of feel that way around you. Maybe you're rubbing off on me." He ran his fingers playfully across her belly, tickling her sides.

"Oh, yeah, I'm rubbing off on you, all right," she said, squirming against his body.

"You better be careful unless you want to go another round." His brow shot up in question. Yes, he was very good at that.

"What makes you think I don't?" Multi-orgasmic sprung to mind, but she didn't say it out loud. Hopefully, they'd discover that special little pleasure together. "I just hope you came well prepared."

And just like that, they were at it again.

CHAPTER 17

B ree awoke spooned against Alex, warm and happy. She glanced out the window then at the clock on the bedside table. "The sun will be up soon. I have chores to do," she said as she turned in his arms to face him.

"Can't you stay a little longer?" he asked without opening his eyes. His grip on her tightened.

"But Sunnyside—"

"Sunnyside can wait. He'll understand. Stay and tell me something about yourself." He opened his eyes enough to look at her.

She snuggled back down beside him. "Like what? What do you want to know?"

"When's your birthday? When were you born?"

Now that was a good question. "My birthday is September 22. I'll be twenty-three years old."

He looked impressed. "Were you born on the fall equinox?" He propped himself up on one elbow, using his free hand to run lazy circles up and down her arm.

It was her turn to be impressed. "Yes, I was. How did you know? I mean, it doesn't always fall on the twenty-second."

"My birthday is March 20. I was born on the spring equinox, right at sunset."

"The moment of balance between day and night."

"Yeah, I always thought that was pretty cool. So did my mom. She liked to say I waited for just the right moment and took my dear sweet time about it. My mother was in labor for over thirty-six hours."

"That poor woman."

"She said I was worth the wait."

"I'd have to agree. Do you miss her?"

"All the time. She was always the cushion between my dad and me. Without her, we've had to learn how to get along on our own. It isn't always easy. He's not an easy man. My sister just chooses to stay away."

Bree drew back. "You've never told me about your sister." It was strange, there was so much she didn't know about him, and yet she knew she loved him. *Loved him!* Mentally, she clamped a lid over that thought. Surly that was only her lust talking.

"Yeah, my younger sister, Janet. She got married pretty young, and Dad didn't approve, so now she just stays away. I go to see her whenever I can."

"Janet MacDonald. You have a sister named Janet MacDonald?" A creepy little feeling began to crawl from the pit of Bree's stomach.

"Yeah, except that's not her name any more. Not since she married Duncan."

"No way! Your sister, Janet MacDonald, married Duncan?" Bree sat up, scrambling to get out of bed.

"Yeah, Duncan McNiell. Do you know them?" Alex sat up on his side.

"Yes. No. I don't know." Holy crap. This had to stop. It was just too creepy, even for her.

Alex's father was Angus MacDonald, the chief of the clan, and his sister, Janet, was married to Duncan. Those were all names from her past—her centuries long-ago past. But she had never heard of an Alex MacDonald. An Arlin MacDonald, yes, but not an Alex.

Please, sweet Mother of God, don't let him be Arlin. Anyone but Arlin. Arlin was the man who had rejected her mother.

Her mind was filling with gibberish. She needed to leave.

"Bree, what's wrong? You look as though you've seen a ghost."

"Good God, I hope not." Before he could stop her, she gathered up her pajamas and sprang for the door. "I've got work to do," she cried and shot out the door.

Naked, she rushed across the hall into the bathroom and locked the door behind her. *This cannot be happening,* she thought. *This cannot be happening to me.*

~*~

Alex lay there, stunned for a moment, wondering what had just happened. Then just as quickly, he climbed out of bed and pulled on his pants. Before he had even finished zipping them up, he was out in the hall. He checked the bathroom door. It was locked.

"Bree, are you all right?" he asked, rapping his knuckles against the wood.

"I'm fine." Her muffled voice came through the closed door. "I need to take a shower."

"Can I come in?" He tested the door knob again. No luck.

"No. Go away. I'm fine."

A door opened down the hall, and Jack stepped out. "Is there a problem?"

"No, no. Everything's fine." Alex stepped away from the bathroom door. "Bree just got to the bathroom before me. You know, ladies first." He could hear the water running on the other side.

"You need to take a piss? There's a half bath off the kitchen behind the mudroom."

"Thanks, I'll go there." Alex went to use the facilities and then retreated back into his bedroom with the door open. He was just going to have to wait for her to come out, because until he got some answers about what just happened, he wasn't going anywhere. So, he sat down on his bed and waited.

Twenty minutes later, Bree came out of the bathroom wrapped in a towel, her damp hair hanging limp around her shoulders in silky ginger waves. She looked damn sexy, but he needed to concentrate.

"Are you okay?" he asked as he met her in the hall.

"Yeah, I'm fine." She shrugged, as though nothing unusual had just happened.

"Do you want to talk about it?" He stood with his hands in his pockets, wanting to touch her, but unsure how she would react.

"There's nothing to talk about." She turned and started walking toward her bedroom.

Alex didn't try to stop her. He just followed her down the hall. She stopped at the door to her room. "I need to get ready for work."

"I don't understand what just happened. You jumped out of my bed as if you'd been bitten by a snake. Is it something I did?"

"No, Alex." She reached out and touched his arm. "Let me get dressed, and we'll have breakfast together. Okay?"

"Fair enough." He took a chance and reached to cup her chin in his hand. When she didn't pull away, he pressed a kiss upon her lips. "I'm here for you, Bree."

He was rewarded with a weak smile before she ducked into her room.

Apparently, she wasn't ready to deal with what happened in the bedroom. He'd have to let it go.

~*~

By the time Bree walked into the kitchen looking for Alex, she was feeling much better. She'd had time to think and relax. Her escape into the shower had given her the space she'd needed to digest what she'd learned. Alex was brewing a fresh pot of coffee when she found him.

"Believe it or not, Jack left us some steak and eggs, if you're interested." Alex pointed to the casserole dish warming in the oven.

"You go ahead and finish them off. I'll just have some cereal." She pulled a box from the cupboard and set it on the counter. "Look, Alex, I'm sorry I freaked out back there. It's just that I've done some research on my clan's history, and one of the great chiefs of the MacNicols was named Duncan. He was married to Janet MacDonald, sister of Angus MacDonald, chief of their clan. When you told me about your sister, it seemed too freaky to be real. But I'm okay now, really I am. That's all ancient history. I've put it all behind me."

It was the closest she could come to telling him the truth. Now wasn't a good time to tell him she'd been alive in 1326 and had traveled through time. Of course, she couldn't imagine a good time would ever come. Not for something like that.

"Are you sure?"

"Yeah, I'm sure. Here, let me help you with that hot pan." She grabbed the oven mitts down from the wall and handed them to him.

"I don't blame you. That's a pretty weird coincidence."

"You're telling me." It was plain something strange was going on. Fate was conspiring to bring her past into the present, and no matter how hard she tried to run and hide, it seemed fate would always find her. Confronting it was the only possible solution.

She handed Alex a plate from the cupboard and brought down a cereal bowl for herself. "Growing up on Skye, I've always known my clan's history. My mother was a MacNicol, and though my dad was English, we always felt our loyalty to the MacNicols. While researching our history, I found the last great battle of the MacNicols was with the MacDonalds. After that, the MacNicol clan scattered and was crushed." She stopped for a moment and shook her head. "I'm sorry. You probably don't want to hear all this."

"No, Bree, please go on. It's part of your history. I want to know." He set two cups of coffee on the kitchen table along with his plate of eggs.

It occurred to Bree if she had any hopes for a future with Alex, he would eventually have to know about her past—all of it. If not, she'd have to spend the rest of her life pretending to be a normal twenty-first-century woman, lying about where she came from. She was a woman with a past, and most of it happened seven hundred years ago.

With Teressa's help, she'd been able to let go of her resentment of the MacDonald name. She might not be ready to forgive and forget, but at least she was willing to let it go. Still, she had one more hurdle to jump over. Faulting Alex for not telling her the truth about his last name was nothing compared to the secrets she was keeping.

Her secrets were huge, much bigger than simply carrying the name of a long-ago feuding clan. She had been born seven hundred years ago, she carried the bloodline of the fae, and her family had a history of traveling through time. Oh yeah, her secrets were huge.

Bree took her bowl of cereal and sat across from him. "There's nothing more to tell. It was a brutal time. People did brutal things. Times have changed. People are more civilized. We take hot showers," she said with a grin, trying to lighten the mood. After pouring on the milk, she began eating her breakfast. This was what normal people did, right? Have breakfast together after a night of passionate sex.

Alex eyed her cautiously before speaking, as though unsure of her meaning. "It would have been nice to have taken that shower together," he said.

Bree laughed, grateful for his jest. "Yeah, my bad. A missed opportunity."

"We'll have to set that right." He reached for her hands across the table. "I get the feeling something bad happened to you in the past. Something more than just an attachment to old clan history. You haven't spoken much about your parents or your family back on Skye. Losing both of your parents when you were just eighteen, I know you've been through a lot, more than I could ever imagine, but I want you to know, I'm here for you now. Bree, you don't have to be alone anymore."

Talk about hitting the nail on its head. She turned her palms up to lace her fingers with his, receiving his strength and giving him her trust. "Are you sure you're not psychic?"

"If being psychic means having a greater connection to someone, then yeah, I'd say I'm psychic where you're concerned. So, do you want to talk about it?"

Bree shook her head, "No. Not right now. I'm trying to leave my past behind." Under her breath, she mumbled, "*Meminisse sed Providere.*"

Alex cocked his head. "Excuse me? Is that Greek?"

Bree chuckled. "No, it's Latin for my clan's current motto. It means remember, but look forward. Something I need to take to heart."

"Listen, Bree, I've been thinking about this, and I'm wondering if you'd be willing to drive up to Sacramento next weekend to join me while I work. I'd love for you to see the stage coach, and Malt and

Barley will be there. They're part of the four-in-hand team we use to pull the coach."

Bree sat silently for a moment, considering his suggestion.

When she didn't answer right away, he pressed on," Even though it's close to home, once we're on the road, we always stay with the rig. I've got a hotel room close to the fair grounds. It's nothing fancy, but you could stay there with me, if you like. Maybe we could take a hot shower together. What do you think?"

She sucked on her lower lip, drawing it between her teeth. Actually, she didn't have any classes scheduled over the Memorial Day weekend. Her students preferred to spend the holiday with their families, so she could be available. Still, she hesitated. "It seems kind of improper, running off to spend the weekend with you."

"Bree, we just spent the night together. You seemed okay with that."

Oh, yes, that had been better than okay, and the idea of repeating the experience was very appealing. But to actually plan for it to happen wasn't something she had considered, at least not until now. And now that she was considering it, she had to admit, she liked the idea. She wondered for a moment what Jenny or Teressa would say. Knowing them, they'd probably tell her to go for it.

"Okay, Alex." She took a deep breath, suppressing her nervous grin. "Yes, I'll meet you in Sacramento."

"Great!" Happiness burst across his handsome face. He pulled her hand to his lips and kissed her fingers. "You won't be sorry. We'll have a good time. Be sure to pack some Western wear, you know, a cowboy hat and boots, stuff like that. I want you up on the driver's seat with me."

She felt herself drawn into his excitement. "I'm thinking I should drive the Mustang."

"Awesome. Maybe I'll get a chance to drive it, too."

Bree laughed. "Alex, you can drive it today if you want. We could drive it into the city, maybe out to lunch."

Alex turned serious. "I'd love to spend the day with you, but I've got to get back to Placerville. We've got a lot to do before we go out on the road. Wayne and I need to clean the coach, check out the harnesses, get all the gear packed and ready for the trip, ..." He began ticking off his task list but then stopped. "I'm so glad you agreed to meet me. I was hoping you would. In June we'll be in Pleasanton for the Alameda County Fair. Maybe you can meet me there. That's a three-week run. What do you say, Bree? Will you agree to run around California with me for the summer?" He looked so excited, like a kid sharing his Christmas wish list with Santa. It broke her heart to have to say no.

"I wish I could, but I'm going to be running the kids' camp with Jack, remember?"

His expression wilted. "Only a day camp, right? During the week?"

"Yes, but it'll take a lot of my time. I can't leave it all to Jack." She pulled her hands away and started to clear the table. "Like you, I have a family business to run. These electric lights cost money, and there's food and feed for the horses—plus taxes. My God, there are always taxes. Aunt Teressa and her brothers might own this farm, but I'm responsible for paying the taxes. After all, I live here."

She set the dishes down in the kitchen sink and turned on the water.

Alex stood and joined her at the counter, wrapping his arms around her. "Bree, slow down; I get the picture. I understand. Trust me, if we want to make this happen, we will. There's nothing that can't be fixed, except maybe death." He turned her in his arms and gave her a lighthearted grin.

She returned his smile, feeling a wee bit better. "Not even death if you believe in reincarnation," she chuckled.

"You don't believe in that sort of thing, do you?" He drew back, and that questioning brow of his shot straight up.

"Well, I believe it's possible," she hedged. She guessed now wasn't a good time to tell him Uncle Robert and Franklin both remembered having lived before. "Anything's possible, right?"

"Maybe," he shrugged, not looking convinced. "I'd rather put my money on doing the best I can with the life I've got. But like you said, anything's possible if you believe, and trust me, Bree, we can make this work."

"Okay, Alex, if you say so." She leaned back against his rock hard chest, taking comfort in the wall of protection he offered. It was lovely to think they had a chance, that they could make this work, but right now she had no idea how on earth they could possibly be together in the long run.

CHAPTER 18

Alex was both persuasive and persistent. Their weekend in Sacramento was better than perfect; it was magical, and thrilling, and beyond anything Bree could have imagined. She sat high above the road bed on the driver's seat with Alex as he drove the stage coach and felt the majestic strength of the Clydesdales as they pulled their load. They were four powerful beasts, and yet Alex controlled his horses with the sure-handed confidence of a seasoned professional. She couldn't help but admire his display of masculine assurance.

She also fell in love with the razzle-dazzle intensity of the county fair with its bright colors, glittery lights, and nonstop noise. Sometimes she was overwhelmed by the heavy scents of sweet desserts and greasy fried foods permeating the air, but those odors were nothing compared to the smells of sweat and horses lingering around the paddocks.

After their first weekend in Sacramento, Bree managed to rearrange her schedule so she could see him again at some of the county fairs closer to her home. With each rendezvous, she felt energized and more productive. She found new and innovative ways to get her work done, running the kids' camp during the weekdays with Jack, to free up time to meet with Alex on the weekends. Between their visits, she became a wiz at texting and emailing. Modern technology! Who knew?

They were halfway through the summer, and Bree was looking forward to another weekend visit with Alex. It was late on a Friday afternoon, and Jack had just left in the van to return their campers to the bus spot near the college. He would stay there and wait until the last camper was picked up by his or her parents. It was time for Bree to pack her overnight bag and get ready to head out to Pleasanton.

Mentally, she ran through her check list to make sure she wasn't missing anything. Jeans, tee shirts, a pair of shorts, a light summer dress, and her prepacked toiletry kit nearly filled the bag. There was barely enough room for one more thing.

Though she hardly wore them, she placed her neatly folded pajamas at the top of the bag, running her hand over them to smooth out the winkles before she zipped up the small duffle. Delicious memories of how good Alex was at taking them off her brought a smile to her face.

Everything was perfect.

Everything except for the nagging guilt gnawing at her gut that she wasn't being completely honest with Alex. Every time she set out to see him, she vowed she would tell him everything, and every time the weekend came and went without one word said about who she was or where she came from.

For the past week, she'd been running through various scenarios, trying to picture how she would tell Alex about her past. So far, she hadn't come up with anything that didn't sound bat shit crazy.

In one scenario, she pictured herself talking to Alex about her mother and working into the conversation that the last time she had seen her mother was right before that fateful battle at Scorrybreac in 1326. In another, she imagined telling him how she had celebrated her eighteenth birthday in the fourteenth century and had turned nineteen seven hundred years later in the twenty-first century. Maybe she could just ask Alex how he felt about dating an older woman, since she was born in 1308. Yeah, that was a good one. Surely he'd love to hear that.

Anytime the subject of her childhood came up in conversation, she managed to be evasive enough to maintain her deception. When he had asked where she went to school, she had answered honestly that she'd been home schooled on Skye. Of course, she had failed to mention that home was actually the MacNicol keep, and the only other students had been members of her immediate family. When he asked about her high school graduation, she told him Aunt Teressa had helped her get an American GED diploma when she arrived in California. She'd even gone on to take a few classes at Diablo Valley College, mostly in animal husbandry. It was all true. She simply failed to mention the reason she had never attended public school on Skye was because in her time, it didn't exist.

Bree shook her head again, thinking how stupid and unrealistic it was to think she could spend the rest of her life with someone who didn't know the truth of her past. There was too much of a possibility that some day, somehow, he would learn of her deception, and her whole world would come crashing down around her. She knew from experience, no one wanted to discover someone they loved had lied to them.

She wondered what she would do if their roles were reversed. Would she be able to believe, much less accept, if Alex had lived most of his life in the past, or perhaps the future, and had traveled through time? It was doubtful. Because it had happened to her and her family, she believed such things were possible, but most people didn't share her experience, or her viewpoint.

She had lived her whole life aware of the spiritual magic present on earth. Since she was a wee child, her mother had told her of their fae heritage and the fae blood flowing through her veins. Her eldest sister, Lorene, like their mother, had the gift of healing. Her sisters Treasa and Glenna both had a gift for second sight. Treasa always seemed to know whether someone could be trusted or whether a couple belonged together. Much like her namesake aunt, Treasa had been a marvelous matchmaker, bringing couples together in unusual ways. Glenna knew the sex of every child before it was born. Bree had often heard the story of how Glenna had been only two years old when she informed their parents she was going to have a new baby sister, well before her mother had even announced her pregnancy.

The ability to communicate with animals was Bree's gift. She'd been able to hear their thoughts and feel their emotions nearly her whole life. Vividly, she still remembered the first time she spoke to her new puppy and understood his thoughts. She thought everyone could speak to animals until her mother explained how blessed their family was to have been gifted with the magic of the fae. Kayla insisted their gifts were treasures to be used for the good of mankind and never abused.

Bree never doubted her father had traveled to the past to meet and marry her mother, or that her mother was half fae, passing the fae bloodline on to her daughters, or that she had traveled through time from the fourteenth century with her father. What was difficult to believe, if not impossible, was that Alex, or any modern man would believe such stories. She came from another time and place, and often felt as alien in this modern world as those extraterrestrial spacemen depicted in movies.

With an effort to put it out of her mind, she tried to focus instead on her eagerness to visit another county fair. She liked being around the animals, the rides, and the bright lights. Each fair was an exciting spectacle, and being there with Alex made it even more magical. Even traveling through time paled compared to going round and round on a large Ferris wheel with Alex by her side, seeing the whole of the fair spread out at her feet. At times like that, she wanted to believe they could go on forever, living life as though they were meant to be together.

That was why she found it so hard to tell him the truth about her past. She was too afraid he'd walk away and all this would end. With each visit, her conscience nagged at her more and more that she was withholding her biggest secrets, and still she worried the knowledge of who she was and where she came from would send him running back to his farm in Placerville, never to return. She couldn't fault him if he did. How could she have been so reckless as to allow herself to become so vulnerable and exposed to pain when he finally learned the truth?

As Bree lugged her suitcase toward the back door of the house, she heard a car come down the lane and pull into the driveway. Glancing out the kitchen window, she recognized her aunt's little red MINI Cooper parked next to her equally red Mustang. Bree knew Teressa was expected for dinner with Jack and Jenny, but her aunt's early arrival was a perfect opportunity for Bree to get a little one-on-one counseling from the experienced relationship coach. She set her bag down in the living room and went to open the kitchen door for Teressa.

"Hey, Auntie, perfect timing. I was just getting ready to head out to Pleasanton. But I'm glad I caught you." She greeted her aunt with a big hug.

"It's my luck, I'm sure. I've been hoping to hear how things are going with you and Alex. Jenny tells me you're planning another weekend away with him." Teressa glanced over to the suitcase waiting by the door. "Things must be going well from the looks of it."

"Better than I could have imagined. Can I get you some tea or something to drink?" Bree lead the way into the kitchen and began filling the tea kettle.

"I'd rather have soda water if you have any," Teressa said before taking a seat at the café table in the adjoining breakfast nook.

"Jenny always keeps us stocked." Bree pulled a cold bottle of sparkling mineral water from the refrigerator and handed it to her aunt along with a tall plastic tumbler from the cupboard. She took her favorite sunflower mug down from the shelf, plopped a tea bag in it, and then leaned against the kitchen counter while she waited for the water to boil.

"There is something I've wanted to talk to you about." Bree took the string from the tea bag and began winding it around her index finger.

"Okay, Bree, I'm listening. Is everything all right?" Teressa poured her sparkling water into the tumbler and let the bubbles settle before she took a sip.

"Yeah, everything's fine. Like I said, better than I could have imagined. It's just that, well, I haven't told Alex about my past." She unwound and rewound the string from the tea bag around her finger.

"Hmm, yes, I can see how that might be a problem if you let it." Teressa took a sip of her soda water, leaning forward in her chair.

"Do I have a choice?" Bree stopped playing with the string.

"I can understand why you haven't said anything to Alex before now. It's not something you want to blurt out on the first or second date."

"Right. Exactly. But don't you think it's something he should know?" Bree poured hot water from the kettle into her cup then took a seat across from Teressa.

"Eventually, yes, and probably soon. But I'd advise you not to worry about it. When the time is right, you'll know. And until then, I say, don't worry."

It was amazing how calm her aunt could be when faced with a relationship problem. "But I feel so bad not telling him." She cupped her hands around the warm mug, waiting for the tea to brew.

"Okay, then tell him, but don't make it into something bigger than it is. This is who you are, Bree. If he wants to be with you, it won't make a difference. And if it does, then he doesn't really want to be with you. Not the real you. He might only want an image he's created of you, and if that's the case, it's best to know. I'm not saying it won't be painful, but short-term pain from a quick breakup is a heck of a lot better than a lifetime of lies. You're going to have to trust Alex wants to be with *you*, the real you, or not at all. Do you get what I mean?"

"I think I do, but you're making it sound so simple." It certainly didn't feel that way to Bree.

"And you're making it seem so hard; am I right?"

"Well, maybe." Bree shrugged her shoulders before taking a sip of her tea. Hot tea always made her relax.

"Trust, Bree. It's all a matter of trust. Do you know what makes up trust?" Teressa asked.

Bree shook her head; fairly certain her aunt was going to tell her.

"Truth, respect, understanding, support, and togetherness," her aunt ticked off the letters of the word on her fingers. "But the first thing is truth. And I feel certain when the time is right to tell Alex, you'll know. Don't force it, and don't fight it. Just let it come and trust all will be well."

"Won't he be mad that I lied?"

"That's very possible. Remember, it wasn't too long ago when you misjudged him because he's a MacDonald. Don't be surprised if you get a taste of your own medicine."

Bree drew back in horror, remembering her angry dismissal of Alex when she learned his last name. Teressa was right, karma had a nasty way of biting you on the backside when you least desired.

"Try not to worry, Bree. I'm sure he'll understand you had to wait for the right time. That's what you should tell him; you were waiting for the right time. When I traveled back in time and met Rory, he didn't know I was from the future. I wasn't allowed to tell him, or I risked not being able to go home. Trust me, as much as I was falling in love with Rory, I wanted to come back home. I don't have to tell you, after living in modern times, thirteenth-century Scotland wasn't exactly a barrel of laughs."

"I know. No hot showers." Bree grinned gleefully, thinking of all the hot showers she had shared with Alex.

"And no grocery stores, or toilet paper."

"Oh, yeah, how could I forget toilet paper?"

Both women laughed before Teressa continued. "It was funny how I accepted magic had taken me back in time and I believed magic would take me back home, but I hadn't been able to believe magic would somehow, someway, keep us together. I felt like I had found the love of my life, only to lose him. But I didn't. Love, or magic, or whatever you want to call it, kept us together. When Rory asked me to believe, I did. He told me love is the strongest magic of them all. Love kept us together. If what you have with Alex is love, than all you need is a little faith, and things will work out."

"That's what Alex keeps saying."

"Don't you believe him?"

Bree sat for a moment, digesting Teressa's words. All she needed was faith, and love, and the right timing. Slowly, a satisfied smile spread across her face as she sat back in her chair. "You know, Auntie, I love the way you put everything into perspective. It saves a lot of wear and tear on my nerves."

Teressa raised her glass in a salute. "Glad I could help. That's what I'm here for."

CHAPTER 19

Alex woke with a start, looking about to see where he was. When he recognized the nondescript walls of another hotel room, he fell back against the pillow and heaved a sigh of relief. Thankfully, he was back, safe in this lousy hotel bed, no longer battling for his life.

For the past few weeks, these dreams—the Scottish dreams— had been getting stronger and stronger. The only time they stopped was when Bree was with him. But this time, the vision was too real, too vivid to have only been a dream.

He had observed every detail of the battle, and felt every nuance. He'd seen the expressions of pain, anger, and fear etched deep on the faces of the men and women around him. He'd heard their cries for help and their agonizing screams. The scent of blood and human sweat had filled his nostrils, making it hard to draw a breath. Gagging, he'd forced back the bile rising from the pit of his stomach. Every muscle, every bone in his body had reacted with brutal instinct to fight for his life and defend his loved ones. And it all had felt real. So much so, every muscle in his body now ached.

Unlike other dreams in which he had felt hopelessly lost, in these recent dreams, he had known exactly where he was, and when. He'd been in Scotland, on the Isle of Skye, in the year 1326. The MacNicols were defending their home against the MacDonalds, and he'd been there, smack dab in the middle of the violence. Only he hadn't been fighting *with* the MacDonalds. He had been fighting *against* them, alongside the MacNicols. What was up with that?

An older woman—he knew her name was Kayla—had called for help, but he hadn't been able to reach her. No matter how hard he had tried, he couldn't save her from the rough and ugly men attacking everyone he loved.

No, not everyone. There had been one glimmer of hope, one thought that rose above all others. His lady love was safe, far away from the impending doom surrounding him.

Then the sharp blade had hit him. The attacking warrior's claymore had sliced through his back and into his gut, ripping his flesh. He'd felt the sword enter his body and felt his legs crumple beneath him as the hard steel withdrew, leaving him lifeless. Only the sheer force of his dying scream had pulled him from the terrorizing vision.

Still shaking and drenched in sweat, he threw off his blankets and crawled from the bed. Stumbling, he made his way into the bathroom. When he looked in the mirror, for one brief second, the face he saw was not his own. Startled, he blinked, and his own face appeared. He bent over the sink to splash cold water on his face, grateful to wake from the cold, harsh reality of his dream.

Alex stood there for several long minutes, struggling to regain his bearings. He tried to recall what day it was. Friday, yes, he was sure it was Friday. He'd gone to bed thinking of Bree, grateful tonight she would be with him and the dreams would stop, if only for a night or two.

~*~

Their timing was perfect. The sun was just getting ready to touch down in the Pacific and dusk would soon be upon them. Lights of the fair were already glowing bright, ready to compete with the spreading darkness. Alex had already spoken to Marty, the Ferris wheel attendant, to arrange for a little extra hang time at the top of the wheel with Bree. He knew the Ferris wheel was her favorite, and he wanted to impress her with a special ride at sunset.

"Step right up, car number twelve, one of my favorites," Marty said. He signaled Alex with a wink as he ushered them into the lemon-yellow cab of the ride. As soon as they were settled, Marty fastened down the safety bar, locking them into place.

Bree giggled nervously as she nestled against Alex with his arm wrapped tight around her shoulder. "Ready for another ride?" he asked, smiling down at her upturned face.

"I love these things. I want to ride one at every fair."

"Then that's what you should do. Ride one at every fair, with me."

Instead of answering, she snuggled deeper against his chest. It felt so right with her at his side.

Up they climbed, higher and higher, until they reached the top, cresting for one brief second at the height of the huge mechanical circle before they plunged downward, sweeping out then back before beginning the ascent, once again. After their third spin around, the wheel slowed and came to a stop just as their car reached the peak. Alex leaned over the side to take a brief look down at Marty. The ride attendant gave him the thumbs up sign. Alex turned his attention back to Bree and heard her sigh.

"This all seems so magical," Bree said, looking out over the fairgrounds.

His gaze followed hers, taking in the glorious view stretching off into the distance. "Sitting up here with you, I'd have to agree. You seem like the kind of person who believes in magic."

"Yes, I guess you could say that."

"I mean the way you can talk to animals and all."

"I guess some people might call that magic. I call it my gift." He felt Bree shrug her shoulder before sitting up to take a better look around, putting a bit of space between them.

"You know, when you first told me about your, umm, gift, I didn't believe you."

She turned and gave him a questioning look. "I know. Do you believe me now?"

"I've seen what you can do. I might not understand it, but I'm convinced by the results."

"Most people think seeing is believing, but I think sometimes you first need to believe to see."

"Are you telling me you could believe in something you can't see?"

"Sure, and so can you. You believe in love, even when you can't see it. You can only feel the effects of it. Right?"

"I'm not sure that's the same thing."

"Most people don't, but I believe there's a whole other world, a world of magic where anything is possible."

Alex wasn't quite sure what she meant, but then again, it wasn't unusual for Bree to say things he didn't understand. He didn't let it worry him, figuring it was just one of those endearing little quirks that made her so unique.

He took a deep breath. Maybe now was a good time to talk about his little problem. "So if someone told you they were having strange dreams, you'd probably be okay with that."

"Strange dreams? You mean like fantasies?" Bree's brows shot up toward her hairline.

Alex gently chuckled. "No, not that I haven't had my fair share of those where you're involved." He grinned, delighted by the pinkness he saw spreading across her cheeks, but then, just as quickly, his smile waned. "No. I'm talking about dreams that seem so real it's hard to believe they didn't really happen."

"You mean like virtual dreaming? I've heard Franklin talk about that."

"No, I mean like memories."

Bree's expression turned serious, thoughtful. "I've had some pretty vivid dreams, but none that seemed like memories. Usually my dreams don't make a lot of sense. Why do you ask?"

Alex took another deep breath, hoping beyond belief Bree would provide him with some answers, and not tell him he was out of his ever-loving mind. Cutting right to the heart of the matter, he asked, "Have you ever heard of a guy named William Gregory?"

~~~

Bree's heart thumped hard and fast in her chest, spreading angst to every cell of her body. "How do you know about William?"

"I've been dreaming about him. Dreaming I'm *him*. It's freaking me out."

"But you're not. You can't be." Bree stared at his stunning hazel-green eyes that reminded her so much of William and trembled. She suddenly felt chilled, though the air still held the heat of the day.

"But what if I were?" Alex persisted.

"How can you say such a thing? You don't even know who William was."

"William Gregory, son of Tavish and Mari, grandnephew of a druid named Souyer. He lived on Skye and died defending your mother, Kayla MacNicol. Am I right?"

Of course, he was right, but that was from her pervious life, a time and place far removed from here and now. "How could you possibly know all that?"

"Because every night, when I go to sleep, I *become* William Gregory, a loyal defender of the MacNicol clan in the early thirteen hundreds."

Her eyes widened with shock. "Holy crap."

She immediately remembered her Uncle Robert had once been Rory in another life, and Franklin had once been Souyer. Was it possible Alex had once been William? The idea was daunting, impossible, and frightfully alluring. If Alex and William were one and the same, it answered an awful lot of questions, like why they shared the same mesmerizing hazel-green eyes, why she'd been so attracted to him so soon after meeting him, and why he felt so familiar. But it also raised a whole new set of questions, most notably, why the hell did he come back as an effing MacDonald?

Alex continued to stare at her, his eyes locked on hers. "But that's not all, Bree. I remember you. When I'm William, I remember being with you on Skye. I called you Breanna."

"William?" She clamped her hand over her mouth, dumbfounded by her outburst.

"Bree, you've got to help me here. I don't understand how I can remember being a guy named William in the thirteen hundreds, but more than that, how the hell could I have known *you* seven hundred years ago."

"Oh, my God," she muttered sheepishly. There was no use denying her blunder. She had all but admitted to knowing William—seven hundred years ago. *Dang.* This was going to take some explaining.

She felt the Ferris wheel start to move again, plunging them down and around the gigantic circle.

"So you don't deny it?" she heard him shout. His words were nearly lost in a rush of air as the Ferris wheel picked up speed, whipping them back toward the top of the ride. Her stomach was having a hard time keeping up.

He looked at her expectantly, almost as if he hoped she would deny they had known each other before. But she couldn't do that. She couldn't lie to him, not if she had any hope of maintaining their relationship. This was the moment of truth her Aunt Teressa had told her to expect.

"Alex, we need to talk," she shouted into the wind. "Maybe we should wait until we're back on solid ground."

Alex made a chopping motion as they neared the ride attendant and their car came to a screeching halt. "Hope you enjoyed your ride," the attendant said with a cocky grin as he unlocked their safety bar.

"Grand, Marty. It was absolutely grand. Thanks for your help." Alex reached for her hand to help her out of the car. "Let me know when you want that free ride on the stage coach. I owe you."

As he led her away from the fair's crowded and noisy midway, Alex continued to hold her hand. She felt pulled along as she rushed to keep up with his long strides, not sure where he was taking her. Along the way, her mind whirled and buzzed like a hummingbird in flight, unable to light upon any one thought long enough to make sense.

How could Alex have dreams, maybe even memories, of being William, unless he had been William? And why was this happening now? Had their meeting somehow released his memories from his past life? Or was Moezell somehow connected to all this? She hadn't heard from her fae cousin in over a year. Was fae magic at work behind the scenes? Bree couldn't begin to guess how Moezell might be involved, but from past experience, it seemed highly likely.

Alex flashed his access pass to the security guard stationed at the staging entrance to the paddocks then proceeded on until they reached the stables. Night had settled in, but the area was well lit, providing a safe, but private space. When he reached the stalls holding his horses, he stopped and turned to her.

"I really need you to help me, Bree, because I need some answers. I need to know what the hell is going on before I go effing nuts."

Though she had run through various scenarios several times in her head, now that she was confronted with the opportunity to explain, she was at a loss for words. "I'm sorry, Alex. I don't know where to start. There's so much to say, and a lot I don't understand."

"Try starting with how you know William Gregory. Or even who the hell he is, or was. Why am I having dreams from fourteenth-century Scotland? And why are you in them? I mean, I can understand dreaming about you, but these aren't exactly what I would call fantasies. And even so, why would I mix a modern-day fantasy with what feels like ancient memories?"

Fear gurgled and stewed in her belly. She was about to discuss something that had never been spoken of outside her immediate and trusted family. Only Teressa, Robert, and Franklin had ever been told the whole story about who she was and where she came from. Even Jenny and Jack hadn't been told about her time travel. Like everyone else, they believed she was a long-lost niece of Robert MacNicol and the adopted daughter of Daniel Ellers.

"William Gregory was the young man I loved back on Skye. The one I lost right before I came to America."

"You mean four years ago, right?"

"Well, yes, but..." She sucked on her lower lip, pulling it between her teeth.

"Not seven hundred?" he interrupted her.

"Alex, I need to start at the beginning. Umm, how do you feel about sitting down?" Bree eyed the wooden bench in front of the stables, thinking she was going to need its support before their discussion was done.

"I'd rather stand."

"Yeah, I figured as much." She ran her fingers through her hair, pushing it away from her face. "Do you mind if I sit down? I think I'll feel better." Without waiting for him to answer, she took a step toward the bench.

"Okay, fine," he grumbled. Rather than taking a seat beside her, he pulled out one of the storage boxes holding his gear and sat across from her. Apparently, he wanted a clear view of her face. Or maybe he just didn't trust himself to sit next to her. Either way, she couldn't blame him. If someone was about to tell her they came from another time, she was pretty sure she'd want to get a good look at their eyes.

"First off, I want you to know, I don't have all the answers, but everything I'm about to tell you is true. I won't lie to you, Alex."

"Fair enough. That's all I ask." He nodded, waiting for her to proceed.

"I knew William Gregory when I lived on Skye. We grew up together at Scorrybreac. His family was part of the MacNicol clan. He was my first love, and I always thought someday we would get married, but that never happened. He was less than twenty-one years old when he died in battle. I was only eighteen."

"That all sounds about right, just like I've been dreaming, but we can't be talking about the same guy here. I'm dreaming about being a guy who lived in the fourteenth century. It's like I lived, breathed, ate, drank, and slept, even died, in another time. That was the weirdest part, remembering my own death. I mean, how can someone remember dying?"

"I know what you mean. I was there, I mean, all except for the dying part."

He looked at her skeptically, as though she had lost half her marbles. It was time to let it all hang out and hope for the best. Alex would either accept her for who she was, or he would walk away. Now was as good of a time as any to find out which it would be.

"Dang it, Alex, you've got to believe me. I was born in 1308. When I left Skye, it was 1326."

Alex pushed back on the crate, knocking it over as he stood. "Holy crap. You've got to be kidding. And here I thought *I* was nuts."

Bree hung her head in her hands, too deflated to cry. "I knew you wouldn't believe me." She shook her head and stood up, prepared to leave. There was nothing more to say.

"Whoa there, hold on." Alex grabbed her arm. "Let's just wait a minute. I'm not saying I don't believe you. But that's a lot to throw at a guy, don't you think?" Bree heard the frustration in his voice. She couldn't blame him. Who wouldn't be confused by all this?

He sat her back down on the bench, this time, taking a seat beside her. "Let's just try this again. So, you believe you've lived in another time?"

"I know I did. And I knew William Gregory. We were in love, and we were going to be married. But after the MacDonalds killed William and my mother, my father wanted to return to the future to tell his sister what had happened. I had no reason to stay in the past, so I came to the future with him." She was pretty sure she wasn't handling this well, but this wasn't an easy story to tell.

"Your father is also from the past?" His brow shot up toward his hairline.

"No, he was from the future, I mean from these times. My father, Daniel Ellers, was Aunt Teressa's brother. Four years ago, when he

237

was thirty-two years old, he was swept back in time to the thirteenth century. He met my mother, fell in love, and lived out his life—in the past. They had five children together, one boy and four girls. I'm the youngest. My dad always knew if he wanted, he could return to the future, to the exact same moment as when he had left."

"How the hell—" Alex started to ask.

Bree held up her hand to stop him. "Just let me finish. It doesn't matter how this all happened. I'm not even sure I can explain it if I tried, which I am doing. My dad was an old man when he returned to this time, and he died a few months later. Before he died, he told Aunt Teressa everything that had happened to him, and she agreed to take me in."

Alex looked at her as though he weren't buying it. "When did all this happen?"

"Four years ago. Back on Skye."

Folding his arms across his chest, Alex peered at her with skepticism. "If you were born seven hundred years ago, how the hell did you get a passport to come to America?"

Details, Bree thought. He was hung up on the dang details. "Simple. Moezell took my dad's passport and turned it into one for me."

"Moezell? Who the hell is Moezell?"

"Umm, she's a faerie?" Bree said, not sure Alex would believe her. But then again, why should he believe anything she was saying? It all sounded like a load of horse manure.

Obviously deep in thought, he acted as if he hadn't heard her. A second later, he snapped his fingers. "Wait a minute. I met a woman named Moezell at a bar back in Placerville, at least, I think her name was Moezell. She went on and on about the history of the MacDonalds and the MacNicols. I thought it was pretty darn strange at the time, but now, it's starting to make sense."

"You met Moezell?" It was Bree's turn to be surprised. "Did she have long blond hair and ice-blue eyes that could see right through you?"

"Yeah." Alex nodded, as if remembering.

"And was she wearing a pale blue dress that seemed to mold to her body like flowing water?" From the look in his eyes she had a fairly good clue her description was accurate.

"Well, yeah, at first, but then she seemed to change into "little girl lost," like Dorothy from the *Wizard of Oz*. I felt sorry for her, so I let her talk, but when she started talking about our two clans, it sort of freaked me out, and I left as soon as I could."

"That sounds like Moezell, all right. She'd do whatever it took to gain your confidence."

"You're saying I met a faerie?"

"It sounds like you did."

"You've got to be kidding." Alex started to laugh. Hard. She didn't know what he thought was so funny.

"I told you I wouldn't lie, but since you already think I'm crazy, it doesn't matter what I tell you."

It took a moment for Alex to rein in his laughter. "I don't think you're crazy."

"But you just said . . ."

"I know what I said. But you're no crazier than I am. Listen to me, Bree, this is serious. When you're not here, the dreams come back, night after night. They started soon after I met you. Last night, I dreamed I died in that other life. I'm not sure I'm ready to see what tonight will bring if you're not there."

"You saw yourself die?" This was a new one for Bree. She had never heard of anyone remembering their own death. Even Uncle Robert's memories from his past life stopped long before he met his death. Her father, Daniel Ellers, had filled him in on that part of his life.

"Not only that, I hated the MacDonalds, and they hated me. It was awful."

"You remember hating the MacDonalds?"

"Yes, I wanted to kill them, all of them, but they killed me first."

Bree stared at him for a long, hard moment, then she started to chuckle, doing all she could to hold back the hysterical laughter building just below the surface. It was accompanied by a glorious moment of understanding; everything was exactly the way it was meant to be.

William had hated the MacDonalds much more than she had. He resented the threat they presented to the MacNicol clan and her safety. And now, to think William had reincarnated as a MacDonald; she just had to laugh. She didn't know if it were the irony of fate or the simple logic of karma, but either way, William, or now Alex, was experiencing firsthand the old saying what goes around, comes around. Resent someone in one lifetime and you'll be resented in another. All it took to stop the karmic wheel from turning was love. If you loved life, it loved you back.

"I'm glad you think this is funny," Alex said, pulling her back from her thoughts.

"No, it's not like that. But think about it. Let's go with the idea you were William Gregory in another life. You hated the MacDonalds. Now you come back as Alex MacDonald, and when you tell me your last name, I don't want to have anything to do with you. Kinda that taste of your own medicine thing. I had to set aside my hatred of the MacDonalds so I could work with you to heal your horses. Healing your horses was more important than hating you for being a MacDonald. Then, the more I got to know you, the more I fell in love. I stopped caring about your last name because I cared too much about you."

"You fell in love? With me?" He reached out and took hold of her hands between his own.

"Yes, Alex. Surely you know by now. I couldn't have given you my body and soul, and my trust, if I didn't love you the way I do. Now that I think about it, it kinda makes sense to know I loved you before in another lifetime. I love you too much for it to be only once."

"Dang, that's a lot to think about."

Bree chuckled again, relieved Alex was taking this so well.

"Bree, I'm not going to pretend I believe or even understand everything you're saying. All I know is what I see, and what my gut tells me. I might not know how you're able to communicate with animals, but I've seen the results. Somehow, you were able to get inside their heads and figure out my horses had developed a fear of skateboarders, crazy as that may seem. And I know I feel better when I'm with you. I don't know if it's because I knew you in another life or if you traveled through time, and frankly, I don't care."

Bree started to speak, but he held up a hand to stop her.

"Don't get me wrong, I'm not saying none of it's possible, I'm saying it doesn't matter. What matters is here and now. I'm grateful for whatever brought us together, be it fate, or karma, or even Frank's damn efforts at matchmaking. All I know is I feel a lot better when you're around. In fact, I feel more like myself. Like I can be who I really am, and you get me. But more than that, Bree, right now, I've got a feeling if I lose you, I'll be making the mistake of a lifetime. From what you say, I've already done it once. And I damn well know I don't want to do it again."

"Losing my family, traveling through time, all those things make me feel as if I've lived through more than one life and I'm only twenty-two. I may not have died and been reborn, but I've experienced things most people can't even imagine."

"Believe me, I know. Before I met you, I wouldn't have imagined any of this was possible. Now I can't imagine living my life without you. I love you too much to lose you again. Even if it means I have to believe in wizards and faeries, and time travel, or even reincarnation. Hells bells, Bree, I'll believe in it all if it means I get to stay with you. Maybe I don't understand a lot of this, but I do know I loved you then and I love you now, and some things never change."

"You're not going to lose me, Alex. It's like you said; all that matters is here and now. All that's happened before was only there to bring us to this moment."

"Will you stay with me, Bree? Please say you'll stay."

"Of course I'll stay. There's no place I'd rather be."

He gathered her up in his arms and held her tight. "Your place or mine?" he whispered in her ear.

Slipping her arms around him, she answered, "Either one's fine with me, as long as you're there." A feeling of confidence washed over her, knowing this time they were meant to stay together forever.

The End

I hope you've enjoyed the MacNicol Clan Through Time series as much as I enjoyed writing it. If you're looking for more historical, time-slip romance, I invite you to take a peek at my
fairy tale fantasy,
Dreaming In Moonlight.
It takes place in a fictional European duchy and involves an immortal male seeking self-redemption.

Sometimes we wish upon a star . . .

Sometimes we dream in moonlight.

What he thought was the blessing of a lifetime becomes an unimaginable curse when Lord Gavin Richard Montague, the Grand Duke of Maninberg, agrees to accept immortality from Tazire, a powerful wizard, in exchange for complete control of his kingdom. Now he can never leave.

Besides being Tazire's great granddaughter, Lady Tara Zanders, is an experienced dream weaver who would rather travel the world than submit to seeking a husband. When she finds herself attracted to the charming spellbound duke, her curiosity is aroused and her wanderlust falters. She quickly realizes Lord Gavin is trapped in his kingdom, but she doesn't know why.

There's a battle brewing just outside Lord Gavin's kingdom that threatens Tara's safety. He wants to protect her. She wants to uncover his secrets.

Each feels the pull of their passion, but will their well-guarded secrets destroy any hope they may have of finding mutual happiness and truly lasting love?

Dreaming In Moonlight

A small duchy in Central Europe 1692

There wasn't time to think about the pain burning through his shoulder from the heft of a sword he'd held for too long, or the weight of the armor chaffing against his flesh. There wasn't time to worry about the loss of his helmet, or to brush away the hanks of bloodied hair hanging over his forehead. There wasn't even time to consider the horror of the lives being lost. There was only time to fight against the foe advancing upon his kingdom.

The warrior prince had barely a moment to survey the devastation surrounding him before the next wave of barbarians descended upon his army like a black plague of angry rodents. The invaders, dark, dirty, hairy men, appeared as faceless beasts to his eyes, no longer human. And much like swarming vermin, they carried the stench of death and destruction with them into battle. Even the rain, pouring from grey, overcast skies, could not wash away the filth they inflicted upon his land.

With scarcely a moment to breathe, Lord Gavin Richard Montague, heir-apparent to the Maninberg throne, shouted to the heavens, "This madness must stop! These are my people, this is my land. I must maintain control. By the gods and all the powers that rule, my kingdom must not fall to these undeserving beasts."

His father had already fallen under the enemy's sword. It was incumbent upon Lord Gavin to save his kingdom, or what was left of it. The sharp clank of metal against metal rang out, followed by the sickening sounds of crushed bones and tearing flesh. The smell of blood, death, and fear assailed his senses. He cut and slashed at the invading horde, only to be met with wave upon wave of attackers. Driving rain and rivers of mud turned the battlefield into a horrid bloodbath.

"My kingdom must be preserved!" Lord Gavin shouted skyward as his broadsword once again connected with deadly force against his foe. He ducked and dodged sideways to avoid the blade of his opponent as he swung his sword to strike the man. His blade sliced through leather and flesh, drawing blood as Gavin delivered a disabling blow. The barbarian fell to the earth, only to be replaced by another.

With fierce determination he fought against his attackers, spearing another faceless man with the blade of his sword. He needed a miracle to save his kingdom. All appeared hopeless, but he would not yield. With his last dying breath he would fight for is kingdom, he would not yield.

"By the gods above, I demand my kingdom be preserved," Lord Gavin cried out again, his voice thundering above the din of the fighting. "I demand my birthright."

The battle raging around him suddenly stilled. Every drop of rain, every breath of man, was held in place, unmoving, except for Lord Gavin. In awe, the warrior prince lowered his sword, stunned by the power holding the ferocious battle at bay.

A voice as powerful as the wind pierced the stillness. "Say ye true, what demands do ye place upon the powers of this land?"

"I demand nothing less than the safekeeping of my kingdom and my people," Lord Gavin replied, turning his head from side to side. His eyes searched through the rain soaked skies as he sought the source of the voice. Adrenalin pumped through his veins, driving his arrogance to overrule his apprehension.

"By what right do ye make this demand?" A strange-looking figure appeared in the mists. His long robe, the color of polished gunmetal, was belted at his waist by thick braided cords of black leather. Thick, dark hair with strands of silver hung in waves to his powerful shoulders, framing a long narrow face highlighted by piercing grey eyes.

Lord Gavin drew in a sharp breath. There was no mistaking the identity of this ghostly apparition. He was too familiar with the myths and legends told throughout his land to doubt that standing before him was Tazire, an ancient and powerful wizard.

Standing steadfast and proud, Lord Gavin held his head high and faced the wizard. "By the right of my birth," he replied. "By the blood of my father and his father before him. By the generations of my family who have ruled this kingdom in peace."

"Your birthright?" Tazire glared at him. "Do you really believe your *birth* grants you the right to seek control of men's destinies?"

"It's my birthright to seek control of this kingdom and all who live here." Gavin refused to back down. The reason for his birth, the very purpose of his life, was to rule his father's kingdom. He would do anything to secure his rule.

"How far does this birthright extend?" the wizard asked.

"I ask only for the control of Maninberg, my rightful kingdom."

"Your rightful kingdom? Ha! Tell me, how long does this birthright exist?" A wicked smile graced Tazire's lips, but his eyes remained hard.

"For as long as I have breath in my body." Gavin shifted his stance, raising his sword before him.

"And if you were to live forever, would this birthright still hold true?" Tazire's dark, grey eyes bore deep into Gavin, as if seeking his soul.

"Yes. Forever." Lord Gavin returned the wizard's steely gaze, inflexible in his demands, unyielding in his beliefs.

"Beware, young prince. Would you truly agree to accept immortality in exchange for total control of your kingdom – and only your kingdom?" A note of caution crept into Tazire's voice.

"I would accept nothing less," Lord Gavin stated confidently, ignoring the wizard's warning.

Tazire cocked his head, studying the young prince. "Such arrogance shall be rewarded." The wizard lifted his hands to the heavens. "Granted," he shouted, loud and clear. "Thy will be done." And with the wind, he was gone.

Tricia Linden, author of timeless romance with a touch of magic.

In this lifetime, Tricia has lived in five states, on two islands, and on a farm, and is now living with her soulmate in Northern California. Her travels have taken her to Canada, Mexico, Australia, Hong Kong, Guam, England, Scotland, several countries in Europe, and several states in the US. Besides her love of reading and writing romance, she has a great fondness for Pink Flamingos. Over the years, she's gathered a rather large collection of the fun pink birds.

Website: https://tricia-linden.com/

Facebook: https://www.facebook.com/TriciaLindenAuthor/

Tweeter: @TriciaLinden69

Email: Tricia.Linden@ymail.com

www.ingramcontent.com/pod-product-compliance
Lightning Source LLC
Chambersburg PA
CBHW030132180626
46812CB00002B/657